CONFESSIONS OF A PREACHER'S WIFE

CONFESSIONS OF A PREACHER'S WIFE

MIKASENOJA

URBAN CHRISTIAN

www.urbanchristianonline.net

Urban Books
1199 Straight Path
West Babylon, NY 11704

ISBN-13: 978-1-60162-961-6
ISBN-10: 1-60162-961-3

First Printing May 2008

Printed in the United States of America

10 9 8 7 6 5 4 3 2 1

*This is a work of fiction. Any references or similarities to actual events, real
people, living, or dead, or to real locales are intended to give the novel a sense of
reality. Any similarity in other names, characters, places, and incidents is entirely coincidental.*

Submit Wholesale Orders to:
Kensington Publishing Corp.
C/O Penguin Group (USA) Inc.
Attention: Order Processing
405 Murray Hill Parkway
East Rutherford, NJ 07073-2316
Phone: 1-800-526-0275
Fax: 1-800-227-9604

What people are saying about the Mikasenoja's debut novel "Confessions of a Preacher's Wife"

"I was mesmerized and captivated *by CONFESSIONS OF A PREACHER'S WIFE.* I think the story of life as a ministry family will be a revelation to quite a few readers who believe that the wife and children live a spiritual fairy tale existence."
Donna Williams, Senior Pastor's wife for over 25 years in San Francisco, CA.

"*Confessions of a Preacher's Wife* is a great reality check, and learning tool for current and future preacher's wives. It shows the discerning growth and trust in God needed for this special spot for God's first ladies to uphold His leading man."
Camellia Johnson, Dallas, Texas, author of "What Now?"

"Finally . . . a heart-felt, passionate treatment by a real pastor's wife for the real pastor's wife. Like Queen Esther, Mikasenoja has been anointed to deliver such a word of brilliance and breakthrough to the most neglected and often most wounded area of the church . . . the pastor's wife. Read with determination, read with discernment, and read for divine deliverance!"
Pastor Mike Stevens, University City Church, Charlotte, North Carolina, Author of Straight Up: The Church's Official Response to Down-Low Living

Dedicated to my parents,
Minister Fred Jones 1949-1997
&
Lois Henderson Jones
You both gave me the love of life and laughter and
taught me to always make the best of any situation.
Even in this . . . always give praise to God! This debut is
dedicated to the both of you!

Acknowledgments

"For with God nothing shall be impossible," Luke 1:37. This scripture has propelled me to discover my full potential in Christ Jesus, who without Him this literary work would not be possible. I give Jesus all of the praise and adoration for choosing me to deliver a message of hope, forgiveness, love, and restoration.

I want to thank my husband, Pastor C.L. Yancy, Sr. for all of your unconditional love and unwavering support toward my literary career and other ministry opportunities. You are the wind beneath my wings! I adore your honesty and your desire to help me reach my destiny in Christ.

To my children, Joshua, William Caleb, Jennifer, and Clinton Jr.: my precious treasures—thank you for allowing Mommy to share her gift with the world and for your patience with me while I was "away" writing. Remember, only what you do for Christ will last.

To my parents, the late Minister Fred Jones and my mother, Lois Jones, I thank you both for instilling the gift of service and love toward Kingdom Building. Though you are gone, Daddy, you were my best friend and the first man I truly loved. I love you, Mom, for instilling the importance of a consistent and persistent prayer life. This book is for you! You are the epitome of a WOW woman; a Woman of the Word, a Woman of Wisdom and a Woman of Worship. I love you!

To my only sibling and younger brother, Minister Fred Jones II and family, thank you for always believing in your older sister and giving me countless words of wisdom. You are a phenomenal man in Christ! I am waiting on your book to come out!

To the Henderson, Jones, Stevens, Mays, Mercer, Prosser, Clark, Yancy, Greenhouse, Thomas and Haddock families, thank you for the strong rich Christian heritage that I have gained from all of you.

To my favorite aunt, who never stops believing in me, Elnita Simmons & family—you are my strength and I love you! Thanks for always doing my hair, even when I didn't have an appointment, at the best "Healthy Hair" salon, Hair Quarters in Dickinson, Texas.

To my father-in-law, the late Pastor Dr. W.C. Yancy—you left us too soon. Thanks for your listening ear, your constant love and for always believing in Clint and me and what we were created to bring to the Body of Christ. We miss you dearly.

To my mother-in-law, Robbie Yancy (Quiet Storm), a pastor's wife who challenged me to stand strong, thank you! You taught me how to be tough. You were the first to introduce me to the world of Christian fiction!

To my armor bearer, Sister Gussie Dawsey, thank you for covering me in prayer through the years, and encouraging me to stay true to my purpose. You are a cheerleader for the Christian faith!

To Ron DeShay, Arvis Watts, Dedrick Johnson, Bryan Keyth Wilson, and Kiki Jones for helping me to discover the gift of purpose within me and pushing me out here to tell the story and to give God Glory.

To my late godmother, Mildred Vorsburgh: thank you for always making me feel special, anointed and appointed for a time such as this.

To Sharon Johnson, my faithful prayer warrior, you seemed to fill the void after the passing of my precious godmother. You all are my inspiration!

To my sorors of Delta Sigma Theta Sorority, Inc., thank you so much for your continued support of my efforts.

To all of my University of Texas at Austin alumni, students, faculty, and staff, thank you for your standard of excellence in all things.

To the best agent in America, Kimberly Matthews, you are the best kept secret on the East Coast! To my editor, Joylynn M. Jossel and the entire Urban Christian family, thanks for staying true to our craft of uplifting the Christ. To my literary friends across the nation who counseled me, prayed for me and encouraged me. Thank you so much!

I want to give a personal thanks to my "literary angels" Linda Beed, Victoria Christopher Murray, Jacquelin Thomas, the Faith Based Literary Conference, and Jeannette Hill. To my first team of editors, Wanda Lartique, Arvis Watts, Tamara Gillespie, the late Sandra Clayton, and Canditha Davis, I appreciate your time and patience. To my current personal wardrobe stylist Patrice Coleman, owner of Patrice Boutique in La Marque, Texas and Orange, Texas (www.patriceboutique. com), thanks so much for your excellent customer service, and sincere heart.

To Minister Gaston and family of La Marque, Texas, thanks for your creative fashion tips and making sure I am on point. Thanks to Marilyn Long of Vision Ink LLC, who invested so much of her time and wisdom toward this project. God directed you into my life just in the nick of time! Thanks to the Pageturner.net network, and Pamela Williams for your excellent web and networking services. Thank you, Bishop Terry and the Gospel Magazine family for the opportunity to write for the Lord.

To my Houston brother, Kerry Douglas, thanks for your encouragement, networking through *Gospel Truth Magazine* and your other ventures that promote Jesus Christ. To my gospel music friends and gospel announcers across the nation who I had the pleasure of sharing my life with, thank you so much for your music inspiration, which is the back drop of this project. To all of my high school English teachers and college professors, thank you for recognizing a gift of prose in me and challenging me to reach new heights in writing. To my colleagues and students of La Marque ISD, especially Joyce Bell (finish your book!), thank you so much for your unfailing support and encouragement toward this labor of love.

To the church families that I have been blessed to share affiliation with from Munger Avenue in Dallas, Texas, Mt. Carmel In Dickinson, Texas, Mt. Sinai in Austin, Texas, and New Hope, thank you for the medium of the church where I have found peace, deliverance, joy and sometimes pain, but ultimately I found the truth; that there is a reality in serving a true and living God. To all of my church families, senior pastors, and wise first ladies, I sincerely love you!

Thanks in advance to all of the persons, book clubs, bookstore owners, and librarians, who will read this literary work and pass on the good news! To Tia Ross and the Black Writers Reunion Conference Planning Team, thanks for your support and genuine encouragement. To the creative team of KimBry Productions, thanks for your love and I can't wait to see this novel on the stage and on film! Get ready for the tour!

And, to all of the ministers' wives and clergy who shared their endorsement and their labor of love, thank you for your encouragement. To the attendees of Yancy Ministries Powershop Clergy Wives conferences, thank you for your support toward the purpose of this ministry literary work.

And again, I want to thank God for the power of the pen to restore and heal. I want to thank Him for the cross and salvation!

Witnessing to Win,
Mikasenoja

FOREWORD

"What Is Our Crime?"

The Senior Pastor's wife has been accused of being too bold, because she has healthy self esteem. And, she's been accused of being too standoffish, because she suffers from an unhealthy self esteem. But, the truth of the matter is she will never receive an honest chance, because she's the pastor's wife.

It is a sad and tragic fact that so many innocent women are targeted and made miserable, because they are married to the pastor. Is this supposed to be her crime? Why? Should a pastor's wife be mistreated because she married a preacher? Should we expect pastor's wives to mistreat members because of their choices? Some members believe they are exempt from heeding what the Word says. But, God's Word states, "They that plow iniquity, and sow wickedness, reap the same (Job 4:8)." It says in Galatians 6:7, "Be not deceived; God is not mocked: for whatsoever a man soweth, that shall he also reap." If these members were not under such an impression, then they would not spend countless hours striving to make the pastor's wife's life miserable.

The saddest thing of all is that some women are under the impression that they will be the replacement. What they fail to realize is the pastor's wife has grown through years of dealing with such games. She's gained a lot of experience and wisdom from the games that have been played. The games are easy to spot and the players are recognizable, too. It is amazing that it doesn't change from one church to another. The game is the same, even though the players may change. Satan has not put into play a new or different game that pastor's wives haven't already been exposed to.

The majority of pastor's wives have learned more about political strategies in the churches where their husbands have served than anywhere else. They have been exposed to the oldest, the latest, and the most cleaver games played. Yet, God has kept them sane even though they have seen and heard it all: from the bringing in of women to entice the pastor, to the using of associate minister's wives to spite and hurt her. The pastor's wife is made a target as soon as she arrives at the church. And, it does not matter how sweet or pleasant she may be. It is truly sad that so many pastor's wives have to suffer at the hands of church folks for so long.

Some have chosen to leave their husbands rather than put up with such nonsense. Others have suffered ill health and mental anguish. But, there are some who have decided to uncover and expose the bad treatment of pastor's wives, and our hats are off to them. The ultimate question that pastor's wives are asking all over this country is: "What is our crime?"

The heroine of this novel, Jacqueline Stevens, reminds us that there is hope for the pastor's wife if we stay with God and stay the course.

Written From the Heart,
by First Lady Fannie P. Mays, a Senior Pastor's wife for over 35 years.

Chapter One

A Fresh Start

I walked into the church and peeked at the pale green pews, the nostalgic pipe organ, the fresh green carpet and the newly polished pulpit. Then, I prayed that this experience would be different. My husband was appointed pastor of the New Light Church in Southlake, Texas, right outside the Dallas/Fort Worth area. This was our first official visit as pastor and pastor's wife. My husband has been pastoring for over twelve years now, and we have both had our ups and downs. Funny, I never thought it would have been this way. I never envisioned my life like this; A life under constant scrutiny, where people are looking in and I am captured in a bowl of unspoken boundaries.

While I was growing up, before I lost my naïve "church innocence," church was a place of safety and refuge, and a place away from the world's darts and fears. Since becoming a pastor's wife, during the past twelve years, I have run away from the church many times, sometimes in spirit and sometimes physically. I have run away from its accusations, its definitions, and its people. Bitterness would call my name, while I wrestled with sleep from the constant bickering and infighting that would find its way in the fellowship. After all, the church is defined as "a body of believers." Well, those so called Bible packing believers have run many people away from the church house, including me, the pastor's wife.

"Well, Mrs. Stevens, we have heard so much about you and all of your many talents. We are so excited to have you as our first lady," said a middle-aged woman as she approached me wearing a tight pink hat, with matching pink gloves and a pink suit. "My name is Sarah Finley and my husband is Deacon Abraham Finley. We are one of the founding families of the New Light Church. I was six years old, or maybe two years old, you know I rarely discuss my age, when New Light was founded by my great grandfather, Pastor S. L. Robinson. Yes, I remember those struggles to keep these church doors open, and all those chickens that were slaughtered for dinner plates. I think New Light sold every part of the chicken to bring some money into the Lord's house," said Sister Finley with a look of nostalgia and sweet memories as she thought about New Light's historic past.

"Is there anything that you need at this time? How do you like your parsonage?" she continued. "The deacons' wives and I took the time, last month, to decorate the house, just to let you know how much we are looking forward to having you, Pastor Stevens and your children. You do know, Mrs. Stevens, not every pastoral family has a parsonage to call home. We purchased that property about five years ago. We wanted a nice home for our pastor, and his family to live in. So, we are very proud of that property. I personally picked the house out myself for our last pastoral family. Was everything the way you like it, Mrs. Stevens, or would you like me to call you, First Lady?" said Sister Finley.

"Oh, Mrs. Finley the house is beautiful, and Sister Stevens would be just fine," I nodded to her in respect. I smoothed out my size twelve peach linen A-line dress, which hung slightly below my knees, with matching two and a half inch peach Fioni high heeled sandals. I wore my shoulder length, dyed jet blue-black hair, in a slicked back bun to appear more conservative as this was only my second time meeting with Sister Finley. I wanted to make sure to always leave a good impression, so I wore my Tiffany inspired faux peach Indian jewelry with matching earrings, necklace, and bracelet. I topped the look off with a peach clutch Fendi bag, which I held stiffly by my side. The peach dress and matching accessories gave my brown chestnut skin a gorgeous glow.

"I must say, First Lady, you are looking quite dainty today. I like your sense of style. It is just what our New Light needs; a pastor's wife with some class," said Sister Finley.

"Thank you so much, Sister Finley. And please, please, you can call me Sister Stevens," I insisted.

Though I was most honored by being called First Lady, I knew and understood that it is just a term of endearment and in many ways it is paradoxical anyway. Typically the term "First Lady" is used for formal occasions, and besides, the way Sister Finley had just said First Lady, it sounded more like a sarcastic question.

"Please tell the Deacons' Wives Ministry how grateful I am for their assistance."

The church ladies had decorated the parsonage in a soft baby blue and pastel green. Last night, my husband and I almost had a "slight disagreement", because the first thing I wanted him to do was to call a contractor to paint the parsonage a color that I could live with. Baby blue and pastel green . . . Yuck!

Lord, please give me patience and forgive me for lying in this church house that everything was beautiful with our parsonage. I have learned that it is better to be grateful for what you have. Hence, the politically correct response with a Star Jones smile, "Everything was beautiful, and thanks so much."

* * *

I pray for a time, when we can purchase our own house, choose our own colors and have our own furniture. The first parsonage we had was in Cypress Creek, Texas, where Lance pastured the Mt. Bethel Church. That house had a roof full of leaks, and during the first three months of our tenure, every time it rained, which was at least once a week, we had to put pots all over the house. It took the deacons of Mt. Bethel forever to get a contractor to come out and fix the leaks in the roof. And Lord, bless my husband, but he is truly just a preacher and not a maintenance man.

My husband's name is Lance McClain Stevens. He has been preaching the gospel, since he was twenty-three years old. He is a third generation preacher. His father and grandfather were both preachers. He has pastored two churches, and now he is beginning his third pastorate. We have three children: Connie, Jaylyn, and Lance Jr., ages 7, 10, and 13. Lance and I have been married for sixteen years. We met at the University of Texas at Austin. He was director of the gospel choir, and I sang a mean first soprano

I never dreamt of being a pastor's wife or minister's wife. I just dreamed of falling in love with a man who loved Christ as much as I did. At first, when Lance asked me for a date, I declined, because everybody knew that Lance would be a preacher/pastor one day and I didn't want that life. Too many times I had seen pastors' wives give up their dreams and lose themselves for the sake of the ministry and their husband's ambitious ministry goals. Besides, I felt that pastors' wives were either too skinny or too fat, and point blank, I didn't want to be one of them.

I know I had a stereotypical view of pastors' wives, but I never wanted to be in their sorority. So, I ran away from Lance's offers of courtship for over a year and a half. He was very persistent, so I finally went on a date with him. I found him very easy to talk to about God and we had so much in common. After the first date, I was hooked on his character and integrity, so we started dating. Now, here we are over nineteen years later, married with three children and a church to lead.

"Sister Stevens, Sister Stevens," said Sister Finley.

"Oh, I am sorry, Sister Finley, I guess I just dazed off. What were you saying?"

"We are sponsoring a 'Meet the First Lady' tea next month, and we want to know what your favorite colors are?"

"Well, I am partial to royal purple or lavender and millennium silver."

"Don't you think that purple is too strong of a color, my dear?"

"Pastel lavender will do just fine, Sister Finley."

"My thoughts exactly, First Lady, oops, I mean Sister Stevens. Well, I must be going. My Cadillac has to be serviced today, and I can't be late."

Sister Finley placed her French manicured hand in her pink purse, and gently handed me a business card and with a quick wink, she said, "If there is anything else you need, here is my card with my home number, cell phone, and pager. Welcome, First Lady, to our beloved New Light."

"Thank you, Sister Finley." I watched her as she strutted down the aisle of the church as if she had done her duty and now was off to the next matter at hand.

After she walked out of the sanctuary, I saw my husband walk in with his eye looking up into the high vaulted ceilings of New Light.

"How do you like the church, honey? Isn't it beautiful?" said Lance, walking down the center aisle of the sanctuary with his arms outstretched.

I looked at my forty-year-old, 6'3, 215 lbs, ebony king and quietly exhaled. After all these years, this mahogany creature could still light my fire. Lance looked like he was born to lead this church. This morning, he was wearing a linen Sean John brown casual outfit with a white tank underneath and brown sandals that displayed his size thirteen shoe. Lance could have easily donned the covers of *Ebony* and *GQ* with his tall stature, and gorgeous pearly white teeth that he meticulously brushed at least twice a day. He still jogged at least four miles a week to maintain his physical contour. I draped my arms around his neck, and kissed him lightly on the lips.

"Yes, sweetheart, New Light is beautiful. I love the wooden interiors of the church. It makes it look so classic," I said.

We looked at the interior of the church sanctuary, which could easily seat 400 parishioners. Its pews were draped in rustic velvet gold. The choir stand could hold up to 75 choir members, and the pulpit could seat six preachers comfortably. The church had a fellowship hall, family activity room, eight classrooms, one board meeting room, two administrative offices, and four bathrooms. The church was constructed with a white steeple, that was in the form of a light house. The red and white brick of the church made it seem like a home away from home. On the top of the front doors it read, "New Light, where the light of God's love ever shines!"

The pastor's study was draped in carved wood, and was equipped with a shower, bathroom, small kitchen area, counseling room, computer niche, and a small library. Lance's new office quarters spanned over 800 square feet. It reminded me of the hotel rooms that came equipped with a kitchen area. This was the nicest pastoral office space that Lance ever had.

Upon his hire at New Light, we learned that the previous pastor requested that his office be remodeled and a member donated over $15,000 to honor his request. Oddly enough, four months after the renovations, the pastor resigned. Lance had yet to tell me the details of why the previous pastor resigned.

"What do you think of dear Sister Finley?" asked Lance as he looked into my eyes to watch the expression on my face.

"Well, she is friendly enough, a bit pushy, but she is okay, I guess."

"I hear that she is over 70 years old. But no one knows for sure," Lance said.

"No, she can't be! That lady doesn't look a day over 50!" I said.

"They say that she walks a mile a day, attends a day spa once a week, and eats vegetables like they are going out of style. Her family inherited a lot of land in Southlake, and made a fortune selling their land to incoming businesses. She's helped many businesses get on their feet and she has influence within the community as well. She is part of one of the founding families of New Light."

"Yes, she told me."

"Well, New Light is just over 70 years old."

"Wow!"

"Her great grandfather was the founder of New Light and her grandfather was the next pastor after him. Her father probably would have been next in line to pastor New Light, but he had a huge drinking problem that he just couldn't conquer, not even for the ministry."

"Babe, I pray that this time will be different for us," I said, while I turned to put my arms around his neck. I leaned toward him, and laid my head upon his chest. I inhaled his Perry Ellis cologne, which seemed to mesmerize my senses. I knew that we were in a church, but I couldn't wait to get my man to our home, where it could be just the two of us.

"Hey, just listen and observe. Don't be so quick to give your opinion or volunteer for anything just yet," said Lance as he gently raised my chin to look into my eyes.

"I've done that before, remember? Then I was called stuck-up and 'seemingly uninterested in God's work' as they said at Little Zion Church," I stated with one hand on my hip. "And, when I did get involved, in the words of the members of Mt.

Bethel, 'I was overbearing and a little too opinionated'." I had a hint of bitterness.

"I know sweetheart, just be patient and try to feel them out first. Sister Finley certainly wants us to know who has been in charge in the interim, since they have been without a pastor for thirteen months now."

"Wow! Speaking of their previous pastor, where is he now?"

"Well, the brother is no longer in the ministry. He and his wife are separated and the preacher's circles say he will probably be retiring from the ministry."

"Retiring! Isn't he only fifty-three years old?"

"Yes. But, let's just say he may have another child on the way, and it is not his wife's. On top of that, he felt he needed to reevaluate his calling."

"Was the other woman a member of this church?"

"No. It is a woman he met during one of his annual revival trips. Apparently, they were having an affair for over ten years. They have a seven-year-old, and now another child is on the way. I hear they live in West Texas now. He married his mistress."

"What? How old is the other woman?"

"Well, she is old enough to know better. I heard that she is around thirty-five years old."

"Does the membership of New Light know about this scandal?"

"I'm not sure. The deacons just found out about this scandal late last month. They thought he wanted to retire early, and spend more time with his family. However, his wife found out about the 'other family' last year, and she threatened to destroy him with the information. He felt he should retire, and not have her blackmail him with his sin. The sad thing, though, is that the man is a powerful pastor and teacher; however, he just had a weakness for this woman and never could get over it."

"If he was such a powerful pastor and teacher, he should

have been able to learn from his own sermons and control his lusts and sinful temptations. Right?" I quipped.

"Oh no," Lance said, rolling his head and letting go of our embrace.

"I don't know why I tell you things like this because you go right on your pedestal about pastors being righteous men 24/7, but the reality is no one is righteous but God Himself. We are just striving to be holy, and working daily on right-eousness. Really, the fact of the matter is that all men at times can be weak. We bleed red blood too, sweetheart. That's why I constantly need you to pray for me; for it is only Christ that keeps me holy."

"Excuses are monuments of nothingness," I said.

In my heart, I wondered if he had any "weak moments" during our marriage. Lord knows that some women can be predators for men of the pulpit.

"Alright, Jacqueline, get off of your soapbox and change this subject quick."

"Lance, have you thought about your first sermon as pas-tor?" I asked, obliging to his request to change the subject.

"Now, you know I rarely share my sermon titles before preaching," he said.

"Yes, I know, but not even a hint?" I questioned.

"Well, let's just say, Mission Possible: A Purpose Driven Church."

"Oh, sweetheart, that sounds interesting. Do you need help with the church programs for Sunday morning?"

"No, I have an interview scheduled for a new church ad-ministrative assistant."

"Oh, what happened to uh, what's her name, . . . Mrs. Franklin?"

"The deacons determined that it was time to hire a new church assistant. Mrs. Franklin has been church assistant for twenty-five years, and she has not kept up with computer technology. Furthermore, she sleeps at her desk."

"How old is she?" I asked.

"Mrs. Franklin should be around 78 years old."

"Then, I can fill in around the church until you hire a new assistant," I said.

"Sweetie, I don't think that is a good idea."

"Why not? This is a new city for me. I don't know the people well. The kids will soon be active in their school and extracurricular activities. I am accustomed to working with you in ministry."

"I know, baby, but let's take it slow. This is a huge opportunity for me, for us, and I don't want to be hasty about anything. You just rest and I'll take you out to dinner tonight; just you and me," Lance promised.

We walked out of the church arm in arm. He drove me back home, and returned to the church. I went upstairs to our bedroom, and gathered the journal that had been a constant friend and a reminder of God's goodness. I opened my journal and began to read the testimonies of my life and the showcases of God's glory in our lives. An hour or so later, Lance arrived to take me to dinner.

For the last ten years, I have kept a journal. I named my journal "The First Lady: Joy for the Journey." Over the years, I have chronicled my family's ups and our downs. I have a scrapbook full of paper programs from our past churches, special days, special joys, and testimonies enclosed in my journal. I have a prayer life map where God has answered our prayer requests. It will be my testimony for our descendants to discover the joy of serving Jesus. When I am writing, I am able to express my joy, my sorrow and even my pain. Often times, I address my journal notes to Jesus. Other times, I write to the first lady when I need to pull off the coat of high expectations that dominate the life of a clergy wife. That night, I wrote about the newest experience in my Christian journey as a pastor's wife, the assignment the Lord has given me.

Dear Jesus,

It's 10:30 p.m. The kids are in the bed. Well, Lance took me out to dinner, but as soon as we arrived at the restaurant, he received a call to go to the hospital to visit an elderly member who had a sudden slight heart attack. Bless his heart, he stayed with me for twenty minutes to keep me company, and I guess try to keep both the church and me (his two wives) happy. Oops, Lance reminds me that I am his wife, and Jesus is the bridegroom that is talked about in the Bible record of Revelation who will return for His church. In his words, "I made a covenant vow with you and God in marriage,, and I have a charge and call at this particular church in this season of my Christian journey as God's messenger. Churches come and go, but my marriage is supposed to last until death do us part."

As I watch Lance sleep, I thank You for his love for me and our family. He tries to be superman, but I am grateful, Lord, that You gave him to me. He is not perfect, but he strives to be more like You. Jesus, as you already know, we are at a new church and new things abound for us. Protect us, Jesus, like only You can. Help me find purpose in this church. Help me to be slow to speak, and to love, unconditionally, the members of our church. Lord, finally I pray for my husband's strength during any "weak moments."

Love,
Jacqueline Renee Stevens, my confession

Chapter Two

Preparation

"Jacqueline, hurry up. It's 3:45 and I don't want you to be late for this tea party." Lance called up the stairs with a slight giggle. My husband really liked to tease me when the ladies of the church would have these finer womanhood type gatherings where we would sit around in our best hats and sip tea. Hmph, I would be laughing too if I didn't have to attend.

I took a quick glance at myself in the mirror. Okay, my hair was in place. I decided to wear it conservatively with a slight upward curl at the tips. I licked my lips, which had gone dry from my nervousness of attending the tea that the ladies of New Light were sponsoring. It was being billed as "Come out and meet the new first lady at New Light." I felt like a circus attraction. Come on out and see the fat lady dance or put roaring flames of fire in her mouth on a dancing monkey.

Sister Finley insisted the Deacon Wives host the First Lady Tea to welcome me into the Christian sisterhood. She requested all of the ladies in attendance wear a hat to the event, and that there was going to be a parade of hats. I wore my mauve and burgundy wide brimmed hat with a matching mauve and burgundy silk pant suit. I took another quick glance in the mirror after I dressed and thought to myself, "Girl, you look good!" I walked down the stairs and Lance gave me that special look that said, "That is my baby's mama, right there!" But, his look went to disapproval as he followed my legs.

"Uh, Jackie, do you think you should wear pants to a tea party or a function at church?" asked Lance.

"Is the tea party in the sanctuary?" I asked. "I thought it was in the fellowship hall."

"Well no, but I would think that this is your first impression for some of the women and you shouldn't try to buck or challenge the way they have done things in the church. You know how some of these traditional church women of the South can be."

"Is there a sign or an unspoken rule that women can't wear pants in the fellowship hall at New Light? I've seen some of the women wear pants suits to New Light during the week. Or is it a rule that I can't wear pants in the fellowship hall?"

"Well, you are the pastor's wife," Lance said.

"Okay, so is there a special heaven just for pastor's wives?" I replied. "Because if there is, I might need to check it out to make sure none of those angelic choir members hadn't planted a secret bomb in our special heaven and blast us out," I said with a laugh as I turned back up the stairs to change.

It wasn't worth the fight with Lance to argue over other people's expectations of us. Pants was not a salvation issue and I was not about to let that issue divide my house. It was easier to change my clothes and deal with it later without time constraints, when my stomach wasn't turning with nervous pangs as to what to expect from this tea party that was supposed to "welcome" me into New Light.

I had a strange feeling this special called gathering was to let me know the ground rules and what they expected of me as their pastor's wife.

I felt my heart feeling anxious all of a sudden and I counted backward from ten . . . nine . . . eight . . . seven . . . six . . . five

. . . four . . . three . . . two . . . one . . . now   exhale . . . AAAH-HHH!!

I have got to stop doing this to myself. I looked in the mirror and pointed to my reflection. I told myself to get it together. . This church would be different from the rest. I needed to calm down and relax my nerves. I told myself to change clothes and kiss and support that fine husband that God had blessed me with. I knew God would send angels to protect me; everyone was not out to destroy me. I needed to open up my heart, put my confidence in man, but put my total trust in God. I thought to myself, not to let bitter moments of my past, cloud my future.

I changed into a blue flowery dress with a wide white belt and a slanted wide brimmed hat that I customized to match the dress to perfection. I grabbed my white knock-off Gucci bag and joined my husband down stairs.

"Jackie, you look gorgeous. The women of New Light are going to love you!" Lance said.

My husband had a lot to learn about women, especially church women. I smiled and joined him in the car and we drove to the church where my destiny awaited.

Chapter Three

The First Lady Tea

Lance and I walked into the fellowship hall and the ladies were dressed in black dresses with big pink flowers pinned on the front side of their dresses. Not a single woman in the church was wearing a hat. I instantly felt uncomfortable and overdressed. Okay, someone had set me up. About twenty ladies sat in a circle formation behind the tables and there was one chair at the front facing them.

Sister Finley walked toward us and grabbed me by the hand, looking at Lance and sarcastically said, "Okay, Pastor Stevenson, thank you so much for bringing our first lady to our tea. Now you can dismiss yourself and leave us girls to ourselves."

Lance looked at me, cleared his throat, lowered his eyes and walked toward his office. After a few uneasy moments, he turned around and said, "Sister Stevens, can I talk to you real quick," motioning toward me with a look of concern in his eye.

I saw his uneasiness and I replied, "Go ahead and study, sweetheart. I'll be okay." I winked my eye and turned toward Sister Finley with a new determination.

"I guess you didn't get the message that we decided to change the theme of the Tea from hats to celebrating breast cancer survivors. We thought it was more important to honor survivors and those who have passed on to cancer than to parade in our hats," said Sister Finley with a smirk on her face.

Well, now I knew who had set me up; dear Sister Finley. Alrighty then. I could see that I was going to have to pray extra hard that God worked on her.

I removed my hat while one of the ladies pinned me with one of the pink flowers to my dress.

"Hear ye, hear ye, we are calling this meeting to order to welcome our dear sister, Sister Stevens, to our fellowship and fold."

I looked at the ladies. It was about twenty-five of them who sat in a semi-circle. They eyed me with admiration, I hoped. One lady looked me over, smiling the whole way until she saw my legs. I decided not to wear stockings in this summer heat. I was wearing three-inch heeled white sandals. My dress was at least three inches past my knees so I knew she couldn't have scoffed at the length of my dress. Or maybe she did. Oh well.

I walked to the front of the room, where the only available chair stood. "Good afternoon, ladies," I greeted.

"Good afternoon," they responded in unison. A petite pudgy woman stood and came to the wooden podium, which was near the front where my seat was placed. I felt like I was about to give a review over the Sunday School lesson or something.

"We want to welcome you to our First Lady Tea. We are so proud that you came and you adhered to what we asked you all to wear," said the petite pudgy woman.

I thought to myself, *Strike one.*

"We are so happy Sister Stevens is a part of New Light. Pastor Stevens has blessed our souls the last two months with his sermons. My favorite sermon so far was the one called, "I'm

Just Blessed Like That!" Now that was a good sermon. It carried my soul all through the week."

By now, I recognized this woman as Sister Sable. Her husband was a deacon at New Light.

"So again, thank you all for coming out today to welcome the new pastor's wife to our church."

All of the ladies applauded as she took her seat.

⁂ Mrs. Finley strolled to the podium next, or should I say she elegantly glided to the podium in her long wraparound black dress that seductively hung on her frame. I could not believe she was over 65 years old. I know she and Dianne Carroll could have passed for sisters. The woman did not have a gray hair in sight, and her hair was always stiff with perfection. I know she had to spend some change to stifle that gray hair from peeking around her hair edges.

"At this time, we would like to share with Sister Stevens the history and traditions of our church so that she can learn to love New Light as much as we do. Since I am already at the podium, I will go first," said Sister Finley.

"My family was one of the founding families of this church. The original church was started at 2325 Round Rock Street in Southlake. It was the only black church within thrity miles of the Southlake metro area. We took great pride in it. Most of the founders of this church were teachers, masons, and brick layers. They were hardworking people who loved the land of Southlake. We were a self-sufficient multicultural community and we survived by the sweat of our brow and our faith in the Lord. We weathered the storm of segregation, civil unrest of the 60's, the broken promises of the 70's and 80's, and the good times in the 90's. And we are still here," Sister Finley said. "We are surviving. No one has stopped this ministry; not dirty cops or politicians and not even money hungry, skirt chasing so called men of the cloth," said Sister Finley as she turned her head to look at me.

Strike Two—that was meant to let me know that I need to satisfy my husband in more ways than one. Maybe that's not a strike after all, I thought. *I definitely can take care of that.*

"The people, we are New Light." Everyone in the room, except me, broke out in applause.

Uh, oh. I thought to myself. This woman had charisma and control. I needed to start praying for my husband now.

One by one, the women got up and shared a piece concerning the historic past of New Light and what they remembered about the "Good Ole Days" of New Light.

Strike Three. And they are out of there!

My husband was not one who lived in the past. Nope. I think I better go on a three day fast, and prayer festival for my husband next week.

Lance had always taught that when you stop talking about the future, you have lost hope. He preached it was important to respect the past, but not to live in it. And, church folks are notorious for living in the past.

The tea lasted for two hours. The women poured their tea, ate their tea cakes, and fellowshipped before someone said, "Oh, Sister Stevens, we have welcome gifts for you in the back. We were so busy talking about New Light, we almost forgot about your gifts." It was a lady named Betty Jean Pepperdine, who had spoken.

"Thank you so much," I replied. I gathered the gifts and carried all three of them to the car. Lance was outside talking with one of the church custodians and saw me struggling with the gifts and assisted me. All of the ladies were inside talking and gossiping, that they didn't see that I needed some assistance.

"How was it, Jackie? How did it go? Wow, they gave you some gifts. You see, I told you that you would like it here. In time, they are going to love you!"

I looked at my husband who so desperately wanted us to be happy in our new city, and church and I said, "Yes, sweetheart, you are so right. The tea went well, and I am so glad that I came."

Lance smiled with satisfaction and gently kissed me on my cheek. I have learned from this journey that some things are not even worth discussing. I have to let go and let God have His way. Good thing my scripture this morning was Proverbs 16:24, "Pleasant words are like honeycomb, sweet to the soul and healing to the bones," Or else I might have had to "share" some things with Lance about his precious, New Light. Lord, hold my tongue.

Chapter Four

The Visionary

"Jackie, wake up," Lance said as I reluctantly rolled over in our bed to face him. "Did, I tell you that you are beautiful in the morning?" Lance said with seductive eyes.

"Yes, you have, and I have a headache," I said with a smile and bad morning breath.

"The Lord has given me a vision for New Light" Lance said. "I want to share it with you."

"How long have you been up?" I asked as I noticed his Bible and a notepad next to him.

"At least three hours. I couldn't sleep. I have been praying that God give me a clear picture, a vision, for this church, and He has answered my prayer."

Lance had taught me through his ministry that vision is a clear picture of a better future for people from God's perspective.

"Lance, I am so excited." I sat up in bed. "I am listening."

"Our motto will be: A church moving from our trials and tribulations to triumph in Christ!" Lance said.

I must admit I wasn't really moved by the motto, but I decided to keep quiet. I didn't want to attack his vision. I learned that when you attack a preacher's vision, it feels as if you have attacked his very calling to the ministry.

"God has me focusing on the twenty-two things believers should do until Christ returns in First Thessalonians. This past week, every time I opened my Bible, it would open at First Thessalonians," Lance continued.

Now, to myself, I was thinking that could have been just an eerie coincidence. But, I remained silent and listened. I reminded myself to never attack the vision, but try to reaffirm it. I have learned in First Peter 3:1 to fit into my husband's plans. I looked at him and smiled in anticipation as he continued.

"Then, I heard God say, 'Preach Jesus, preach Jesus.' I kept hearing that in my dream last night," Lance said.

"What do you believe God is saying by that statement?" I carefully asked.

"We must get back to the basics of our beliefs. Show the people where the power of spirituality is; and it's in the cross of Jesus, not in the prosperity gospel that focuses only on money or a Houdini Jesus name it and claim it philosophy. Power is not found in who can scream the loudest, shout the most, do victory laps around the church, or who can throw the most money at the preacher's feet. These are just expressions. The power of Jesus is the Word of God and the power of the resurrected cross!

❧ "I envision young people coming to New Light, members participating in foreign missions, schools of ministry and training our members how to represent Christ in the workplace. In my dream, God showed me apartment complexes for our elderly, where we can care for them respectfully and with dignity.

"Jackie, the Lord revealed to me that He needs this generation to serve Him. Too many are falling by the wayside, and we are not evangelizing in this country the way we used to. This is the first un-churched generation in America, we must teach the basics. We must preach Jesus."

Lance was getting worked up talking about the vision and the plan the Lord had given him.

"Jackie, we must not allow the people to become apathetic to the things that matter most to God. We must minister to the people with HIV/AIDS. We can no longer ignore this epidemic. God is holding us responsible to preach Jesus to sick folk," Lance said as he looked at me pleadingly. "Jesus is calling for us to be filled with compassion and not revulsion for people with AIDS. For those with leprosy, Jesus simply asked, 'How can I help you?' He never asked them how they caught the disease. Jesus touched the sick and He wasn't afraid to be around them. He healed them. The Lord told me AIDS is a treatable disease and *it's a preventable 100% behavioral disease.* The church has the moral authority to talk about behavioral changes and lifestyles that are honorable before God. We must teach New Light members that apathy to this crisis is like arsenic. It can weaken the body of Christ slowly over time," said Lance. "The Bible says in Amos 6:1, 'Woe to the man who is at ease at Zion.'

"God is calling us to a great work here. I need you to pray, Jackie."

I thought to myself, but *you* said, Pastor Lance McClain Stevens, that I need to take it slow and not get involved in anything at the church right away. I told myself to listen and smile. So I did.

Lance continued without missing a beat. "I see the church ministering to prison families and helping with the rehabilitation to restore broken families. I see a church service for families who feel dejected by society because of a record. I see drug rehab services and counseling for families ravaged by the disease of addiction. We need to submit to this vision," Lance said. "We can't just commit, but we must submit to the vision that God wants to perform here. We can't be dedicated, but we have to submit to the vision wherever it may lead us; total submission.

"Most of all, I see men and women of all colors worshipping together and giving God total praise. We will bow down before the most high God and worship Him in His sanctuary." Lance said as he stood up on the bed with his arms outstretched before heaven.

I wept as I watched this man, this frail creature lose himself in the vision of hope that God had given him. I wept, because I really knew now that Satan himself would do anything to block this vision from coming to pass. Great vision is always accompanied with great difficulty. With a vision this big, I knew that our experience at New Light would be full of fruitful frustration.

Chapter Five

A New & Improved Ministry

It's been four months now, and we have acquainted ourselves quite well with the New Light Church. It's Tuesday evening, and we had choir rehearsal tonight. Only twelve choir members remained in the choir, after my husband decided to search for another worship leader. Thirty-five members left the choir in protest. They sit in the pews now. One of the ex-choir members had the nerve to bring a newspaper to church and commenced to reading it when my husband mounted the pulpit last Sunday. Well, the previous musician, Brother Ray Joseph, never came to rehearsals or church on time. Worship services began promptly at 11:00 a.m., and he would stroll in at 11:15 and cause everything to be late.

My husband counseled this young man many times, and even docked his pay a few times. But, he refused to obey my husband's leadership. Rumor has it that he may have been gay. One particular Sunday, he came to church wearing a yellow three-piece Armani inspired knock off suit with matching Stacy Adam shoes and a top hat to match. He marched in at 11:20 a.m., walked right up to the organ, and commenced to singing with the Praise & Worship Team who were trying their best to sing a cappella.

"Good morning, New Light!" Ray said from the organ. "Please excuse my tardiness. You know I had a late night last night, but my grandma always taught me that if you party all night long, you betta' have your behind in church Sunday morning! Can I get an Amen, somebody?"

I almost fell off of my seat when I heard the congregation, Amen, to this mad man in a yellow top hat with clear lip gloss on his lips, polished lightly clear French manicured short pink nails, and a cute white bow tie. He looked like a fruity banana in all of that yellow glory.

Brother Ray Joseph was a supremely gifted musician and seemed to make a B3 Hammond organ speak in tongues. The problem was, he knew he was good. He was a cocky and arrogant musician who felt the church would not survive without his skills.

"Matter of fact, I feel like singing one of my grandma's favorite songs right now, 'God Has Smiled On Me.' Will y'all help me this morning and sing my grandma's song?" Ray asked the congregation, as he rang his fingers on the B3 Hammond organ.

The sad part of this fiasco was Ray's personal life was upside down, and it seemed like he sacrificed time with the Lord. His gift kept him so busy doing the work of ministry at the cost of losing fellowship with the Lord.

Brother Joseph continued the song loudly and boisterously. He was oblivious to what was really going on around him. The choir members were fanning their noses, because of the musty liquor air that Brother Joseph exuded from his body that two peppermints could not fix. Lord have mercy! The boy was stone drunk playing the organ in God's house. The Praise & Worship team seemed lost and bewildered as they didn't know what Brother Joseph would do next.

My husband, who had just walked out into the congregation from his office, just glared in disbelief at him. My husband was going to allow Brother Joseph to hang himself with all of his antics.

"Sweet Jesus, you are so good to me!" Ray hollered as he worked his way into a shout, tuning his own sing song sermon. "Yes, Lord, you are smiling on me! You're going to set me free! You are going to protect me from the devil that is pouncing on us in this church! Yes, you will, Jesus!" he said as he turned and looked at my husband.

Oh, wee, I thought to myself. Lance McClain is about to go gorilla ape in this joint with anger!

"That is enough, Brother Joseph!" my husband said as he stood up behind the pulpit. "Deacon Jenkins can you please help Brother Joseph to my office."

Deacon Jenkins quickly received the message, and walked to the organ just as Brother Joseph broke out into a shout!

"Help me, Jesus! The devil is trying to take me out! Lord, don't let him!" He shouted until his body went stiff as a board, and two deacons carried him out.

After church, my husband met with Brother Joseph along with the deacon chairman in his office. My husband told me about the meeting that went something like this:

"Brother Joseph, what was all that about in worship today?" Lance asked.

"Well, there has been a lot of talk about me lately and I am sick and tired of it," Ray responded.

"Are you gay?" Lance bluntly asked.

"What does that mean?" Ray said defiantly, looking at Chairman Jenkins and Lance.

"Are you gay? Are you participating in the sin of homosexuality?" Chairman Jenkins clarified.

"Personally, I don't think that is your business!" Ray exclaimed.

"It is my business. I am pastor of this church. It is important that the leaders of this church represent Christ, and participate in an outwardly fashion. Now, I can offer a counselor for you to speak with, and I am recommending a brief sabbatical to help you deal with this immorality," Lance said. "And, it smells like you may be abusing alcohol too."

"Oh no, you won't!" Ray shouted pointing at Lance. "Counseling! I don't need a counselor. And I am not a drunk!" Brother Ray Joseph said just as a burp escaped from his lips.

"I quit! Believe me, when word gets out, that I am no longer playing for New Light, there will be at least five churches calling me by the end of the week offering me a job! Your day is coming, Pastor Stevens! You have not heard the last from Brother Ray Joseph!"

When my husband asked him if he was gay, he promptly responded no, rolled his eyes, and strutted out the door. Now, I know most male musicians in the church are stereotyped as being gay or the complete opposite; highly sexually charged, hence, "a playa'" just as some preachers' wives are stereotyped as being fat, materialistic, and supremely talented in the gift of music. Yet, this young man never attended Bible study, he was pompous, he was not a continuous tither, and he was constantly bragging about going to shady nightclubs in Dallas. We should all love everyone regardless of their sin; however, the male role model we display in front of our boys is important. My husband advised this young man that if he did not agree to counseling, and take a sabbatical from participating as Minister of Music and a restoration plan that included weekly Bible study and continuous tithing, he would not play at the New Light Church.

Apparently, this young man had played at New Light since he was fifteen years old. It was a fiasco, when he was let go in writing. He demanded that his uncle, Mr. Chambers, a respected deacon of the church, expel my husband from the pulpit because he was a dictator, without a heart for all of God's children. He was fired, even though he told others in New

Light he quit from being worship leader. My husband encouraged him to remain a member of the church. Brother Joseph refused. We haven't heard from him in the last two months.

We know there is a riff of division, because Deacon Chambers has refused to pray with my husband and the other deacons before church ever since his nephew was officially fired. My husband had a meeting scheduled to talk about healing the division and bringing some biblical clarity on the issue. Lance pointed out that the church has the moral authority to talk about behavioral changes, and if the pastors wouldn't or couldn't try to give people the Word of God and explain the barriers of good and evil behaviors , then who would do it?

Deacon Chambers' wife, Jezzie Chambers had joined with Sister Finley in ignoring me during the fellowship time during worship, as they briskly walked past me to hug other parishioners. I was accustomed to members who were upset about something my husband did in the church, and tried to take it out on me. But, I refused to let people's ignorance hinder me from worshipping the Lord. Lance and I have both learned to pray for the promise and not focus on the problem. God promised He would never leave nor forsake us and that nothing could separate us from His love; not even mean and hateful church folks.

Lance quickly worked and prayed to find a suitable replacement and within three weeks, God had answered his prayer. I went with Lance to choir rehearsal as he introduced the new musician team, just in case he was going to need an extra prayer warrior.

The new worship leader would be Marcus Graves. Brother Graves is a recent graduate of one of the nearby universities. He has been married for seven years, and is the father of two young boys. He and his wife are both talented musicians and soloists in their own right.

My husband proudly announced, "Good evening choir, I am excited about what God has in store for New Light's Music

Ministry. I want you to meet Brother Marcus Graves, our new worship leader. This young man has come highly recommended, and most of all, he is saved and he loves Jesus. It is a pleasure to introduce New Light's new worship leader and coordinator, Brother Marcus Graves."

As Marcus stood at his grand introduction, he looked at all the faces in the choir. Some of them smiled in return, others dared not look him in the eye, and others had the silently sarcastic question, "What does he think he is going to do?"

Marcus exhaled. He opened up his first rehearsal with a prayer for the choir that past wounds and hurts would be healed with complete and total restoration for the choir. After the prayer, the eyes that seemed to avoid his eyes, gave him a, "He might just know what we need right now." He introduced his wife, Sister Juanita Graves, who slowly stood up as her husband spoke of her many musical gifts.

"This is my lovely wife of seven years, Sister Juanita Graves. She is a fine musician and soloist in her own right. But most of all, she is a prayer warrior and trusted confidante. We are both grateful that God has led us to New Light and we intend to give the Lord our all in our service to Him."

The pair made a handsome couple and their two small children were absolutely gorgeous.

Marcus Graves was six feet tall with dark brown skin, and curly black hair that formed soft short trinkets around his face. He had a lean, medium build, which illustrated that basketball might have been his favorite sport. Juanita was an ebony skinned, petite woman, and she was no more than 5'2", and probably weighing 120 pounds in a wet rain coat. She wore a short stylish brown and golden-streaked bob haircut that completed her oval frame face and a smile that could coo any little baby to sleep.

"Honey, would you like to say anything?" asked Brother Graves. Juanita quickly shook her head, waved, lowered her eyes, and returned to her seat without uttering a single word.

I thought to myself, *Girlfriend, you better get some guts, or these people will eat you alive. First impressions are everything in the church.* I needed to start praying for her strength.

Pastor and I watched as Brother Graves worked his magic with the New Light choir. First, he listened to every voice in the choir and made necessary adjustments, such as switching a soprano to alto, a tenor to baritone, etc. This young man had skills in music and organization. The choir was mesmerized by his natural tenor voice and pianist skills. His wife accompanied him on the piano, while he played the organ.

This just might work. I looked at my husband; he winked his eye at me and smiled. Lord, I prayed that my husband could finally get some peace. Lately, he'd been so restless due to all the talk surrounding why he fired Brother Joseph. Throughout his ministry, Lance would suffer through his "Jeremiah Experiences" where his soul would lament over the troubles of his church. He would become, at times, the weeping prophet and he wrestled spiritually with how to minister and reach the children of God. Those "Jeremiah Experiences" could wreck havoc on the clergy couple as the preacher would just shut down, cave in, become silent and wallow until, like the prophet Jeremiah in the Old Testament, find the fire and the passion again of renewal and hope to preach and teach God's sheep. I just hoped that everything will work out.

The following Sunday, the new and improved music ministry rocked the church house with Chester D.T. Baldwin's signature song, "God is Good." Brother and Sister Graves were awesome with their new style of praise and worship, which seemed to energize the young members in our church. They even introduced a new church theme song entitled, "The Light at New Light."

My husband preached a sermon entitled, "Knocked Down, but Not Out!" from the text of Second Corinthians 4:8-9, which states: "We are hard pressed on every side, but not crushed; perplexed, but not in despair; persecuted, but not abandoned; struck down, but not destroyed." Ten people joined Jesus and became members of our church on that Sunday! After five months at New Light, things were finally starting to come together. Thirteen people signed up to attend the next choir rehearsal with the new musician team. There was a new energy and an exciting flavor of worship emerging at New Light, and Lance and I began to rest in God's glory for all the new things He was doing within the church body.

Chapter Six

You Betta Watch & Pray

Lance was in the den watching another televangelist broadcast on Christian TV. I heard him throw a book at the TV. "How do these crooks, get on TV?" he yelled. "All they want to show on TV is a cross-less Christ that will bring them wealth. Where are all the preachers of the truth?" he said.

"Apparently, they are sitting at home just like you, on their easy chair complaining about the preachers on TV. Lance, you are so tied to the local church that you miss your broader ministry," I yelled back from the bedroom. I walked into the den. "Have you ever thought about a TV ministry? You could first start with the local cable company here in Southlake to air some of the worship services."

"I asked Sister Finley and Sister Chambers to look into that for me. I'm sure they will get us a reasonable price," Lance said with confidence as he put in a DVD of his latest sermon that was videoed at New Light.

He can forget that! Those two traditional ladies are not trying to do anything new and fresh. They wanted their ministry all to themselves. I learned that from the latest Women Ministry meeting held last week. I remember that meeting so clearly, because it defined for me where the heart of the tradition was at New Light and it wasn't about Christ.

"I am glad that our dear New Light is growing. But, I don't think it's necessary for us to have too many persons in our church. I like my seat," Sister Finley said in the meeting with a chuckle. *"Now, I have to get here fifteen minutes earlier just to get my parking spot and you know I cannot park my pink Cadillac on the street,"* she continued.

One of the newer members of the church, Julie Fresno, responded, *"Sister Finley, didn't Jesus say in His Word in Luke 14:23, 'Go out into the highways and hedges, and compel them to come in, that my house may be full'? So, wouldn't we become an enemy of God if we try to stop people from coming to Him?"*

"Hush, chile. What do you know about the Bible? You just joined our church!"

"Yes, ma'am, but I have been saved since the age of . . . " said Julie.

"That's fine," Sister Finley said cutting her off. *"We all know that we are to evangelize for Jesus. I am just not used to this new stuff coming in to New Light, but yes, we must tell others about Him."*

I held my tongue that night for the remainder of the Women Ministry meeting. I went home, and prayed for our church and its leadership. I slipped a note to dear old Sister Finley, concerning The Message Bible translation version of Luke 14:23 which says, "The master said, 'Then go to the country roads. Whoever you find, drag them in. I want my house full! Let me tell you, not one of those originally invited is going to get so much as a bite at my dinner party.'" I wonder if she would be trying to fight evangelism and winning souls for Christ then. She would still find a way to complain. Let me stop trying to focus on those church folks' handicaps, which I can't change, but focus on how the Lord can change me.

I looked at myself in the mirror. I gained fifteen pounds since we've been here. My Lord, who knows what I'll look like two years from now at the rate I'd been gaining weight. Our one year Pastor & Family's appreciation service was in six months. I don't want to walk down that aisle in a size 14-16 dress. What happened to me? Here I am, looking like I feared I would: a pudgy preacher's wife.

Lance hasn't complained about my recent weight gain. Last week, we had three young, beautiful, single women join our church, and the men did a double take on one woman in the red dress suit, with matching hat, purse, and shoes. Her bone straight jet black hair was down to her behind. I know she was sporting a 38-28-38 figure that she strutted down that aisle after giving her life to Christ. I heard she works at Verizon or something like that. She is 34 years old, and she had never been baptized or ever stepped into a church until she came to New Light.

Her testimony in church last Sunday was a definite tear-jerker. The Lady in Red strolled up the middle aisle, as the invitation to join Jesus was given. She sat in the chair, and crossed her legs, where the split in her skirt exposed her very shapely golden light brown legs. As Lance approached her to give her remarks to the congregation, a huge smile escaped from her face in the midst of her tears. She slowly rose from her chair and said, "To the good people of New Light, I am so glad to be here today. Pastor Stevens, your sermon touched my heart today. I am new to the community, and I am seeking a spiritual counselor and a new spiritual family. You see, I have obtained a good education, and good money but there is still a void. I know now, today, what that void was. I needed the love of Jesus to recapture my soul. I need to do more for the Lord and work with His people to build up His Kingdom and lead others to the Lord. I am finally ready to make a change in my life and I would like to be baptized, Pastor. I am ready to go in the water!"

People all over the church were crying and lifting up their hands in praise for God's power in bringing her to New Light.

Sister Peterson, the church mother and the oldest active member in the church, wrote me a note in church and scribbled, "First Lady, you betta' watch that woman in that red suit. She means us no good at New Light and you betta' pray. You betta' watch and pray! That woman belongs to the W.A.P group; Women After Preachers. Watch my word, you are going to have to WAP her real good!"

Sister Peterson was seventy-nine years old. She was always writing notes in church, and giving people warnings and advice. When I first came to New Light, I thought she was some type of voodoo woman because she always bragged about her mama's Louisiana roots and upbringing. She was known to walk into church with her beaded cane, and purple feather hat. Since then, I see her as a church mother. Unfortunately, this wasn't the first time Sister Peterson insinuated that I needed to watch that woman or this woman. Any time a halfway decent single woman under the age of 45 joined New Light, Sister Peterson would give me "the eye," which said "Watch this one too." She had an old Southern traditional hymn that I called her code word hymn. If she was trying to give me a warning about another sister in the church. Sister Peterson would walk by and sing:

"I don't know what Jesus is to you.

But I hope He is to you what He is to me. He's my all, my all, and all.

He's my chief cornerstone.

I don't know what Jesus is to you, but I hope He is to you what He is to me."

If I heard Sister Peterson singing this song, sure enough there would be an attractive woman in the room. When we first arrived at New Light, she used to scare my children to death singing that song all the time as she walked about doing her church work.

Sister Peterson had a time with "other women", when dealing with her late preacher husband, Pastor Henry Peterson.

Personal experience can hinder anyone's fair judgment of people. As a result, Sister Peterson was always "looking out" for her pastor's wife. She loved to tell me that, just like some women are groupies around NFL or NBA bound men, there are women predators Women After Prayers groupies within the church who would stop at nothing to attract the wandering eye of a preacher. Well, that's Sister Peterson and all of her insecurities and her so called prophesies.

Sometimes, it bothered me. I learned early in my life as a preacher's wife that you shouldn't let people use your head for a trash can, by bringing me all of the junk or gossip in church.

I knew every woman in the church didn't desire my husband. Most were attracted to my husband because of his favor from God. Have you even seen a knock out, drop dead gorgeous pastor? Most pastors look like your classic "big brother" type fellows; not really someone you would like to look at twice if you saw them walking down the street. But, it is a preacher's sensitivity toward people and love for God that is attractive for most women. Lord knows if they knew what I know now, they might reconsider. Don't get me wrong. I love my husband. I remember the first time we met in the University College Choir.

I had walked in choir rehearsal wearing a pink silk blouse, black chiffon skirt, and heeled pink sandals. My hair then was light brown and fell just beneath my shoulders. I boasted a trimmed down size eight. I felt and looked good. I wanted to make a good first impression with the choir music staff. I was so excited that the University of Texas had a gospel choir for its students. I had been singing gospel music in the church since I was three years old. My first public solo was, "Oh, How I Love Jesus." I looked forward to meeting other college students, who loved gospel music as much as I did. It was the initial rehearsal for the choir that year. I walked into a room of over fifty African-American faces, and I was so grateful to see others on campus that looked like me. I realized I was home.

Everyone was so nice and kind, welcoming all of the new freshmen to rehearsal. We started singing and the choir director requested all of the sopranos to sing an A flat note. I belted out my customary soprano voice, and the entire choir seemed to turn to me with a look on their faces that exclaimed, "Who is that?" In the midst of their faces, I noticed a dark mahogany colored brother in the tenor section, who gave me the sweetest smile from across the room, then nodded his head in a way that seemed to say, "Welcome." Toward the end of rehearsal, everyone introduced themselves.

And then it was my turn to introduce myself:

"Hello, my name is Jacqueline Montgomery and I am a freshman. My major is journalism with a minor in marketing. I am originally from Richmond, Texas, and I graduated from Richmond High School. I am really happy to be here. I have been singing in the church since I was three years old and I know now that I have finally found some Christian friends here at the University of Texas who love gospel music just like I do." I gave them my best smile and quickly took my seat.

And then it was his turn:

"Hello. Welcome to The University of Texas. My name is Lance McClain Stevens. I am a returning junior. Yes, I made it through those first two years. Thank you, Jesus! I am originally from Houston, Texas, and I graduated from Jack Yates High School. I am currently majoring in Business with a minor in Philosophy. I am one of the newly elected choir directors of UT's Gospel Choir. We have great expectations for this choir, not just musically, but spiritually as well. Welcome to the University of Texas! Hook 'em Horns!"

He sat down and winked his eye at me from across the room. I was immediately uncomfortable and looked away from his gaze. A philosophy major? Who was he fooling? I figured he was preparing to preach. Lord knows, I didn't want to be a preacher's wife.

After rehearsal, Lance found his way to the soprano section, our eyes met and I made a dash to the door. Just as I was about to grab the doorknob, a short pudgy alto crossed me off, "Hi, my name is Amanda Deshay. Welcome to the University. I noticed that you live across the hall from me. I'm a sophomore originally from Houston, Texas. Are you on your way back to the dorm?

"Uh, yes," I replied.

"Hey, let's walk together," Amanda volunteered.

"Excuse me, Ms. Montgomery."

I turned around and there he was with this big wide Denzel Washington-like smile. It was Lance McClain Stevens.

"I noticed that you sing first soprano quite well and we could really use your voice as one of our choir soloist and section leader. Our last soprano section leader graduated last year. What do you think?" he asked.

"Uh, well, I guess that'll be okay," I nervously answered. I don't know why I was so easily intimidated by this upperclassman. It must have been his broad shoulders, his 6'3 football player built frame and his cute deep dimples that caused me to feel so uncomfortable. Or perhaps it was his absolutely perfect pearly white teeth that caused my dizziness. I loved a man with a great set of beautiful white teeth. I thought I was about to faint for a moment.

"Great, our first rehearsal for the section leaders is this Thursday at 7 p.m. in this same place. It was really nice meeting you," said Lance with a gleam in his eye. He put out his hand, and I gave him mine. He had the strongest and firmest handshake. I like a man with a firm handshake. My grandfather always told me a man with a firm handshake had character, inner strength and integrity.

Amanda and I watched him as he turned and walked away to meet with the other musicians and choir leaders.

"Girl, did you see the way he looked at you?" exclaimed Amanda as we walked toward our dormitory.

"He was just being nice," I said.

"Girl, you better recognize the difference between, nice and *nice*, if you know what I mean. Lance Stevens has never looked at any girl in the choir the way he looked at you tonight. Girl, you just might be Mrs. Lance McClain Stevens."

"What do you mean?" I asked.

"I mean he has been too fixated on his music and his studies to even give any of the girls in the choir the time of day. That boy has seen some women obsess over him and he wouldn't even look at them twice. Have you heard him sing?"

"No," I said.

"Girl, the boy has a gospel Sam Cook sound. And he has range like gospel singers John P. Kee and Fred Hammond. Simply put, the boy has mad singing skills."

"Then why is he majoring in business?" I asked.

"Well, he's a brainy guy too and he follows God's purpose for his life, and right now, it's to get an education."

"Sounds like you know a lot about him."

"Lance is my second cousin. Our grandmothers were sisters. So, I do know a lot about him. During my freshman year, all of these junior and senior girls from the choir were trying to befriend me just to get closer to him."

"That must have been devastating."

"I received what I wanted out of my connection with Lance as well. Instantly, I was popular on campus because of my relationships with so many people. But, I haven't seen my cousin look at another female the way he looked at you tonight."

"I am not interested," I said, looking away.

Amanda looked surprised.

"Oh, I get it, someone back home? Yeah, me too. But, don't you want someone locally too? Why can't you have your cake and eat it too? The guys around here do it all the time."

"I want to concentrate on my studies, and I am not interested in dating a preacher."

"Lance is not preaching right now."

"He may not be now, but he will be. I discerned that the moment he introduced himself. My purpose in life is to not be a preacher's wife. I want to be my own woman and own my own public relations/marketing firm."

"Yeah, you are probably right about Lance. My grandmother said that he is just running from the pulpit. She said that Lance started preaching when he was two years old. He would mimic our old Pastor Barnes at our family's home church in Houston. They said Lance would spit, holler and wave his arms in a chicken dance when he was so-called "preaching." And my grandma said Lance loved to go to church and would fall out if his grandmother didn't take him to Sunday school. He did that from the age of two until he was five-years-old."

"He seems like a decent guy and I am sure we can be friends," I said.

"Well, you are now my new friend," Amanda said as we turned to enter our separate hall rooms. "Listen if you need anything, just let me know."

"I will. Thanks, Amanda, for walking home with me," I told her.

"Oh, girl, it's okay. We live in the same dorm, so we might as well keep each other company."

"Okay, Amanda, you have a nice night. And let your cousin, know I said goodnight as well."

With that, she turned around with excitement in her eye and said, "You can bet on that."

Chapter Seven

A Time to Pray

It was dawn. The birds were chirping, and the smell of spring was in the air. But, something wasn't quite right. I got out of bed, found my robe, and headed to my prayer corner. I am grateful that Lance is a man who believes in the power of prayer. After Lance called in a contractor to paint the parsonage walls a neutral light brown, he had them build a nook and special altar that faced the window.

The house was quiet as I made my way to our place of prayer. Lance was in Austin preaching a three day revival. The children were in bed asleep, so this was my precious time alone with Jesus. A pang of sadness overwhelmed me. I am not sure where it came from, but I felt a sincere need to intercede for our church, and for my husband. I fell on my knees in prayer.

"Dear God, the most High and Omnipotent. You are the Holiest of Holies. I adore your name, Jesus. I thank you for all of your blessings. I thank you for my family, and the church that you have blessed us with. Lord, I come interceding for my precious husband. Lord, protect him from all hurt and danger. Keep him in your loving arms. Keep him humble, oh God.

Speak to him so that he may speak to your people. Cleanse him from any sin and restore his spirit. Give him the joy of our salvation. Watch over our babies and show them your way; direct them and guide them. Lord, I pray for the sick in our church; the spiritually sick and the physically sick. Give us all a hunger for your Word and a desire to do your will. Watch over New Light and every church that stands open in your name. Let us all possess a kingdom building spirit to overtake the world for Christ. And I pray that Sister Mary Temple will one day be restored to her right mind, and her trust in you completely restored. I praise you, Jesus, for all that you have done for our family, our church, and our friends. In Jesus name, I do pray right now, that your perfect, divine will be done. Amen."

I always pray for Mary Temple, a senior pastor's wife I met just five years earlier at a Ministers' Wives Conference in Galveston, Texas. Mary was a brilliant speaker at the conference. She testified about her 15 years as a senior pastor's wife with a 3,000 plus member congregation. She was a marvelous speaker, who testified about her Christian journey in the role of a minister's wife. She shared her mistakes, her bitterness, her anger, and then her joy. Mary was now seeing a psychiatrist, after suffering an exhaustive breakdown two years ago.

After eighteen years of marriage, she discovered her husband was having an affair with a fellow male parishioner, and he suffered from sexual addiction. He had sex with men and women. Mary was devastated and humiliated as news of her husband's indecent affairs became public knowledge. They watched as the church membership fell to under 100 members in just eight short months.

Everything sacrificed for was stripped away by a total confession from her husband. He confessed he had a life-threatening sexually transmitted disease. Her husband died three years ago with Mary by his side. She forgave her husband, but she failed to address her own emotional and mental needs. So, one day her mind just snapped.

"Lord, I wonder if I would be able to handle everything she had to go through," I said out loud. My heart still ached for Mary Temple. At that moment, my spirit longed for my husband to return by my side. I miss him so much when he is gone. I walked to the phone to dial his hotel number.

"Hello," he said with a groggy voice.

"Hey, babe, I just wanted to hear your voice," I said. "How was service last night?"

"We had a great time. The Holy Spirit was in the place. What time is it?"

"It's about 5:45 a.m. I'm sorry to call you so early, but I miss you when you are gone." I paused to measure my next words. "Is everything okay, sweetie? I woke up with a strong urge to pray for you this morning."

"Did you pray for me?" Lance asked.

"Of course, sweetie. Is everything okay?"

"I got a phone call from the chairman, Deacon Jenkins, late last night. We're going to have a meeting soon."

"What about?" I asked.

"I am not too sure, but it may have to do with our former musician. I heard that he has been sabotaging me with the ministers in the area, and he is making accusations against me."

"Accusations? That boy hardly knows you! What kind of accusations?"

"Honey, we'll talk about it when I return. I don't want to focus on that while I am trying to focus on the message for this revival. I don't want Satan to distract me."

"I know, baby."

"What food do you want me to prepare for you when you come home?" I asked.

"I will probably go with Pastor West and some of the other preachers to dinner Thursday night. But, I look forward to breakfast in bed with you, Goldie."

I loved it when he called me Goldie!

"Alright, babe, you got it! Should I have the honey ready?" I asked in my sexy whispering voice.

"Yes, yes, get it ready for me!"

I love that we still have the passion to satisfy one another in more ways than one.

"I love you, baby," I said.

"I love you too, Goldie. Give my children a big hug from their daddy, and let Junior know I will be at his game on Friday. That is a promise!"

"Okay, get some rest, bye."

I hung up the phone and sighed, grateful that my husband loved me and his family. I thanked God for waking me up to say a prayer for him. I knew something wasn't quite right. Over the years, I have learned to pray for my husband and my family.

I believe it is something that God gives the Christian woman, to be in tune with her family. It is the still small voice or the gut feeling of a woman's instinct to guard and protect her family. Big Mama Thompson always said if I could not sleep at night, then God was waking me up to pray and ask Him to cover my situations, family, and friends with prayer. I remember as a little girl, waking up to my grandmother's prayers. "Lord, bless my family, keep us together, make us strong and bold for your glory." Yes, Johnnie Mae Thompson could pray, and I loved hearing her talk to her God.

Big Mama T, as her grandchildren still affectionately call her, taught us to strive for our dreams and keep God first in our life. I thanked God we are blessed to still have her on this earth to give us her wisdom. Big Mama T is a go-getter. She and Big Daddy owned two restaurants and the first black nursing home in the small city of Richmond, Texas. They had over 30 rent houses, and were very active in local politics and the church. They were also financial lenders to the black community, loaning money and charging thirty-five percent interest. Yes, you heard me right, thirty-five percent interest! Big

Mama T said she charged thirty-five percent because it was to discourage everybody from seeking a loan from them. Typically, they loaned money for emergencies when the family could not get a loan from the local white-owned bank or from family members. But, she prided herself in loaning her people money because she gave them up to five years to pay them back. My maternal grandparents did very well for themselves. It wasn't their houses and land that impressed me; it was their devotion to prayer, God, and His church.

Big Daddy only had a sixth grade education and he couldn't read very well. So every week, I had to read the Sunday School lesson to him, and he would memorize the words so that he could teach it on Sunday. He was the chairman of the deacon board, and the Sunday School superintendent. Very few of the church folks knew that he couldn't read that well. However, reading the Bible and the Sunday School lessons for my big daddy gave me a love for God's Word.

My parents lived across town in Richmond, Texas on family inherited land called Montgomery Quarters. It was family legacy that my paternal great-great-great grandfather was a famous southern carpenter and he saved his monies from his work to buy over 100 acres of land that he divided up among his family members. He named this acreage "Montgomery Quarters." For over 75 years the Montgomery descendants lived and retired on this land.

In the 1970s my great-uncle, Robert Montgomery, who was an architect, redeveloped the land and developed a 50-house plot subdivision which was aptly named Montgomery Estates. Each four bedroom house sat on at least three acres of land. Each plot consisted of sidewalks, curbed streets, three parks, and a recreation center. This is where my parents built their dream home while I was still in high school. Frankly, I thought our five bedroom farm house on ten acres was a great place, but my daddy agreed to let Uncle Robert redevelop our land and make it a part of Montgomery Estates. Uncle Robert turned it into a seven bedroom-four bathroom, and three car garage with beautiful green landscaping paradise. I still re-member my mother's face when our new home was complete.

A small tear of joy fell from her face, as my mother looked at me and said, "One day, this will be yours. This is our family legacy. Our family's sweat, tears and hard work defines this land. Never forget the sacrifice." I was the oldest of three girls, and my mother was always talking to me about taking care of my younger sisters and honoring the family legacy of land and prosperity.

You can imagine her disappointment, when I married a smart, intelligent, working class preacher. My mother was Eva Montgomery, wife of Attorney John Montgomery and daugh-ter to Edward and Johnnie Mae Thompson. Both affiliations gave her great pride and she was considered to be a blessed woman of prosperity in our small town of Richmond. Eva wanted nothing, but the best for her three daughters. My mother was a woman who loved the Lord, but I wondered if she just attended church because it was considered to be a "proper" thing for women of prestige. Going to church in the South was an unspoken rule for most women of money, black or white. I still recall an article in *Jet Magazine* I saw my mother reading, which said most middle class people attend church. She remarked after completing the article, "If our people in the ghettos would just attend church, it just may take them out of poverty. But they would rather wait for their monthly government check. It's so sad, so sad."

That was my mama. She attended our local family church, Mount Moriah Church, founded by my maternal great, great uncle. My mom was a deaconess, a youth matron, member of the Local Links Chapter, charter member of the local Jack-N-Jill, charter member of Delta Sigma Theta Sorority Alumnae in Richmond and a graduate of Texas Southern University where she obtained her B.S. and Masters in education in the 1960's. She married John Montgomery, then a law student at

Texas Southern University and heir to vast land in the Montgomery Quarters in Richmond.

I absolutely adored my daddy. He was the balance that our family needed. He was quiet, strong, and humble. He loved his daughters. He taught us strength, ambition, and the love of Jesus. In the eyes of our father, his daughters could do no wrong. However, he was a strong disciplinarian who taught us about hard work and efficiency. He would work us like boys on the ranch. He taught us how to change a tire on a car, and unclog a sink drain, and then my daddy would cuddle his girls like his little darlings. John Montgomery was a bear in the courtroom. He was one of the few black attorneys in the local Richmond area. Furthermore, Houston area judges and attorneys of all nationalities respected him.

He served as a deacon at Mt. Moriah. I believe he passed up his calling as a minister due to my mama's absolute objections to being a minister's wife. She did not want to be called a minister's wife and experience all of the restrictions that came along with it. I would hear my parents argue many times about my daddy's desire to preach, and my mama telling him that he was doing fine as just a deacon in the church. She was afraid of the pulpit and its demands. Besides, she felt like he had more control in the church as a deacon. She loved my daddy so much that she didn't want to share him with anyone, especially not any of the sisters in Richmond, who eyed her husband every Sunday. She did not want to leave their precious land if daddy was given a call to pastor a church in a new city. She loved her life in Richmond.

Daddy died of a heart attack at age fifty-six. I was devastated. I rushed home from our small church in Cypress, Texas to be by my daddy's side as he whispered his last breaths. He died in my mother's arms as she sang, "Yes, Jesus loves you." We made the difficult decision to remove him from life support as the doctors told us that he was legally brain dead. It seemed as if my whole world was falling apart. Daddy was my strength. The one who made me laugh, who held me in his arms, and said everything would be okay, was gone.

He died two years after Lance received the call to pastor a small church in Cypress, Texas, named Mt. Bethel Church. His pastorate lasted only four years. He resigned due to the deacon board's desire to tell him what to preach and what not to preach. Their wives refused to speak to me and pretty much acted like I didn't even exist. That was, until my son spilled some crackers on their beloved carpeted church floors.

I'll never forget that Sunday morning, Sister Newsome noticed that my eight-month-old son, who was teething at the time, dropped some crackers on the floor. She got all in my face, stating, "It's people like you who give the saints of God so much to worry about. Did you not see your baby dropping these crumbs on the floor? Are you blind, Sister Stevens? I don't care if he is a baby, thou shall not eat in the Holy Sanctuary of the Most High God! And that goes for your baby too! You are supposed to be setting a good example for the young women of Mt. Bethel, but instead you don't have any respect for our God. And to think, He chose you to be a minister's wife!"

As she screamed, spit from her crazy verbal rampage landed on my dress. I chose not to respond. I grabbed my baby, my Bible, politely smiled, rolled my eyes, turned my heels, and walked away. You know, it is those legalistic Christians who will be sour about not receiving any rewards when they get to heaven due to how they treated others. Sister Newsome never asked me how my baby was doing, neither did she know that he was having a terrible time teething, and was on medication to relieve his pain. All she saw were the crackers on the floor. It was just a crazy situation, and I was grateful to God when Lance resigned from Mt. Bethel and we moved to Tyler, Texas to pastor Little Mt. Zion Church for eight and a half years.

I shook away the demons of my past, and walked upstairs to grab my journal. If I focused too much on the negative people in my life, I would spiral into a tornado of bitterness. I returned to the prayer nook with my journal and wrote.

Dear Jesus,

As I kneel here and reflect, Lord, you have brought us a mighty long way and you have protected us throughout the entire process of ministry. Thank you, Lord, for your mercy and goodness toward my family. I thank you for my strong Christian heritage. Help me to instill the love of family and faith in my children. Lord, I thank you and praise you for our present condition. Help me evolve and strive to be more like you, Jesus. I long to be like you. Help me celebrate and suffer in you. Thank You, Jesus, you have been good to us in spite of what others may have done or said to us. Thank you for always leading us from trials and tribulations to triumph. Now, Lord, protect Lance and move like only you can with this new dilemma. Stop the accusations; hold the tongue of Brother Ray Joseph. Release your angels of power to control his actions. I pray for that young man's salvation and restoration, dear Jesus. I pray for the preached Word that Lance will bring during Revival, that sinners will be saved, and saints restored and encouraged. Protect my husband from any danger, and return him safely home to his family.

I looked out of the window of our prayer nook as the dawn peeked beneath the shadows. God's morning was approaching. This subtle picture of beauty assured me that all was well with my soul. Tears of joy fell gently down my face. God, thank you, for joy in this journey.

Chapter Eight

Traditions

It was early Sunday morning on a beautiful spring Texas day. New Light Fellowship Hall was littered with the early bird saints who arrived at 6:45 a.m. for prayer, coffee and conversation. This tradition of the deacons, ministers and their wives meeting in the early Sunday morning started at New Light over fifty years ago as the leaders of the church would meet to fellowship and start planning for morning worship. It was during this time that the deacons and ministers would sit at the table, drink coffee, and talk about community happenings and plans for the church. This fellowship time was equivalent to businessmen who met on the golf course to secure their business dealings and ventures. This was also a time where the deacons' and ministers' wives would fellowship and spend time encouraging one another. This particular Sunday morning, Sister Peterson arrived at 6:45 a.m. with her beige winter hat, beige matching cane, purse, and a winter white pearl lace dress that fell to her ankles. The only thing that spoke to Sister Peterson's beginning dementia were her white stockings and red sandal shoes that she wore with this outfit.

"Good morning, Sister Stevens," said Sister Peterson. "I

haven't seen you at the morning gathering for quite some time."

"Good morning, Sister. The children stayed at the Caldwell's last night, so I am able to come and join the fellowship this morning. How are you feeling, Sister Peterson?" I asked.

"The Good Lawd has blessed me to see another Sunday morning! I will be eighty years old on July 14th, and I praise God for every new day! Hallelujah!"

"I am grateful too, Sister Peterson, for a new morning that I have never seen before," I said.

Sister Peterson sat her lean frame down at the table, kindly placing her cane and Bible by her side. It was quiet in the fellowship hall as Sister Peterson looked around to see who was around us.

"Sister Stevens," she said.

"Yes," I replied.

"Why do you let these folks call you First Lady? When my husband was pasturing, he told me that I wasn't the first lady. He was adamant that the church was his first lady, and he would outright denounce that saying. I didn't like it either, and would tell off any member that called me First Lady."

"I consider it a term of endearment. You know, it's a phrase of respect. It doesn't hurt my feelings when they call me that, Sister Peterson. At first, I didn't embrace it. But, I don't hinder anyone from calling me that now. I see it as the same type of respect that preachers give each other when they call each other "Doc." Now you and I both know that a lot of black preachers with "Dr." in front of their name haven't completed any type of accredited doctoral program. So the title "First Lady" is also equivalent to the fact that we call preachers Reverend as a term of endearment or a sign of respect. The exact word reverend is not even mentioned in the Bible when speaking concerning ministers, preachers, or elders, but it is a word that was developed by men taken from the word reverence as a token of respect. We are to respect and give double honor to the man of God. Therefore, First Lady and Reverend are terms of respect and endearment."

"Chile, it seems like you did your homework on that. Well, I have to confess. I told some members to stop calling you First Lady, because you weren't anybody's first lady. You were a member just like the rest of us."

"I am a member, Sister Peterson. I come to church, participate, and pay my tithes just like you do," I said.

"I know. I guess I'm just stuck in tradition that's all," said Sister Peterson.

"Don't worry, it is not a salvation issue," I said with a smile.

"I remember all the sacrifices I made for our church. My Henry put everything before his family. He truly believed the church came before his family. He put the church, his money and his women before us. You know I can't be upset that two of our six children have not set foot in a church in over twenty years. They resented the church for taking their daddy away from them. Your husband preached a sermon just two months ago about prioritizing in your Christian journey. He called that sermon, 'The Right Order.' I recall him saying that it's: God, family, and church in that order. If only my Henry would have had that type of order in his life. Sometimes, I think the man married me just so he could pastor a church."

"Oh, Sister Peterson, don't say that," I said.

"It's probably true. We were married over forty years, and he never really let me in his heart until his last few years. He loved the church so much. She was his first lady. Yeah, his first lady . . . He let the women in the church just treat me any kind of way. You know, I had a fight on the church steps with one of his women!"

"Sister Peterson, you have got to be kidding."

"Naw, chile. I whooped that woman up something good. She came flaunting up to me and whispered in my ear, 'He sure was good last night.' Before I knew it, I whacked that heifer with my purse and my Bible. It took three deacons to get me off of her. My Henry just stayed in his office the next two hours, too embarrassed to preach that morning. The poor fool had to pick me up from jail after church that evening. All he kept saying was that he was so sorry. One time he even had the nerve to tell me that he had a three-week revival in upstate New York. Baby, by this time we were married for about twenty-five years and I was sick of the lies and his games. I had never flown on an airplane before, but I bought a ticket and flew to his so called three-week revival," said Sister Peterson.

"Well, was your Henry at a revival?" I asked.

"That was one time I caught him at his game. He did have a revival. It was a four-day revival. But I caught him with a twenty-three-year-old gal just living the life in the summertime of upper New York. You would have thought the man had a heart attack when he saw me walking up to him on that beach."

"What made me you stay by his side?" I quizzed Sister Peterson.

"You see, the man loved his church so much, that he was afraid that I would let the church members know. I hired a private investigator to take pictures of him and his woman before I caught him red handed on that beach. And, I played my own game. I told him I wanted to become a full-time house-wife and retire. At the time, I was working two jobs as a teacher and an after school counselor to send our babies to college. I made him promise to send all of our children to the college or trade school of their choice and that I would quit my jobs to support him in ministry, travel with him or else those photos would find their way to his beloved church deacon board."

"Oh no, you didn't, Sister Peterson!" I said with a hearty laugh.

"Yes I did. I was too old and I wasn't trying to find another man, so I could train him too. I made that Henry do right by me, because he had a greater love for the church, but loved the adoration that the church gave him and he put them before God and his family. So honey, if I sometimes sound like a bitter woman, I probably am at times. I am praying that God takes this bitterness away from me completely. I know what Proverbs says about bitterness in 17:22, 'A merry heart does good like medicine, but a broken spirit dries the bones.' So I am learning to have a merry heart in spite of what has occurred in my life, because I don't want these bones of mine to become brittle and my heart cold.

"I learned to forgive my Henry with a merry heart. You know I have cooled down some. I didn't trust any woman with an hour-glass figure and bone straight hair that walked in our church. But, I just didn't trust my Henry around any good-looking woman. They made that man weak in the knees. Everyone has a weakness or sin they have to overcome, including a few of our preacher men. My Henry once said that a sermon should be just like a skirt, long enough to cover the most important stuff and short enough to still be interesting. Yes, indeed, my Henry loved to chase after them skirts, but that pretty yella' Negro could preach!" chuckled Sister Peterson.

"Excuse me for asking, Sister Peterson, but what happened to him?"

"Ten years ago, he died of a prostate cancer at the age of seventy-two. You know he was player in his day, but the last twelve years of his life, that man was completely loyal to me. He retired from the church at the age of sixty-five and I think Godly wisdom taught him the error of his ways. All of our children have professional degrees, thanks to their daddy's promise to send them to college, and three of them are active in their church and community."

I often wondered why Sister Peterson came to church alone, so I was surprised to learn that she had so many children.

"Where are your children now, Sister Peterson?" I asked.

"My oldest boy lives in New York City. He is an accountant and a minister. He has two children. The rest of my children live in Atlanta, Georgia. One is an attorney, the other a college professor, and two of them are engineers. My baby boy is a pastor in Decatur, Georgia. We are all so proud of him. All together they have given me twelve beautiful grandchildren and two great grandchildren. Yes, chile the Lord blessed me with my family! My Henry would be so proud of his children."

"What brought you to Texas, Sister Peterson?"

"Why this is my father's family's home, I inherited a house from my paternal grandmother in Southlake. Henry and I retired here after he retired from the church. He promised me that we would move to northeast Texas and spend our last days together."

"Do you think Mr. Henry loved you?" I carefully quipped.

"I think Henry learned to love me. I don't know if it was that, or the onset of prostate cancer he developed that actually slowed his playing days down. You know this time was before the days of Viagra," laughed Sister Peterson.

"I don't think his motivations were pure when we first married, but the good Lord, after many years, turned Henry's heart toward me. I think it's because I always prayed that God would grant me favor and give Henry a genuine love for me. So in our old age, he fell in love with me for the first time. You know, one person may not mean a lot to the world, but one person can be a world to someone else. My Henry, well, he was my world. Though our times were tough, I loved that man and I know he opened his heart to love me. I've learned that most people don't know how to love others, they just want to be loved by someone else. Yet Henry learned how to truly love me, by witnessing my love for him and seeing God's love of forgiveness and longsuffering through me. I knew that God would teach Henry how to truly love others and not try to seek satisfaction from empty places. Our lives are void, when we never learn how to love others. Yes, sister, my Henry learned how to love and stopped trying to seek love and acceptance from others to justify his purpose and existence."

"Sister Peterson, that is a beautiful story!!"

"God knows what he is doing," said Sister Peterson, grabbing her cane while looking around to see the young children coming into the fellowship hall to start their Sunday School class. Sister Peterson wobbled her way up to a stance.

With a sparkle in her eye and a wink, Sister Peterson said, "I guess it's time for us to stop talking and prepare to learn about the Lord. Come on, First Lady. Let's get ready for class."

I looked at her, when she called me First Lady. It was a term she never used to refer to me. However, her wink let me know that she shared something special with me. She opened up her chest of treasures, and allowed me to look inside her past history to help me understand the Sister Peterson she is today. I watched as this nostalgic seventy-nine year old woman made her way to her Sunday School class and I then admired her dedication to God to serve Him in spite of her own disappointments and pitfalls in her life.

Without missing a beat, Sister Peterson turned around and said, "First Lady, you need to watch them young women around your husband. Treat your husband like a king and he will treat you like the queen. They don't necessarily want your husband they just want the favor that God has on his life. Pray for your husband that he won't be weak in the knees for those young thangs like my Henry. But, if those sisters mess with ya' just give em' one good left hook. That'll teach them to leave ya' alone."

"Yes, ma'am," I replied.

I grabbed my Bible and purse and joined her walking toward the Adult Women's Sunday School class. I thought to myself, this woman is still somewhat crazy and thinks that every woman is after the preacher man. It was sad that in her old age she characterized every single woman in the church under the age of fifty-five as a roaming predator of married preacher men. I shook my head, and smiled as the image of Sister Peterson fighting a woman on the church steps entered my mind. If dementia did take her good mind, she still did have her fighting spirit and a good left hook.

Chapter Nine

The "Heavenly Hands" Experience

Upon relocating to northeast Texas, I loved, and at times hated, going to Vivian's Heavenly Hands Beauty Salon. This was where the women of Southlake gathered together for community gossip. Often, the people and the good church folks of Southlake were the top discussions. I think the conversation often turned to church because of Vivian's bitterness over the church.

Vivian Daniels, the owner and operator of Heavenly Hands, was an accomplished organist who had played at various churches within the county since the age of twelve. However, she and her then pastor had a disagreement and she left the church for good. She hasn't played a church organ in over ten years.

At the age of forty-seven, Vivian lived a carefree life, free of the demand of playing in church Sunday after Sunday. She traveled extensively and loved to watch those televangelists who taught prosperity and finance. Vivian believed in the principle of prosperity so much that it led her to the Louisiana casinos and the Houston horse tracks on a monthly basis. So naturally, she loved when folks came into the shop with their share of church news-namely bad news.

Vivian was known for her expensive taste, and her salon was always decorated to a tee. Every three months, she changed the color scheme of her salon. Today, it was decorated in pink and green. Ms. Vivian loved to pamper her customers, so today she catered from her cousin, Thelma Henderson's, restaurant. The spread included fried catfish and shrimp for her afternoon customers.

I walked into the salon to see Ms. Vivian's tall 5'9, voluptuous frame walk elegantly toward me to give me her trademark bear hug, which was the customary greeting for all of her customers. Ms. Vivian could have easily been a model with her oval mahogany shaped face and her lean but strong frame. She was wearing long golden micro braids in a Japanese twist up do. Her spring green linen dress and matching green sandals were a great accent to her recently redecorated salon draperies and accessories.

"Good afternoon, Sister Stevens. How are you doing?" asked Vivian.

"I am fine, Ms. Vivian," I said.

"How is the preacher and those beautiful children?"

"The Lord is blessing us. I love your pink and green decorations this quarter."

I noticed a pink and green elephant on the salon shelf and I thought to myself, if my Mother Dear, who was a faithful member of Delta Sigma Theta, were to see this pink and green elephant, she would faint.

"Sister Stevens, what can I do for you today?" asked Ms. Vivian.

"I think I need a relaxer, and I'll take one of your classic Ms. Vivian French rolls."

People from as far away as 100 miles came to Ms. Vivian's Heavenly Hands to receive one of her signature French rolls.

Lance loved when I had my hair in one of those up 'dos. He said that Ms. Vivian's French rolls made me look like a princess. So I thought that I would get a nice up do for his return on Thursday night.

I made an appointment for him at our local Total Wellness Spa to receive a massage and a pedicure. I pray nothing interrupts this appointment for Lance. I constantly encourage him to take care of himself physically, or I would be a widow at fifty years old if he didn't learn to relax and pamper himself.

Interrupting my thoughts, Vivian said, "Come have a seat. I am ready for you now." I followed her to her chair as she continued to speak. "So how is the great New Light Church?" she asked in her customary sarcastic tone.

I sat down in the chair, while Vivian began to brush my hair and spray some soft sheen on my scalp to prepare for the application of my relaxer. "The church is doing fine. The Lord is blessing us," I replied.

I learned early in the days of being a pastor's wife that people loved to "pick" the pastor's wife to find out if certain rumors or gossip being circulated was true. Preachers' wives were automatically deemed credible as if they had a 411 on the truth of a matter.

"I heard you all got rid of your former musician and the Lord has blessed you with a dynamic duo in Marcus and Juanita Graves," said Vivian.

"Yes, the Lord has blessed us with a great musical team in the Graveses," I said, purposefully not trying to answer the first comment about our former musician. I had learned that short and sweet responses were key to getting persons to feel uncomfortable enough to eventually change a subject.

I looked at Vivian's reflection in the mirror as she applied my relaxer. She was probably trying to figure out what question to ask me next. I heard that the youngest pastor's wife of Southlake, Sister Patricia Wiley, had been in Heavenly Hands and Vivian gave her an onslaught of questions about her church.

Sister Wiley, at thirty-one years of age, resented the demands and the fishbowl experience of being a preacher's wife. Every week, she came into Heavenly Hands and gave her own brand of church gossip and her own hurts within the church. I heard Sister Wiley fell for every "pick" that Vivian and her local customers asked of her. On the other hand, I was a seasoned preacher's wife who understood credibility and being discreet. I knew I could win Vivian's respect, by illustrating discretion in protecting my family and church. After all, you can't misquote silence.

"Have you talked to Sister Wiley lately?" Vivian asked.

"I haven't seen or spoken to Sister Wiley in over a month," I carefully responded. I thought to myself that I probably wouldn't be speaking to her any time soon since I hadn't heard from her after calling her up and cautioning her about her tongue.

Two months ago, Sister Wiley came into the salon to drop off some money she owed to Vivian and stayed over an hour gossiping about the women and the deacons in her husband's church. The poor girl fell for every question they asked her and then some information she volunteered for free.

After Sister Wiley had left the salon, Ms. Vivian said, "Now there is a preacher's wife who talks entirely too much." They laughed at her, when they thought I was under the hair dryer, but didn't realize my dryer turned off and I heard their entire conversation about Sister Wiley. I called Sister Wiley and cautioned her about sharing too much inside information and shared a verse in Proverbs 17:28, "Even a fool is thought wise if he keeps silent, and discerning if he holds his tongue."

She listened to me, but I think she resented me for giving her any counsel, so she hasn't called or dropped by the salon on my customary salon days. Sister Wiley had only been a pastor's wife for eighteen months, so she was presently being schooled on the do's and the don'ts of the First Lady Sorority.

This was her first marriage, and she was still learning how to be a good wife.

Pastor Wiley married her after his second wife died of a massive stroke. It was the talk of Southlake, when Pastor Wiley at age fifty-eight, married a twenty-nine year old young nightclub singer by the name of Patricia Carry. After they married, Pastor Wiley baptized her and welcomed her into his church as his new bride, Sister Patricia Carry Wiley. I don't understand why some pastors marry women who do not know the Lord. When their wife acts a fool, does and says things uncustomary to the church, the pastor wonders why. One time, Sister Wiley told a customer in the salon she knew Pastor Wiley had affairs on the former, deceased second Sister Wiley, and the first Sister Wiley who died giving birth to their first son. I looked at her and wondered: *Why on earth would she share that information with anyone? Was she trying to ruin her husband?*

I believed she liked the attention of being a somewhat automatic, credible representative, because she was now a pastor's wife. Or, Sister Wiley was just young, stupid, and naïve about people's motivations. If she was ever to experience joy in the journey of being a minister's wife, she would have to learn to control her tongue and pray for wisdom to discern others' true motivations.

"I hear that old man Wiley and his new young wife may be on the rocks right now. She came in here yesterday complaining that she wants to have a baby and the old man told her that he was done having babies with anyone," Vivian said. "She was just crying in front of everybody because she desires to be a mother. I could hardly complete her hair because she was crying so hard. My customers just looked at me like, 'Something is not right with this woman.' They all looked at her like she was a manic-depressive or something. Some days she comes in the salon on a high, and other times she is downright depressed and bawling all over the place."

Ms. Vivian was known to over exaggerate a situation, so I knew that Sister Wiley had simply needed a place to vent her frustrations so she choose the salon and she might have only cried once.

"Has she cried in here before, Ms. Vivian?" I asked.

"No, that was the first time she broke down like that. It made my customers uncomfortable, so I finished her hair and led her to my back office where she slept for a few hours and I called Pastor Wiley to come pick her up. He was so embarrassed when he walked in and had to lead his weeping wife out of a salon filled with at least three women from his church watching him. You know it was the talk at their church that next Sunday. By the way, what is the name of their church?"

I knew Ms. Vivian knew the name of the church; she was trying to coax me to comment to her remarks.

"I believe it's Mt. Olivet Church," I replied and hastily ended my comment.

After about two minutes of silence, Ms. Vivian said, "Yes, it is Mt. Olivet Church."

"Okay, Sister Stevens, let's go to the shampoo chair and wash this relaxer out of your hair," said Vivian.

Good God! I thought to myself. *I thought the woman was going to burn my hair off with that lye relaxer!* She was trying to get me to talk about some mess, and I had crossed my legs the entire time to not focus on the pain of the lye relaxer she was applying to my hair or her silence to get me to talk. My worst nightmare was an atomic bomb or catastrophic explosion occurring during a time when I was receiving a lye relaxer in a beauty salon!

After Ms. Vivian washed, dried, and styled my hair into her signature French roll, I made an appointment with her receptionist for my next visit. I went into the salon's women's bathroom, looked at my hair and freshened up my makeup. I looked at the mirror and thought that I didn't look bad for a 38-year-old woman. My sweetheart was going to love my hair.

Now if I could just lose these 15 pounds on my waistline. "Lord, can you please help me lose this weight?" I said as I looked up.

I adjusted my clothes, walked out of the restroom, said my customary good-byes to the other patrons in the salon and issued my monthly invitation to Ms. Vivian to come and visit New Light. "Ms. Vivian, we would love for you to visit New Light. You have been promising me that you would visit. I have lived here now for over six months and you have yet to visit. I tell you what; I am personally inviting you to our First Pastor's & Family Appreciation Sunday in two months."

"Sister Stevens, I am going to check my calendar and I will see if I can make it. I am not promising you anything, but I will see. Are you coming that week to get your hair done as well?"

"Yes," I replied.

"Now, will you be wearing the customary preacher's wife hat? So that means you will get a wash and set that week, right?" Ms. Vivian asked.

I looked around the salon, immediately feeling a little uncomfortable as all eyes were now on me.

"I am not really sure what I will be wearing just yet, but when I do know, I will call you."

I hated that people felt that all preacher's wives needed to wear a hat on the Appreciation Day. I truly liked wearing church hats. My paternal grandmother, Anna Belle Montgomery, introduced me to church hats when I was just 14 years old. I paraded in church hats long before I married a preacher. My Granny Montgomery had a church hat that cost over $2,000. She let me wear it in a most beautiful hat contest held at our church in Richmond when I was 16 years old. I won the coveted award for "Most Stylish Hat."

Granny Montgomery just winked at me when I won, because no one in the church even recognized that it was her hat. She told me I looked beautiful in a church hat and only a certain kind of woman knew how to strut in a church hat. I remember practicing my walk with her hat on my head. Some of her hats were wide brimmed, while others were coifed and short. Whatever the occasion, Granny Montgomery had a church hat to match. My daddy once said she spent an average of $10,000 a year on purchasing church hats and matching shoes and purses. When Granny Montgomery died, she willed her church hats to me. So I have a stash of over 100 church hats in our outside storage house. As a result, some people have often referred to me as "The Hat Lady." I have chosen not to join the choir at New Light so I am able to really sport my church hats a lot more than I used to. Choir members aren't allowed to wear hats while singing unless it's for a special occasion and every one was going to wear a hat. Uniformity was important in a good church choir.

"Well, ladies, I will see you all later. Thanks, Ms. Vivian. I love my hair."

"Yes, it is beautiful on you, Sister Stevens. Tell the family I said hello and you have a good night."

"Good night, Sister Stevens," echoed the other patrons who were being serviced by Ms. Vivian's other hair operators.

"You too," I replied.

I knew that my name was going to be the center of their next discussion, as soon as I walked out of the shop.

Chapter Ten

A Wounded Soul and a Bitter Cup

As soon as I exited the front door of Heavenly Hands, the ladies began their gossip about me. One of our newest members, Sister Turner, was in the salon that day and recounted the entire conversation to me. Though I listened to her account, I was wise enough to know that a dog that could bring a bone, can carry a bone. Of course, she came to me in an angle that we need to pray for Sister Vivian and the gossip within her salon walls, and this was why. According to Sister Turner, as soon as I closed the door to leave, the conversation went like this:

"Now Vivian, you know that Sister Stevens knows what she is going to wear to her husband's appreciation service. I don't know why you play with her like that," said Mrs. Woodard, *a fifty-something church deaconess at Rose of Sharon Church who was sitting down in a chair receiving a roller set.*

"I wasn't playing with her. I may have been out of the church for a while, but I do know that the first lady is expected to wear a hat on appreciation day," replied Vivian.

"Now, Viv, why should she wear a hat?" asked Mrs. Woodard.

"Hey, I don't know, you church folks make up all the rules. You know church school on Sunday at 9:30 a.m., worship at 11:00 a.m. You can't wear pants in the church, women are to shut up, don't preach and don't talk, but you can play our piano, cook us dinners and of course, bring all your money. Now, why does church school have to be on Sunday morning? You know that big mega church down the highway that has over 4,000 members? I heard they have church school during the week and worship services only on Wednesdays and they have a seeker service or something like that on Sundays, just for the sinner folks. And they don't have all of these 3:30 p.m. afternoon services and 6 p.m. Sunday evening services that are nearly empty. They are in to do one thing; worship God and then they are out. And that is why they are growing at the seams right now. They are not stuck in tradition like folks in our community," Vivian continued.

"So, honey, I didn't make the rules, those old nasty men made the rules, and one rule is that the first lady is to look like a classy lady and wear a hat," said Vivian with confidence.

"I wonder what color Sister Stevens will be wearing? I may have to help her dress up and find a dress for her, because she is a little plain and it looks like she has gained some weight too."

All of the women and the three hair operators in the shop laughed except Mrs. Woodard.

Sister Turner looked extremely uncomfortable, when she shared that piece of information. I gave her a look as if to say, "So what? Keep going. I can handle that." They weren't exactly lying, I had gained weight. But, I wouldn't be caught dead in the loud colors Vivian wears. I know that fashion sense was a relative term and very opinionated. I smiled at my own sudden humor.

Sister Turner continued her account:

"Vivian, have you joined that big church up the highway since you like them so much?" asked Mrs. Woodard.

"No, I just don't like their song service; it's a little too boring for

my taste. You know I have to have my gospel singing, that good old gospel singing. So I haven't found that kind of church with the flavor that I am looking for."

"Yeah, Vivian, I guess everywhere we go there will be rules," said Mrs. Woodard trying to calm the atmosphere. A small tear fell from Vivian's eye as Vivian quickly began to talk about her latest trip to the Louisiana Casinos and the $2,000 she'd won on the slot machines.

According to Sister Turner, she discovered Vivian hasn't played actively, in a church, for over ten years.

I knew Ms. Vivian would find a way to not go to church and fight her demons. It was easier to focus on someone else, than on her own shortcomings.

During one of my first couple of visits to Heavenly Hands, I remember Vivian telling me that her parents, who were now deceased, might be turning in their graves since she had not played in a church regularly for over ten years.

Vivian recalled how her parents would spend their last ten dollars some weeks to make sure Vivian received piano lessons. Vivian was a gifted musical child. She knew how to play most of the church hymns on the organ and piano by the time she was eleven years old. She could read music and she could play by ear. As a result, by the time she was fourteen years old, she was leading the entire adult choir and the youth choir at her home church, Antioch Church, in Southlake's neighboring town of McKinney. She had a beautiful contralto voice and she could sing with vibrato and belt out acrobatic musical scats and runs with ease, which would move the small congregation of Antioch to tears on Sunday mornings.

Vivian told me she loved getting her paycheck for her services. By the time she was sixteen years old, she was making one hundred dollars a week. Her pastor wanted to make sure that she remained at Antioch for a long time. And she stayed at Antioch as the head musician for over twenty years until she fell out with the new pastor over her church salary. He cut her pay by thirty percent without a deacon vote and notified her when he gave her the weekly check. She was hurt and humiliated that a new pastor could come into Antioch and dismiss her loyalty and faithfulness like a man trying to swat a pesky fly. Not one of the deacons had stood up on her behalf and most of them had known of her dedication to Antioch. The following Sunday, she came to play the organ, but anger and bitterness wouldn't let her get out of her car and she cried in the parking lot as the members passed her up on their way to the church. No one, not a sister, a deacon or even the new pastor came to see if she was okay. Vivian told me that it wasn't about the money, but that she was hurt that her loyalty and commitment to the church over the years was seemingly overlooked. Just as the church requested her services to play an instrument, she needed the church to minister to her emotional needs after being disrespected by church leadership and not given proper notice. An hour later, as she watched the parishioners enter the church, she drove off and she has never stepped foot in another church in over ten years.

I remembered seeing the discomfort on Vivian's face as she recounted this story to me in the salon. I prayed that God would heal her pain and deliver her from resenting the church.

Chapter Eleven

The Balancing Act

It was Wednesday night, and Lance would be home late tomorrow night. I did not feel like going to Bible study tonight. I feel like the church members think I am spying on them if I attend worship or Bible study without Lance. The kids enjoyed the reprieve to stay home from church. I am worried about Lance Jr. He is beginning to show signs of resentment toward the church. Today, he came to me and showed me a D+ English paper. He said if we didn't go to church the night before his paper was due, he would have been able to check his paper and possibly made an A on it.

I looked at him coolly and said, "Sweetie, you knew we were going to church last Wednesday night. We go to church every Wednesday night. Why didn't you properly plan to do your English paper?"

"Mom, I was too busy and church takes up too much of my time. I don't practice baseball as much as we go to church. Why do I have to go to church four times a week?"

Lance insisted that Junior be a part of the junior deacons, usher ministry, and the musical staff because he was a gifted drummer. So yes, Junior did spend a lot of time at the church. He spent more time at the church than I did.

"Besides, they don't like us anyway," Junior said.

"What makes you say that?"

"I overheard Sister Finley and Sister Pepperdine talking about the appreciation services and how they don't think it's necessary to have an appreciation service. They said that Daddy makes enough money during the week and he don't deserve any more money with all the confusion he has caused around New Light. They said that they had a special surprise for Daddy and that it would show him how to lead the church. Then they said they were sick of you parading around in your hats like you were Queen Elizabeth."

"Junior, stop it! Don't repeat such slandering gossip. It is not worth repeating to anyone. Not even to me."

I thought to myself. *What type of surprise are they planning?*

"Well, I think you should know how these folks feel about us. All that fake and phony love they show us. It's not for real. Even I know that, Mama," said Junior.

"Come here," I said as I wrapped my child in my arms. I hugged him real tight and looked him squarely in the eye. "We are here in Southlake, Texas at the New Light Church to serve. We are servants of the Most High God. Sometimes in our service, everyone is not going to be pleased with everything we do, and that's okay. We serve to bring someone to Christ and to give glory to God. I promise you, Junior, your service will not be in vain. But, you have to learn to not let people's opinions of you or your service distract you from serving Jesus. Our goal is to please Christ. Satan wants to cut off your service so that you will not be a key player in kingdom building. I'm sorry you had to hear those two women talking about our family. Just pray for them. See their needs and look beyond their faults."

My fourteen-year-old son, my firstborn, my quiet one,

silently cried in my arms. "Mom, I love Jesus. I do. But, I hate to hear the things they say about you and Dad," he said.

"Part of being a Christian is being able to withstand criticism; good and bad. Junior, never let someone else's opinion of you, or what others say about you, stop you from serving Jesus. It is a trick of the enemy. Look beyond the person and look at the purpose of the words and the spirit behind them. We are in a spiritual battle between good and evil."

I knew it was time to introduce my son to Frank Peretti's debut novel, *In This Present Darkness*, a Christian fiction story that details the spiritual nature of principalities and the consistent battles between good and evil. It is a great read to learn about the forces of good and evil as it relates to the Bible.

"I want you to study Ephesians Chapter six and I want you to focus on the twelfth verse which says, 'For we wrestle not against flesh and blood, but against principalities, against powers, against the rulers of the darkness of this world, against spiritual wickedness in high places'," I said.

"Junior, I want you to prioritize your time. A responsible young adult knows how to set priorities and daily goals to reach their purpose in life. Now, I've watched you spend at least two hours some days playing video games, and another hour and half watching television. That's time where you could be studying your schoolwork, especially if you know it is going to be a busy church week. If you promise me that you will work on prioritizing, I will talk to your dad about all the extra time you spend at church and we will get his opinion on what we can do to help you prioritize."

"Thanks, Mom. I just want to be able to do my very best in school. Most of my friends at school don't even attend church, so they don't know how busy our schedules can be with the church. Most of the time, I feel like I am rushed to complete my work, while my friends have all weekend to chill, relax and spend time researching for our school projects," responded Junior.

"Okay. We will both talk to your father about this," I said.

Here was my oldest child, my beautiful baby boy, learning at the tender age of fourteen to prioritize and make God number one in his life. I learned early the importance of balance. I didn't want Junior to grow up resenting the church and eventually running away from it. This was my fear concerning all of my children. Lance and I worked hard to ensure that our kids were involved in sports and other community events as well as the church. We both felt that it was important to expose our kids to other positive things in the community.

Southlake, fortunately, is a great place to raise a family. The average income in Southlake is over $65,000 a year. There are three golf courses, two country clubs, twelve churches, and one upper scale Mall of Southlake. It boasted a six-year exemplary rating of its school district and a winning sports tradition. Junior loved Southlake Independent School District, when he first enrolled in the eighth grade. He enjoyed being on the football and basketball teams. He was recently voted class president for his upcoming freshman year at Southlake High School. We are all hoping that he goes to the University of Texas at Austin and follow in our footsteps as a fellow Longhorn. This was my baby, my beautiful baby boy. Children grow up so fast. One day we are teaching them how to walk, and then the next day we are teaching them how to iron their clothes.

I've learned to appreciate the time I have with my children. There was a time I took my babies for granted. In the early years of his pastorate, Lance and I were so busy in the church trying to see to the needs of the people, that we soon realized that the television and our baby-sitters were raising our children. We rarely sat at the table to eat together as a family except on Sundays after church.

I remember when Junior was about eight years old and he went to a friend's house for the weekend. Upon his return home, I asked him if he had a good time and he said, 'Yeah, it was alright, except for the fact that Jonathan's parents talk too much. They made us eat at the table for every meal and we couldn't even watch the television while we ate. So we were forced to talk to them."

Needless to say, I was ashamed that my son thought that eating in front of the television was family time. Soon afterward, I made it a goal to cut out TV at least once a week and have dinner and breakfast together as a family at least four times a week. Lance and I were so consumed with the church and the things of the church that we didn't realize that our home life was out of order and our children were being taught that this was normal.

I learned to pay attention to all of our children's needs. Big Mama Thompson would always tell me, "Jackie, you need to learn to build up your house. Do not build your house on sand. Build your house on solid rock. Jesus is that Rock. Chile, you need to teach your children about Jesus, but you need to show them how to make a living for themselves. You have no business being at that church five nights a week with small chillin'. You need to make sure that you are giving them chillin' a healthy balance in their lives. Mary and Joseph did it for their children and you need to do it for your chillin'. Jesus was a carpenter. He had a trade. His Mama and Daddy knew from His birth that He was divine, but they still made sure that He knew how to make a living for Himself. Now, Jesus didn't have to work if He didn't want to because He was God in the flesh, but yet He did. The Bible says, a man that won't work, won't eat. The one thing that I hate to see is lazy, resentful preacher chillin'."

Big Mama T would tell me these things to make sure I invested in my children so that they wouldn't turn into those hellion type preacher kids that are often the gossip of conversations. Big Mama T was concerned that her beloved great-grandchildren would turn into a resentful wild group of children. That reminded me I needed to call her this week. She is turning 84 next month and she did tell me that she had a chauffeur, a deacon from her church, who was going to drive her and my mama up for Lance's first appreciation service at New Light.

If I knew my Big Mama she was probably trying to fix my mama up with that deacon chauffeur. My mama said that if she couldn't rise up my deceased father, John Montgomery, from the dead, then no other man would suffice for her. She'd rather live her life as a widow. Big Mama T knew that time would heal my mama's lonely heart, but it hasn't stopped her from trying to marry off my mama ever since my daddy's death.

Big Mama T was always trying to fix my mama up with one man or another from the Richmond churches or the community. At sixty years old, my mama is a beautiful woman. She is a perfect size ten and stands at 5'6 inches tall. She has natural golden brown hair with a gray streak down the side like the black actress, Della Reese. Men, young and old, still exhale when my mama, Eva Montgomery, walks into a room. My mother still lives in her dream home with my younger sister and her two kids. Now, Mama's world revolves around them.

I told them both about how much nicer the people were at this church than Lance's previous pastorates. I told them how great our children were adjusting to the city of Southlake and how much they liked it. We moved over three different times in the last twelve years and my children were grateful for any stability. I said Lance had fixed up the parsonage and how we were planning to own our first home together in the next five years. I told them that over forty percent of our church members had some type of college degree, professional training or trade school certificate and forty-five percent of our church members were consistent tithers, thanks to Lance introducing an online tithing system, where New Light members by choice, could tithe directly from their banking accounts on pay day. It was very convenient for our members, especially our younger members, who paid most of their monthly payments and gifts on the internet.

I then told her how we had started with only about one

hundred and fifty active members and now we have grown in less than a year to more than three hundred and fifty active members. I have learned that good news traveled faster than bad news sometimes so I have learned to be optimistic particularly with my family. They had a tendency to blame Lance whenever I was unhappy or when I complained. Big Mama T was looking forward to coming to Southlake and I sure was looking forward to her visit. I loved to hear her pray those sing-song prayers and I knew that New Light would love my Big Mama and my mama too.

I was determined not to share with them my concerns about the controlling Sister Finley or the woman in the red suit that recently joined that Sister Peterson had warned me about. For the last two Sundays, that sister in the red suit always had something to say to Lance after service. I would catch her whispering in his ear or stroking his back in a weird, seductive way. Sometimes, I would catch her gazing at Lance, with this dreamy expression on her face. Last Sunday, she accidentally parked her gold Jaguar sports car in my parking space. Someone removed the moniker sign that read, "Pastor's Wife Parking." Lance found the sign in the trash compactor outside. Someone threw it away. I decided it was better just to pray about these things or write them in my journal than to share my deep concerns with anyone, not even my closest relatives. Sometimes when we speak those things to someone else, Satan and his vices will hear it and use it against us in their spiritual warfare, so it's better to keep it in our spirit and talk to the Lord about it. One thing I know is that Satan cannot read our minds, but he has been playing this game long enough to be able to predict or try to set up what can or could occur to stop the saints of God from enjoying our victory. And I was determined to claim my victory. A pretty woman in a red suit was not going to steal my joy or my focus. No matter how many times she put her bosom in my husband's face.

Chapter Twelve

Another Lonely Night

Dear Jesus,

Our one year appreciation services will be here soon. Lord, give me patience to deal with all the issues that can arise out of an appreciation day for the pastoral family. Lance will be in tonight from his revival. Give him safe travel, Jesus. I pray for Lance Jr. that you will help him to find proper balance in his life. Lord, be with us as we prepare to talk to his daddy about his time for school. Watch over Connie, who adores praising you, Jesus. Lord, you have given her such a spirit of praise and worship. Watch over Jaylyn, who is blooming into puberty. I pray tonight for my mother, my sisters and my Big Mama T, keep them in your loving arms.

I also pray for the woman in the red suit. I pray that she will find the counsel she needs and that her motives are pure. Give me peace about her, Lord. I also pray that Sister Peterson stops sending me notes about the woman in the red suit every Sunday. Though it is kind of unnerving that this woman, since the Sunday she joined our church, wears a different variation of a red suit every Sunday. She is clad with a red suit, a matching red hat, red shoes and a red handbag. I must say this woman has style, but I wonder why she loves the color red so much.

I have tried to introduce myself to her but she seems to avoid me or walks away when she sees me heading in her direction. I know Lord that people have their issues, but I wouldn't harm a fly. So as a result of her distance, I have decided that perhaps she wants her privacy and so I will respect that. I pray, Jesus, that you dispatch your angels to provide protection over my family and over our church family. In your name, in your will, I do pray.

Love,
Jackie S.

Lately, the woman in red is beginning to be a bit unnerving for me. I found out her name is Marilyn Steele, and she is originally from Miami, Florida. She is 34 years old, and relocated to Southlake because of a job transfer. She is a software engineer with a Bachelor of Science degree from Florida A&M University and a Master's degree from Brown University. Sister Peterson and I happened to walk by the new member's class one Tuesday night and managed to hear Sister Steele give her introduction to the class.

"My name is Marilyn Steele. I relocated to Southlake to take a job as lead engineer for Verizon. Originally, I am from Miami, Florida. I have no family in Texas. My closest living relative is in Alexandria, Louisiana. I did not grow up in the church. I was only truly converted when I joined New Light. I saw the advertisement about New Light riding in my car; I saw the billboard about seeking the light of Jesus. I left Miami, where I was in a dark place and I came to Texas for some hope and a new direction. I hope I am in the company of new family and friends," she said.

"Amen, my sister. You are home," my husband said.

Sister Peterson just raised her eyebrows and shook her head, as she continued to get their meals ready for the meeting fellowship after their class in the kitchen, which was right next to the new member's classroom. And she said she started singing while she prepared their food.

My husband makes it mandatory that every new member of New Light goes through an eight-week new membership class. Marcus and Juanita Graves were currently enrolled in the class along with about 25 other new members that have joined in the past few months. Sister Peterson routinely made it her business to volunteer to bring food to the new member class sessions. I think she attended just to be nosy and to spy on some of the women folks who joined our church. My husband learned to just put up with old Sister Peterson and her ways of trying to pry into people's lives. Besides, he loved the way she makes her signature sweet potato pies and peach cobblers that she brought to the class fellowship meetings. However, he hated when she started singing her signature song while preparing the food.

My husband will be home tonight from his revival. I bought a sexy red silk pajama set with a matching robe and scarf. I even bought him a purple silk pajama set with matching purple house shoes. I prepared him a bubble bath that was ready with soft music by Marvin Gaye, his favorite secular artist, playing in the background. The kids were fast asleep. I know my Lance is going to love my French roll. I looked myself over in the mirror. At 165 pounds and 5'6, I still looked fairly decent for my age. If only I could lose these love handles around my sides. I was blessed with beautiful hair, teeth and nails all inherited from my mother. I keep them manicured and clean. I made sure to attend a full body spa at least three times a year. I knew my Lance would be pleased with my look. It's 11:30 p.m. and Lance is still not back from Austin. Suddenly the phone rang.

"Hello," I said.

"Hi, sweetheart. Look, I think I am going to spend another night here. I am really tired from preaching and I could use the rest. This last sermon took a lot out of me. I am going to leave tomorrow around 10 a.m. so I should get home about one or two in the afternoon."

"But Lance, what about our night together?" I asked

"Okay, baby, I'll go ahead, get dressed, and check out of this hotel. It's only 4 p.m. It will take me about four hours to get to you. I'll call you when I'm halfway home," Lance said as I heard him getting out of his bed.

"No, honey. I know you are tired," I reluctantly said. "Get some rest and your Goldie will be waiting for you. Of course the kids will be home, but I will still be here."

"Maybe we can go to a nice dinner or something tomorrow night, baby," Lance said.

"Tomorrow is Lance Jr.'s basketball game, did you forget?" I asked

"You are mad with me. I can tell in your voice that you are disappointed with me," Lance said, yawning.

"No; I am okay. I'll see you tomorrow afternoon, sweetie" I said. "You just get some rest. I'll be fine. I probably need some rest too. I love you."

"I love you, too, Goldie. Goodbye," Lance said.

My dear, all of this preparation and he is a no show. I must admit, I have learned to be flexible with Lance's religious vocation and his time. Preaching can be a very draining employment for those who take it seriously. I have seen Lance study at least ten hours a week for one sermon or even more than fifteen hours if he has a week-long revival. After a revival he is usually exhausted, and is not very communicative with anyone for at least a day. When he first started preaching, this routine of Lance's not wanting to communicate almost drove our marriage toward a divorce. My Big Mama T would tell me, "Girl, you just need to learn your husband. Find out what makes him tick. Learn his routine. Stop hollering and screaming, but study that man before you make a move to try to help him."

So that is exactly what I did. I studied my man and I still do at times. I learned that if he has a big church association assignment, he would be like a kid on Christmas day, and sometimes his other priorities, like bill payments, might routinely be forgotten. So it's typically during these times, that I will just pay a little something extra on our bills just in case Lance forgot to pay for them. This was early in his pastoring days and he had to learn how to balance his family and the church. I was tired of coming home and the gas would be off. A couple of times, I came home from work and our phone and lights would be off too. It wasn't always because we didn't have the money or that the church didn't have the money; it was typically because our church board was either too lazy to keep up with the bills and Lance was so involved with his studying for school and his sermons that he didn't check on them to make sure our parsonage bills were paid.

Oh, Lord, here I go again reminiscing about the bad times, because I am disappointed right now. I wish I had more friends to spend time with. My friends are in Austin, Houston, and Richmond, Texas. My best friend lives in Los Angeles, California. I admit I am very lonely here in Southlake. I haven't found one good friend here since we have relocated. The women of New Light are nice to me, but I am hesitant to get close with anyone for fear of betrayal or that others might persecute them because they are my friends. So my husband, my children, my new job and my trusted journal are the persons I spend most of my days with. Recently, Lance would be out of state preaching at least one weekend out of every month and he averaged one revival every month, in Texas. Our times alone together were constantly being circumvented by his growing ministry calendar.

I folded up Lance's new purple pajamas and placed them neatly in his drawer. I went to the heated temperature controlled whirlpool bathtub and let the water drain out. I swept up the red rose petals that I had delicately placed on the floor and I turned off the Marvin Gaye CD that was crooning ever so silently the song, "Distant Lover." I pulled off my sexy nightgown and put a scarf around my hairdo. I washed off my makeup and mechanically brushed my teeth. I then climbed into my familiar cotton pajamas and slipped under the covers until sleep overcame my tears of loneliness.

Chapter Thirteen

My Purpose

Since Lance did not want my secretarial services at the church, we decided four months ago that I would interview to lead the church sponsored part-time temporary agency called, Victorious Workers. I interviewed for the supervisor position and I was hired as director of Victorious Workers. I presently work about twenty-five hours a week in a small office next to the Southlake Outlet Mall. I help train people preparing for interviews and I just contracted out two workers to a local department store in the outlet mall. My specialty is grant writing. I wrote a grant through our 501c3 organization that Lance organized within the first four months of his pastorate at New Light and this grant was enough to pay for my salary, a part time assistant and lease office space. The church members were very impressed with their new pastor's leadership ability, but I don't think they liked the fact that the pastor's wife would be employed through their newly formed organization.

I thought Sister Finley would have a heart attack when Lance announced who would lead the first business our 501c3 would support.

"Good morning, brothers and sisters," Lance said during the 11:00 a.m. morning worship pastoral emphasis period. I sat quietly in the church, on my customary second row pew with my hands folded on my lap. I shifted side to side with nervousness as how the announcement would be perceived by New Light's members.

"The Deacon Board and I are happy to announce that my wife, Sister Jacqueline Stevens, will lead our new venture called Victorious Workers, a temporary agency established to help train and equip our people for quality, successful employment. Sister Stevens is more than able to get this organization off the ground. She has a Bachelor's Degree in Journalism and Marketing from the University of Texas at Austin and a MBA from the University of Phoenix. She also has a certificate in interior design. And, she loves Jesus and this church and community."

I immediately saw Sister Finley throw Deacon Finley a dirty look that said, "How could you not tell me this information!!" Deacon Finley darted his eyes away from her and said, "Amen, Pastor Stevens."

After church, many of the members came up to me and congratulated me for the new position. Of course, Sister Finley lowered her lavender wide-brimmed hat and walked past me without a customary good-bye. I knew Deacon Finley would have to explain why he voted to elect me as Director of Victorious Workers.

Sister Finley wanted her twenty-two- year-old niece, Kayla Barnes, to head this business venture. Kayla was a college senior majoring in education at Southern Methodist University in Dallas and she was trying to find employment upon her graduation in May. Sister Finley felt this job would have been perfect for Kayla and it would keep Kayla active in the church. Rumors were circulating that Kayla had been visiting the newly formed Abundant Joy Fellowship Church in Southlake and Sister Finley was not having any of her family members leave her beloved New Light that was established by her kin-folk. She felt her family had a duty to stay at New Light and to help it prosper despite having a new pastor with a new vision for the church.

Two weeks after my husband's initial announcement of the Victorious Worker's leadership, Sister Finley, dressed in a green and gold suit with matching J. Renee shoes and hat, calmly walked up to me in the sanctuary before church services began one Sunday and said, "Sister First Lady, I am looking forward to seeing what you will do for Victorious Workers. There are not too many times around New Light that our men allow a woman to lead such an unprecedented new ministry. I hope that you will do a great job as the director."

"Yes, ma'am. I am quite honored that our leadership has so much faith in me. With God's help, I pray I will do okay," I replied.

"You know, my Kayla, my deceased sister's child, will be graduating in May and she will be looking for a job. Do you need an assistant to work with you at Victorious Workers?" asked Sister Finley.

"Right now, we are not in a position to hire any additional staff. I recently hired Julie Jones to serve as my assistant," I said.

"You did what? You hired Julie Jones? She just joined our church two months ago! She has three babies by three different men, and she never married any one of them. That woman does not come to any of our teaching ministries at New Light. Why would you hire a woman like that to represent my, I mean our church? But you couldn't hire my Kayla, huh?" Sister Finley fired back.

"After much prayer and the completion of the interview process, I felt led to choose Sister Jones as my assistant. Kayla's application was received a week after the closing dead-line date for the office assistant position. Sister Jones attends school at night, and that is why you have not seen her at the nightly ministries. But, she is enrolled in our church Sunday School," I coolly and carefully responded.

"Do the deacons know about your decision or did you even ask them their opinion?" Sister Finley inquired.

"As Director of Victorious Workers, that decision was left solely up to me," I said.

Sister Finley, calmly walked up to me and whispered in my ear so that no one else in the sanctuary could hear and she proudly said, "Well, that is the problem; you have too much authority. You wait until I get through with you. My Kayla will soon have your job. You just wait and see!" snickered Sister Finley. She walked away with a prance in her step while her golden-green polka dotted hat bobbed from side to side.

I turned around and thought that woman was the picture of evil! I watched her strut away, and I reminded myself to pray a special prayer for her. You know if she said something like that to me during my first few years of being a pastor's wife, I would have either hit her or cried like a baby. Over the years, my skin has become tough and I learned to laugh at ignorance in the church and Sister Finley was definitely ignorant. She was more concerned about power and control than she was about seeing people saved toward Jesus Christ.

Ever since that Sunday, I have learned to kill Sister Finley with kindness. So I was not surprised when Junior told me he overheard Sister Finley talking about us. She is slowly losing her grip on New Light and she is crying like a big fat baby over it. She has seemed to age ten years over the last few months because the lines in her face are beginning to show and the black dye around her hairline was beginning to crust at her nape. The way she has tried to yield power over this church, you would think that her husband was the chairman of the Deacon Board. Deacon Finley is a deacon and a trustee, but has always refused to be chairman, probably because he knows his power hungry wife would go stone crazy if she had the title of "The Chairman's Wife."

New Light's current chairman is Deacon Theodore Jenkins. His wife passed away five years ago. He is sixty-three years old and a visiting philosophy professor at Paul Quinn College and a retired tenured professor from Southern Methodist University. He has been a member of New Light for over forty years and was known as a friend to the preacher man. I love Deacon Jenkins, because he is always trying to encourage Lance and me to reach our full potential in the Lord. If he disagreed with anything, he always met with Lance, one on one, and was very professional and Christian-like at every business and deacon meeting. Lance said that Deacon Jenkins is the kind of deacon that every pastor prays for. He was respectful, intelligent, slow to anger, loved the Word of God, loved God's people, and most of all, was saved and lived a godly life.

When we first moved to Southlake, Deacon Jenkins would call us at least twice a week just to see if we needed anything. We were so amazed by his attentiveness and respect for the man of God. When Lance would be out of town preaching for a revival or mission trip, Deacon Jenkins would always drop by the parsonage to give me a couple of dollars to take the kids out to eat so I wouldn't have to cook. Our kids affectionately call him Uncle Jenkins.

Deacon Jenkins did not have any children of his own, so he liked to come to Junior's basketball games to give him encouragement. That reminds me, I need to call him and remind him about Junior's game tonight. Let me call him right now.

I called Deacon Jenkins's number, which was now imprinted in my memory from calling so many times over this past year. He answered after the third ring.

"Hello, Deacon Jenkins, I was calling to remind you about Junior's game tonight at seven," I said.

"Sister First Lady, I already have my ticket to the game. I'll see you at courtside tonight. Did the good reverend make it in last night?" he asked.

"No, he will be in later on this afternoon. He is planning to attend Junior's game tonight."

"The reverend hasn't come to but four of Junior's games all season and now his season is almost over. We have got to make that man slow down, and spend some time with his boy. A boy needs his father," said Deacon Jenkins.

"Pray for him, Deacon. He has been really pushing himself with all of these revivals and he is often quite drained and tired," I said.

"I know, but I hate Junior to scan the stands looking for his daddy, and all he sees is this old man with peppered gray hair and a graying beard," he said.

"You know, Junior loves when you come to his games. You know how he adores you, Deacon."

"I know, but that boy will be in high school next year and I think he has a real shot to go to a Division I school for college. If he does, that boy is going to need his daddy to help him with that decision."

I was starting to feel uncomfortable as Deacon Jenkins made me seem like a single woman. My husband was out in the field bringing souls to Christ. He was encouraging the saints and providing inspiration. He was kingdom building. But, I longed for my husband to be with my son at every game and every outing. Too many times, I was the only one putting together the birthday parties, going to the school plays, and the sport activities. I had grown accustomed to supporting my children in ways that their father couldn't. I understood that this life was a sacrifice of service. However, when he returned home, he was always keenly interested in anything he had missed that his children were involved in.

"Sister First Lady. Are you okay? I didn't offend you, did I?" asked Deacon Jenkins.

"Oh, Deacon, I am fine"

"I'll see you at the game tonight, 7:00 p.m. straight up. Wear your red, white, and blue for school spirit. The high school coaches from Southlake High will be in attendance tonight, so it is a big game for Junior," I quickly said.

"Okay, sister, I will see you tonight."

I silently wiped a tear away. I was glad he couldn't see my tear drop over the phone.

Just then, the devil began to play tricks in my head. My mind raced as I pictured Lance and Marilyn Steele laughing after church last Sunday as she gently gave him a hug. I remembered seeing her name among his list of counseling sessions in his appointment book for last week. I thought about my lonely night and how lately it seemed my emotional needs were not being met. Lance had been so busy. Our weekly "midnight snacks" in each other arms had dwindled down to once every other week in the last month. Now, that was strange for my husband. I wiped away another tear of insecurity, as I remembered our covenant vow to be faithful to each other. I reminded myself to stay focused on my children tonight and let my prayers fight for us and pull us through.

Chapter Fourteen

The Schemers

I walked to the prayer nook, and silently prayed to God. Thank God for Deacon Jenkins.

One Sunday, when I was having a difficult time with one of the children and we arrived late to church, Deacon Jenkins said, "First Lady, you are looking so awesome today in that crème suit that I know nothing but a smile would go with that gorgeous outfit. I love the way you wear your hats and walk around in your suits on Sunday morning in grand style."

I would always blush and plaster on a smile that I knew was necessary to witness for Christ. I knew he discerned that my eyes had a hint of loneliness in them.

Deacon Jenkins was always kind to me and often defended my honor with his sister, Betty Jean Pepperdine. He would tell me his sister was a sucker for people like Sister Sarah Ann Finley. He shared that Sister Finley and his sister Betty Jean had always been partners in crime since they were fourteen years old. Sister Finley was always manipulating his sister to participate in her schemes.

Jenkins said that Sarah Ann Finley was just upset because

my now famous church hats made her hats look like snake feathers.

During one of our weekly conversations, Deacon Jenkins said that he believed the source of Sister Finley's discontentment with me was that she secretly felt that I was trying to always upstage her fashion sense. I had over one hundred hats, and I rarely wore the same hat two times a year.

"I'm so sick of these old women in church trying to compete with these younger women in the church," said Deacon Jenkins as we both shared a cup of coffee at my home. Lance was attending a church conference in Houston that morning. Deacon Jenkins recounted an earlier luncheon with his sister Betty Jean a few days earlier.

"Where are all the women found in the book of Titus, who are supposed to be supportive and teaching these young women?" said Jenkins out loud to himself as he thought about the state of women in our society.

"Boy, who were you talking to?" asked Betty Jean, who was Deacon Jenkins' older sister and had moved in with him after his beloved wife passed away. She came into the kitchen and began to prepare their afternoon meal.

"I was thinking about how we need more Titus women in our church to train up our young women in the church," said Deacon Jenkins.

"What are you saying, Jenkins? We don't have any Titus women at New Light? We have plenty of Titus women at the church. Sister Finley, Sister Chambers, and I are classic examples of the Titus women talked about in the Holy Bible, Titus chapter two. We can't help it if those young thangs out there won't listen to us. I know I tried to counsel them at our church about 'shacking and smacking,' but do they listen? No! They go right ahead and let them young men live with them without the sanctity of marriage. They just let the man have his milk and drink it too. He doesn't have to buy the cow,

because the milk has been given to him freely on a daily basis," ex-
plained Sister Pepperdine.

Deacon Jenkins told with me that his sixty-eight year old
sister was a life long member of New Light. She was a retired
school teacher of the Southlake Independent School District,
and served on the Usher Ministry and Senior Mission group.
She was affectionately known as Mama Pepperdine by the
children of New Light, because she did not have children of
her own and over the years, she was a strong supporter of the
New Light Youth Department and their community events. It
was not odd to see Mama Pepperdine at a Southlake football
or basketball game cheering one of New Light's kids on. She
made it her business to find out their games and events so she
could cheer them on and encourage them. She had served as
one of the Youth matrons for over forty years.

"Betty Jean and Sarah Ann were high school classmates and
best friends. They were there for each other for their wed-
dings, the births of Sister Finley's children, and Sister Pepperdine's husband's funeral ten years ago," said Deacon Jenkins.
"Betty Jean and I decided to move in together about a year
ago, to cut extra expenses during our retirement years, since
we were both now widowed. We are still getting used to the
idea of living under the same roof again. Believe me, it's a real
challenge," he said.

Deacon Jenkins recalled how bossy his sister was when they
were growing up together. She was the oldest of the five Jenkins children and let her siblings know who was left in charge
during their childhood days. Deacon disclosed the brewing
discussion he shared with Betty Jean concerning Titus Women
at New Light.

"All I am saying Betty Jean, is that over seventy-five percent of
the traditional African-American church is now filled with women.
And, we will need more Titus women to teach the women of our
church about dress inside the church walls, how to be good wives, and

good mothers," said Deacon Jenkins. "But it seems that most of you all have Jezebel spirits. You all are not trying to be submissive to anyone, not to your husbands or to those in authority at church."

Walking up to Deacon Jenkins, Betty Jean calmly responded, "Did you see that young woman last Sunday strolling into the church with an orange pantsuit on with no sleeves on her arms? Now that's a Jezebel spirit! I thought Sarah was going to have a heart attack when she saw that woman coming around the offering plate with that on. Or, that other woman who had her skirt hiked up so much in the back that you could see her pink thong. Jenkins, that's a Jezebel spirit. I thought old man Johnson was going to see again through his glaucoma laced eyes he was looking so hard at her," laughed Betty Jean.

"You see, this is what I am talking about. You talk about these women, but have you tried to get close to them to form a relationship? Then, you can minister to them. We get a lot of people in our church who have never been in the church at any other time in their lives. This is the age of the first un-churched generation in America," explained Deacon Jenkins.

"Jenkins don't stand on your coffee can this morning. Leave your philosophy for your college class. I know what you are saying, but they don't want to hear some old woman telling them how to dress in the sanctuary. They probably won't listen, so why waste our time? We just make sure that we set an example before them and that is why you see Sarah and me always decked out in our Sunday best, with our matching designer shoes and hat. Plus, our hair is always coifed or curled to perfection."

"Do you mean, your wigs, Betty Jean?" laughed Deacon Jenkins.

"Wigs, fake buns, whatever! I bought the hair and so it's mine," snapped Betty Jean.

It was church knowledge that Sister Pepperdine hated that her hair had thinned so bad, that she had to resort to wearing wigs to cover up her bald spots.

"The morning of our discussion," Deacon Jenkins offered,

"she was sporting a streaked blond, brown chestnut weave that bounced to her shoulders. She looked a hot mess," he sipped his coffee, laughing at the same time.

It was also church knowledge that Sister Pepperdine walked two miles at least three times a week to maintain her size sixteen build that she's possessed since the age of nineteen. If she wanted to, she could probably still "catch" her a man, but those days were over and her brother's company was all the man she wanted right now. However, she loved to still get the "cat calls" from some of those older men in the church and the Southlake community who had been recharged due to the invention of Viagra.

Deacon Jenkins continued to enlighten me their discussion regarding the state of women today:

"All I am saying Jenkins, is that these young women of Southlake are not into us old women and they don't want to hear what we have to say. Besides, you can let First Lady Stevens talk to them, she needs something to do, something besides wearing her hats on Sunday. Let her talk to those young ladies. She is not much older than most of them. She rarely comes to Sunday School, anymore, and she hardly comes to the Mission group. But yet she wants to be over Victorious Workers. I still haven't figured that one out. So, I guess if she is not running things she doesn't want to participate in them," said Sister Pepperdine.

"Girl, you need to stop listening to Sarah's crap, because now it sounds like you don't care for Sister Stevens," said Deacon Jenkins.

"I know Sarah doesn't care for the first lady, but she does make a point about her. She has been here a year and she hardly says two words to anyone. She doesn't work with our children in the church. She doesn't even try to help us serve in the kitchen or help clean up. She sits there and wears her hat like she is a queen or something. Why do we have to fix the pastor's plates and his family a plate after church fellowships? She is young enough to make her own plate, and fix her family a plate including her husband," explained Sister Pepperdine with her hands on her hips waiting for a response.

"It's not easy being a pastor's wife, Betty Jean. You need to pray for her. Her purpose right now may be to nurture her children and tend to their needs," explained Deacon Jenkins.

I knew Deacon Jenkins was fiercely loyal to any pastor that graced the pulpit of New Light. But, I didn't know how his sister would feel if he was always taking up for me. I wondered why Deacon Jenkins felt it necessary to share this very private conversation with his sister with me. I guess even the chairman of deacons needs a confidant.

"If that is the case, then why is she taking the time to lead Victorious Workers?" quizzed Sister Pepperdine.

"Just pray for them, Betty. Can you do that?" said Deacon Jenkins as he abruptly stood up from the table.

"I don't understand why Kayla Barnes didn't get that Director's job for Victorious Workers," said Sister Pepperdine trying to get some answers from her beloved deacon brother.

"That is official church business, and you don't need to know the reason why she didn't get the job," said Deacon Jenkins.

"Well, I'm a sixty-five year member of New Light, and I pay my tithes every month from my trust fund, pension, and my social security check, so if I want my church to tell me why someone was hired over someone else, I have a right to know. I am sick of you men folk at that church trying to keep everything from us women in the church!" shouted Sister Pepperdine.

"First of all, Betty, y'all talk too much and you can't hold water! That's why we don't tell the women anything. If you all were prayer warriors, maybe just maybe we would give you the inside scoop. But, you women would find a way to gossip even during your public prayers," said Deacon Jenkins.

"All I know is, if it weren't for the women of New Light, you twenty-five, or on a good day fifty men of New Light wouldn't even have a church. Call us what you want; we are still the majority in the church," rebuffed Sister Pepperdine.

"We may be in the minority in the church, but God gave us the authority and some of you, like you and Sister Finley, need to learn to be silent in the church. And, if Sarah wouldn't talk so much in the church, she wouldn't get misquoted so much. One thing about it, you can't misquote silence," said Deacon Jenkins as he straightened his chair and put it underneath the kitchen table.

"I bought two tickets to Lance Jr.'s game tonight," he quickly said, trying to change the subject.

"I already have plans for tonight, so I won't be going," replied Sister Pepperdine.

"What do you mean you are not going to his game? You go to all of the other New Light kids' games, but you have yet to attend any of Lance Jr.'s games. This is his first year playing for Southlake, and you are the kids' favorite youth matron. You know how those kids brag about how you attended one of their games, and screamed the loudest. And, this is the second time I have bought you a ticket and you haven't gone to Junior's game. Are you deliberately trying to hurt Junior?" Deacon Jenkins questioned.

"From what I hear, his daddy hardly attends any of his games, so I know Junior will hardly miss seeing me there tonight," fired Sister Pepperdine. "I told you Jenkins, I have other plans tonight, so just invite someone else to go with you."

"I looked at her with disdain and pity in my eyes," Deacon Jenkins said. "Was my sister that bored at home since her retirement that she was being this vindictive?"

Deacon Jenkins continued to share their conversation.

"I don't know what has gotten into you lately, Jenkins," said Betty Jean. "Every time I say a word about the pastoral family, you get so protective of them. Why should I go to Junior's game? I know he heard Sarah and me talking about his mama and daddy. I saw the boy eavesdropping on us after we had our conversation. Since then, I can't look the boy in the eye. If I went to his game, he would know I wasn't being sincere so why even try to pretend I supported him by attending the game when the boy already heard me gossiping about his parents? I have a funny feeling he told his mama. For the last two Sundays, Sister Stevens has been syrupy sweet to me and mak-

ing a point to smile in my face and hug me, which is something she would normally not bother to do," said Betty Jean.

"Why were you talking about his parents with Sarah Ann? You need to strive to be more holy, Betty," quipped Deacon Jenkins.

Ignoring his comment, "Besides, I have plans tonight. Sarah and I are going to the church and clean, and we hired a contractor to surprise the pastor for his anniversary by buying him a new desk, computer, a color TV and a few other surprises. Sarah thought a soft baby blue was a soothing color for an office that was used to counsel the members. Sarah has an associate degree in Psychology so she is always trying to use her knowledge of colors and its effects in her decorating. I believe she is still upset that that the pastor and first lady had the parsonage repainted in another color. Sarah said that the pastor's new office color, complete with a new desk and accessories, was supposed to be a surprise," Betty Jean carefully said.

"But I pray that it is not pay back toward the pastor and first lady for being ungrateful for her gift of painting the parsonage when they first moved into the house. Surely, Sarah wouldn't stoop that low and still call herself a Christian."

"I need to call her and see what day we are going to meet at the church to begin our surprise extreme makeover of the pastor's office."

Oh, my goodness. Wait until Lance finds out about *this* surprise. While he had an open door policy about his office, he was not comfortable with persons, that included me, going in and out of his office without his express permission. On the other hand, perhaps, they both wanted to bless their pastor.

"Betty Jean, you are not authorized to do any such thing in the church house without the church officers' approval. The pastor may not be comfortable with you in his office," Deacon Jenkins said.

Just then, Betty Jean dialed Sister Finley's number.

"Hello?" answered Sister Finley.

"Betty Jean," Deacon Jenkins interrupted his storytelling to say, "you know, can't hear that well, so the phone receiver was loud enough where anyone could hear the caller on the other end. So I heard everything," Deacon Jenkins said, shaking his head. "I pretended to eat my breakfast and prayed that God would intervene."

"Good morning, Sarah, how are you doing?"

"Girl, the Lord is blessing me this morning. I have the contractor in place, and he is painting as we speak and the pastor's new furniture has arrived by truck this morning. So I let the contractor in the pastor's office this morning at 9:00am and afterward the movers will put the furniture together and trash his old desk. I think he is really going to be surprised!" said Sister Finley.

"How did you get a key to Pastor's office?" Sister Pepperdine asked.

"My sweet, dear Abraham, left his master key to the church in his pants pocket and when I went to wash his pants, the key miraculously fell on the floor, and I miraculously made a copy of it, " laughed Sister Finley. *"My family sacrificed too much for this church for a living member of our family not to have a copy of our sweet beloved New Light master key. I have a right to this key,"* declared Sister Finley. *"And I don't care what Abraham Finley or that new pastor of ours has to say about it."*

"Won't they know that you have a master key after the office makeover?" asked Sister Pepperdine.

"Our pastor may assume that my husband opened up the office for me and believe me, my Abraham will be too embarrassed to tell anyone his wife has her own key to the pastor's office. I can handle my Abraham."

Did you find anything in our pastor's office that might be a little secretive?" quizzed Sister Pepperdine.

"I did find a small safe in his office but I could not crack it open. I tell you, our new pastor is smart. Other than that, the boy is squeaky clean. I did notice that new member, Sister Marilyn Steele's information card on his desk, so I guess they are now communicating. You know I couldn't help but feel that the two of them knew each other when she first joined our church. It was just something in his eyes

when he saw her walk forward to join our church that made me think that our pastor knew this Marilyn Steele woman. My woman's intuition told me that something is familiar between the two of them. I am going to check out a few more things in his office when we return tonight," said Sister Finley.

"Please Sarah, every man in the church is going goo-goo over that woman right now. I am wondering why she has to wear different shades of red to church every Sunday. That girl must be crazy or something," said Sister Pepperdine.

"Maybe she likes the color red, like I like the color pink. Did you know I own over thirty pink hats?" said Sister Finley.

"Yes, Sarah, I am aware of your hat collection. Didn't you like that hat First Lady Stevens wore last Sunday? Now that was a pretty pink hat," said Sister Pepperdine.

"Oh, please; those are her grandmother's hats she wears, so therefore it is not her style, but a style she is emulating. She is not original like I am," proclaimed Sister Finley.

"Well how do you know where her hats are from? You barely even talk to the first lady?"

"Well, when I was really talking to her, she shared with me her little secret. Of course, I wasn't supposed to let the cat out of the bag, but oh, well. She let me know that her grandmother had willed her a collection of hats. So you see, her style is old and imitated," said Sister Finley.

"But you don't know which hat is willed or purchased, so I think she is still classy," Sister Pepperdine chastised.

"Whatever, Betty Jean. You just want to be in the good graces of the pastoral family because you know your brother would want you to pay respect to them and he wouldn't have it any other way," said Sister Finley.

"Need I remind you that Jenkins is not my husband, nor my daddy? He is my younger brother, and I can think what I want about anyone," said Sister Pepperdine proudly through her telephone.

"Jenkins has his opinions, and I have my opinions. We respect each other's differing opinions, Sarah. Stop trying to insinuate that I don't have my own mind or I am being influenced by Jenkins," Sister Pepperdine said.

"Okay, Betty Jean, don't get all worked up. Now, I need you to meet me at the church at 5:30 p.m.. I talked to the first lady earlier today who told me that Pastor won't be in until this afternoon and they are going to Lance Jr.'s game tonight. So, that is enough time for us to tidy up his office. I told the church janitor to take the day off and come back on Saturday afternoon to get the church ready for the Pre-Appreciation service," said Sister Finley.

"Wow, you have a lot of power. When did you start telling church staff to take the day off?" questioned Sister Pepperdine.

"It's easy, when they are too stupid or looking for an excuse not to work. I told him that Pastor told me to tell him to take the day off to spend time with his wife, who is in the hospital battling an episode with her lupus condition," said Sister Finley.

"Girl, you are so bad. God is going to get you for lying on the preacher," said Sister Pepperdine.

"Well it's really not a lie. I overheard Pastor talking to Abraham about letting our church janitor off from work to spend time with his sick wife, and I thought it was perfect timing. I told him to take off Friday, so that we would have time to do our little extreme makeover surprise for the pastor. And, while we are remodeling his office, make sure to remind me to take down the first lady's picture and her personal biography hanging up in his office. I don't understand why she must have her picture and bio up next to the pastor in his office. It's not like we are giving her a salary too. I told our church secretary to take the word 'family' off the programs for the appreciation service. This celebration is for the pastor, not his family or his wife. Does she get up every Sunday and preach to us? Is she held responsible for our souls? No, she is not, and therefore, we should not appreciate her or her children," said Sister Finley, in her customary sarcastic tone.

"I guess you forgot we are giving the first lady a salary now. Remember, she is Director of Victorious Workers," said Sister Pepperdine.

"Oh yes, indeed, how that happened I don't know. I must be losing my grip, because that should not have occurred. That reminds me, I need to give Kayla a call to see how she is doing in her job search. She cried like a baby when she found out that she didn't get the job as Director of Victorious Workers. I bought her a $200 black pants suit for her interview with the panel and she still didn't get it. Did you find out from Jenkins why they didn't hire Kayla?" asked Sister Finley.

"Please, Jenkins is not saying a word to me about that matter. Furthermore, I believe the first lady does sacrifice being married to the pastor. She has to be careful with her words and be discreet while her life is altered by the members' needs as well," noted Sister Pepperdine.

"Does she dress like she is sacrificing for anyone or anything? Is she teaching in the church or even singing in the choir when we all know she can sing? Isn't she and Pastor both dressed to kill every Sunday at church?"

"I guess so, Sarah, but you would talk about them if they weren't dressed to kill," trailed Sister Pepperdine.

"Please, Betty Jean. They have it made. They are living in a parsonage, all bills paid. We give them a housing allowance and he was recently approved for a $50 monthly car allowance. Our pastor's aide agreed to pay for Pastor Stevens' seminary tuition to obtain his accredited doctorate from Dallas Seminary. Sister Stevens is working for the church outreach business, and receiving a nice salary at twelve dollars an hour. They are riding in nice cars, even if those cars are over eight years old. They are rolling. But, wait and see. I bet you the next thing he requests will be a new car. I don't see why they can't go out and buy a new car with their own money. They don't have to be dependent on the church for everything," said Sister Finley, matter-of-factly.

"Is that all the church is paying Sister Stevens is twelve dollars an hour? Are you serious? Why, that lady has two degrees. She could earn over $80,000 a year in the secular world!" said Sister Pepperdine.

"She can work for a secular company and find another church for

all I care. Kayla should have had that job, and if Sister Stevens wasn't the pastor's wife, the job would have been Kayla's," said Sister Finley. *"Meet me at the church around 5:30 and we will talk then."*

"Okay, Sarah, talk to you later," said Sister Pepperdine as she gently laid the phone down on the phone rest.

"Lord, Jesus, I pray I am not guilty by association for this," Sister Pepperdine said out loud to herself.

"I pretended I didn't hear their conversation," said Deacon Jenkins. "I rose up from the table and gave her my last words of that day," he continued.

"Betty Jean, I am going to give you a warning. Stop messing with the church and leave the pastoral family alone. You are asking for trouble. You know how controlling Sarah Ann is. Don't join her in her devilish games. You need to go with me tonight, and forget about meeting up with Sarah Ann. You know this isn't right."

"I told you I have other plans," Betty Jean lowered her eyes and turned toward the stove. *"Besides, you and I know Sarah Ann is all talk. She is not going to do anything to the pastor or his family. I am going to make sure of that. I gave her a listening ear, that's all Jenkins. Sarah is harmless. She is getting old and she is fighting it tooth and nail. She is not trying to pass the torch down to another soul. But, again, I have other plans and I am not comfortable around Junior yet, since he overheard me talking about his family. Now, just leave me alone, Jenkins, I have other plans.*

"Woman, you and I both know you will be sitting here tonight on that phone gossiping with Sarah about the church," said Deacon Jenkins. *"I'm going over to Thelma's Diner for lunch,"* he concluded, slamming the door behind him.

"What about my chicken & dumplings and cabbage I'm slaving over here trying to fix for us?" hollered Betty Jean out of the kitchen window.

"Eat it yourself!" Deacon Jenkins hollered back.

"I drove off in my car and grabbed lunch at Thelma's Diner," said Jenkins with a scowl on his face. "I don't know yet, but I have a funny feeling Sister Finley may be up to something. "Sister Stevens, we have to pray for the both of them. I must make plans to talk to Abraham Finley's about his wife."

"We will be praying, Deacon Jenkins. God will protect His church," I said, assuring him. "Be careful about approaching a man about his wife. Pray on the matter first. Perhaps, your sister will put a stop to this nonsense. Nothing has been done just yet. And of course, this is conversation you overheard and you weren't supposed to be listening. Be careful, Deacon Jenkins. Be careful," I shared with him.

Jesus give me strength. I thought to myself. Surely these women could not be that evil? Or could they?

Chapter Fifteen

A Beautiful Southern Lunch

It was a beautiful April afternoon in Southlake. Birds were chirping, squirrels were playing hide and seek along the curbed streets and there was a clean northeastern Texas breeze flowing through the city. There wasn't a cloud in the sky, and the Texas beauty of the day put a smile on every face that entered Southlake. It was on these days of living in Southlake that I was glad we relocated here. I was on my way to eat at Thelma's Diner since Lance wouldn't be home until mid afternoon from his revival trip. I wore my beige linen A-line pants with a red silk blouse accented with my Indian ruby red jewelry with matching earrings, necklaces and two rings. It was a gift Lance brought back with him from one of his revivals in the state of Florida a few months back.

Today, I felt pretty and professional even if I was now a size 14. I knew it was important to "look" like a pastor's wife wherever I was out and about in the city of Southlake. My hair, nails, and clothes must look polished at all times. People expected their pastor and his family to look good at all times. The first family was a reflection of the church, as Sister Sarah Finley reminded me at least once every other month. I walked into Thelma's Diner to find Deacon Jenkins sitting in a booth by himself reading a paper. Deacon Jenkins looked regal in his khaki pants, Sean John button down maroon shirt and Stacy Adams shoes with a matching maroon kango hat. I walked over to his booth and sat down.

"Would you like some company, old man?" I asked.

He looked at me. "Sister Stevens, how are you doing? I am blessed to see you in here," replied Deacon Stevens, putting his paper down on the table. "You are looking very pretty today. I love your Indian red accessories. That really looks good on you."

"Why, if I didn't know it, I would think you were flirting with me, Deacon," I said with a hint of teasing in my voice and a wink in my eye.

"Girl, I'm old enough to be your daddy, but I have learned to always compliment a good looking woman on a beautiful day like this," said Deacon Jenkins.

The waitress walked over and took our orders.

"I'll have a salad with red-wine vinaigrette dressing, a small baked potato with the works, and a glass of water with lemon," I said.

"I'll have your chicken fried steak meal and a glass of sweet tea," said Deacon Jenkins.

"Thank you."

"I can't believe that you are not home eating one of Sister Pepperdine's famous meals," I said. "Is everything all right?"

"Yes, she and I had one of our little spats again, that's all. I needed some air, and I was hungry so I came here.

"I hope your spat wasn't over her and Sister Finley's surprise for Pastor," I said.

I didn't tell Lance what Jenkins had shared. I was determined to meet it with prayer and God would reveal their true intentions. I didn't want to assume what these women were trying to do.

"No, our spat was over the bathroom toilet seat. I left it up again," laughed Jenkins, "and Betty Jean was having a fit about. She has refused to talk to me about their surprise so I pray that they have abandoned that idea. I walked into Pastor's office last Sunday and I was relieved to see that all was the same and nothing had been changed. You haven't mentioned anything to him about it?" Jenkins asked.

I looked at my hands carefully in my lap and said, "Jenkins, I don't want to worry him, needlessly. If it happens, we will deal with it."

"I hope I didn't share too much with you First Lady about that conversation. I know you are a strong prayer warrior, and there is not anyone else in the church I could entrust with that information. We are in a good swing right now at the church with people turning to Christ, great ministries, our tithes and offerings are doing well. I am the chairman of the Deacon Board, and I support and uplift the ministry of the church."

I looked him in his light brown eyes, aged with creases of wisdom and placed my hand in his hand. "Jenkins, you are an awesome deacon; possibly one of the best that Pastor and I have had the privilege to know."

Jenkins immediately blushed and said, "How often do you come to Thelma's Diner?" asked Deacon Jenkins.

I looked around and saw Vivian Daniels smiling at me from across the room. I put my hand in the lap and continued my conversation with Deacon Jenkins.

"I go once a week and I know Thelma's barbeque ribs are probably the reason I have put on this extra weight."

"You look great, Sister Stevens," Deacon Jenkins said.

The owner of Thelma's Diner, Thelma Henderson, was originally from Karnack, Texas, a small town located in East Texas. Her immediate family was known for their secret family barbeque sauce and their ability to make a great Texas sausage and delicious ribs. Her macaroni and cheese and baked beans could make a grown man slap himself. She opened up her own restaurant in Southlake about ten years ago and the community of Southlake, blue collar and professional folks alike, made her an instant hit in the county.

Today, it was filled with people on their lunch break and tourists who loved to take pictures of her wall of fame which contained pictures of famous Texans, politicians and entertainers that have dined at her restaurant. Thelma was a member of New Light and gave the pastoral family a 50% discount whenever they came to dine at her restaurant. She and Vivian Daniels were second cousins, and the granddaughters of two sisters. They had always supported each other in their business. So today, I noticed that Vivian was eating Thelma's signature barbeque ribs, potato salad and baked beans with a cool margarita.

Vivian was eyeing Deacon Jenkins like a fat man in a candy store. Deacon Jenkins may be 63 years old, but I'm sure any woman like Vivian might feel he was a king of wealth and intelligence. He was 6'4 inches tall, with pepper gray hair, a kingly pepper gray beard, light hazel eyes, and brown majestic skin. Deacon was a nicely built piece of man who owned a slamming Mercedes Benz SUV and lived in the "right" community of Southlake in his 4,000-square-foot home. Deacon Jenkins oozed money, and he was a college professor. He possessed brains, beauty, money, and power. It was a perfect combination.

Vivian was wondering what Deacon Jenkins and I were doing out together from the smirk on her face. I was trying my best to pay attention to his conversation, but Vivian was just outright staring at us now. I smiled back and waved her over to our table.

"Wow, aren't you two the picture of happiness over here?" said Vivian as she walked up to our booth.

Vivian looked beautiful in a pink and green tunic sundress and two inched heeled Star Jones Fioni strap sandals. The smile on her face let me know that this scene would definitely be replayed in her weekly gossip sessions at her salon. Deacon

Jenkins didn't have a clue that he was about to be devoured by this woman of distinction. Her curvy, sexy walk communicated that she was a woman on a mission to plant herself in a potential Boaz's garden.

"Hello, Vivian. It's so good to see you. Yes, the good deacon and I both happen to be here at the same time and we said why eat alone, when we can eat together?" I said with a smile and glow on my face. "This is Deacon Jenkins, our Chairman of Deacons at New Light. Do you two already know one another? I know I am still new to Southlake," I said.

"Hello, Ms. Vivian, you are looking mighty nice today. Pink and green are your colors, young lady. Of course we know each other. I've known Vivian since she was a little girl, playing that organ and making it talk. She was our county's first child musical prodigy," said Deacon Jenkins.

"You are so kind, Jenkins," said Vivian, as she gently stroked Deacon Jenkins' back. "I hope you noticed that I am a grown woman with many needs and wants."

I noticed that Deacon Jenkins was now looking Vivian up and down with his eyes and laughing at her comment at the same time. Okay, the deacon had some moves.

"Mrs. Stevens, you look absolutely fabulous! Girl, red is your color," said Vivian.

"Why, if it wasn't for Heavenly Hands," I said, raising my hands in the air like I was giving a praise shout, "I don't know where I would be."

"Thank you, sister. Well, I just wanted to stop by and say hello. It's time for me to prepare for my next appointment at the salon. I will see you next week for your regular weekly appointment First Lady," said Vivian to me and kissed me on the check.

She faced Deacon Jenkins, "As for you, Jenkins, I hope to be seeing you in the near, not so far future," Vivian said with a wink of her eye. "Good day to both of you," Vivian walked off with a little twist in her step I'm sure just in case the good deacon was still watching her walk off. And he was.

When she arrived at the door of Thelma's Diner to exit, I noticed Vivian peeked at our booth to find Deacon Jenkins still watching her with a huge grin on his face. With that, Vivian swung her golden micro braids and laughed as she strutted out of the door. I knew Vivian may visit New Light real soon after all. Work on her Lord, anyway you can, I thought. I smiled and continued to eat my salad.

Just as Vivian left the restaurant, I noticed Deacon Jenkins' bright eyes and grin went to a look of worry. I saw Brother Ray Joseph coming into Thelma's Diner with an entourage of about three young men who looked no older than 30 years old. They were dressed in loud colors, and when they walked, I noticed that most of them swished their behind more than most women. Brother Ray Joseph sat down with his entourage, but I knew when he noticed us, he would make his way to our table.

"Lord, that is just a shame over there," Deacon Jenkins implied with his eyes as he looked at Ray's encourage gathered all together in a small booth. "Now, that young man didn't start out that way, but something just got a hold of him.

"My mother told me that Satan tries to pervert the gift of worshippers. He tries to pervert the sensitivity of artists, dancers, writers, musicians and persons who praise and worship God in the arts. Satan himself was created as Lucifer, the most beautiful angel in heaven, and yet that honor was not enough for him. Lucifer was created for worship to God, but Lucifer wanted to be worshiped. We become lovers of our own image-vanity; then we lose sight of what God has for our lives. After Lucifer was thrown out of heaven, God created man for worship. Satan wants to stop, deny, and pervert the worship of God. That young man is a true worshipper, but he lost his way," said Deacon Jenkins.

I listened with great intensity as this church deacon ministered to me. I sensed that he loved this young man, yet he did not know how to reach him.

"Sister Stevens, we need to pray for that young man. I've known him all his life, and we need to show him the love of Jesus. This is the only way we are going to win him."

"I will, Deacon," I replied as I watched Brother Joseph walking toward our table. He was wearing his trademark vest, buttoned down long sleeved shirt, faded blue jeans, and black Marco Vicci shoes. Brother Ray Joseph was definitely a man any young female could fall for. He was handsome with his naturally curly hair, cut low to advertise his waves, and his almond colored eyes could move any female.

"If it's not Super Deacon Jenkins and First Lady Stevens," he said.

I was surprised he was wearing bangles on his wrist with three earrings on each ear and that his eyebrows were now arched. What was this young man going through?

"Hello, Brother Joseph," I said. Deacon Jenkins just lowered his eyes.

"Well, are you two going to invite me to sit down or what? I may not be a member of New Light anymore, but you still know me," Ray said as he sat down in the booth next to Deacon Jenkins.

"You are looking mighty pretty today, First Lady. I love your red jewelry. You are going to have to let me borrow those sometimes. Do you like my bangles? I bought these yesterday at Macy's. Girl, they had a sale where you could buy three bangles and get two for free. So you know I loaded up and bought several," Ray said without a thought to his manhood.

"Brother Joseph, I like you without the bangles," I courageously said.

"How is that husband of yours doing?" Ray said with a lot of sarcasm. "Please let him know that I am playing at the big church down the highway and I make $1,000 a Sunday. They let me play my music and stay out of my personal business. As long as I make them shout and be slain in the Spirit by the tuning of the organ, they are satisfied. Some preachers don't care about how their parishioners live. As long as they have a fat pocket full of green paper bills, they are satisfied. They let my friends over there join the church and become a part of the musician team. In *our* community, we believe in giving great amounts of money to the church and other charities. You could say that it's our penance."

I looked over there at his friends in the booth and saw that they were freely drinking beers and smoking cigarettes without a care to their Christian witness and testimony in the public eye.

I guess my face said what I felt. Brother Ray quickly said, "No, First Lady, they don't look or act like the average Christian, but they need salvation too. Unlike your husband, some churches don't judge other folks. They allow us to come as we are, as we really are."

"Brother, no one said you can't come to church, but you must be ready to become holy for Christ. You refused to get counseling and confront your sins. We love you, son," Deacon Jenkins said, turning to really look at Brother Joseph.

"You would love me for who I am, if you truly loved me," Brother Joseph responded.

"We do love you, and that is why this is so difficult. The Bible says to love the sinner but hate the sin. When did sin define you? No one is trying to hurt or judge you. We have something in life to overcome. We have personal sins that we have to face and overcome. However, when we are in positions of leadership in the church, sometimes our sins are more magnified or seen more often because we are in the front. Sin should not become a lifestyle that we accept," I said with caution.

"Oh, the first lady knows Jesus. I couldn't tell if you knew the Man or not, because you sit so quietly on the second pew and smile at everyone," Ray said as he waited for my reply.

"Brother Joseph, I think you need to return to your table with your friends. It was nice seeing you, and I pray that God moves on your heart towards obedience," Deacon Jenkins said."

"Kicked out again! I heard about your new powerful musician team in Brother and Sister Graves. But, from what I hear, there might be trouble in the home. You may want to check it out Super Deacon. Remember, you didn't hear it from me." He places his index finger to his lips signaling us to keep quiet.

"In a couple months, we are putting on a big concert at my new church and I want you both to come and hear our new gospel band. You know our church now has 6,000 members and I may start attending our seminary school that is affiliated with our church. Maybe I'll start my own church and show the world what the church should look like," Ray said with a smirk. "Now that is an idea" he continued as he got up from our table.

"We love you, Ray," Deacon Jenkins said.

There was an uncomfortable silence that followed as the two men looked at each other. "I'm sure you do, but this is who I am and who I choose to be. Love me for that," Ray said. It sounded like he was pleading for acceptance.

"The Bible will not allow me to celebrate sin, but I am called to love you. I have shown you that. Because we love Christ, we must overcome our sins. He will bless us and reward us for obedience. He blesses us when we reject the lust of the flesh and turn to His will and become obedient," Deacon Jenkins ministered.

Brother Ray Joseph turned to walk away and shook his head as he returned to his lively group of friends who were buzzing with glee from drinking their beers.

"You really do care for him, don't you?" I asked Deacon Jenkins.

"He is one of my former students. He was an A student all through school. He could sing and play the piano since the age of ten. Ray is living in a world where black male geniuses are not celebrated, but they are tolerated. He wasn't a thug. He wasn't trying to prove his manhood by fathering multiple babies out of wedlock. He always dressed nice, did his school work, and was always at church during the week. Believe me when I say, he was all boy. But when the alpha males were outside playing football and chasing girls, Ray was inside reading books and writing music. He was teased about it by his neighborhood friends. His parents would encourage him to use his mind and read all he could. His dad would tell him, 'If you chase money, you'll never have to chase women, but if you chase women, you'll always be chasing money.' He dated a young girl once that he was quite serious about. They dated for nearly a year and then she moved away to go to college. I encouraged Ray to go away to college, but he loved playing for New Light's choir. I wanted him to go away to college, and meet more geniuses like him. He went away for three months, but returned before the end of fall semester. He received his degree on line and recently received his MBA from the University of Phoenix. But, music is his first love."

"I didn't know he was so educated," I said.

"Most people don't know. He has never really used his degree for any good length of time. He changes jobs like he changes shoes. In the last ten years, he has been a teacher, a job trainer, a producer, a writer, an accountant, a mortgage broker, construction manager, fast food manager, and a bank teller. Ray is a lost soul, and he can't find anything to fill his void," Jenkins said.

"What is he doing now?" I asked.

"He has this gospel band and they are trying to record a live CD. He substitutes for the local school district, and rumor has it he is trying to open up an after school performing arts academy at the shopping strip where Victorious Workers is located," Jenkins said. "Ray Sr. and I were fraternity brothers. I promised him I would look after his son. Ray Sr. died of cancer seven years ago. Ray Jr.'s mother died when he was just 17 years old. Both of Ray's parents are gone now, so you can say I do feel like an older dad to him. Ray Sr. and Sarah Finley were distant cousins, though a lot of people don't know that."

"Why?" I asked.

"Ray Joseph Sr. was the illegitimate child of Sarah Finley's great uncle, Deacon William Harris."

"You mean the Deacon William Harris that New Light's fellowship hall is named after?"

"Yes. Deacon Harris did a lot to help the African-Americans of Southlake. He was a great tenor, and would sing all over the state of Texas. He donated the money to build the fellowship hall. He would host local gospel concerts and was very active in the state religious conferences and conventions. He donated money to local schools and served as the first African-American councilman in Southlake. He was married for forty years, and had two children. And, then there was Ray Sr. Apparently during one of his travels, he fathered a child who he didn't know existed. Ray Sr. showed up at New Light at the age of 28 to introduce himself to his dad. I still remember that church service when Ray Sr. first visited New Light." Deacon Jenkins went on to tell the story.

"Good morning, New Light. I have traveled here from Tulsa, Oklahoma to find my roots," Ray Sr. said.

"Amen," the church replied.

"I waited for this moment to meet the man who fathered me," Ray Sr. continued. It seemed like a third of the men in the church crouched down on their pew. *"I tried to contact him but to no avail. I set up times to talk with him, but he refuses to speak to me. This may be the only way to hold my father accountable. I have to announce this to his church."* The preacher began to crouch in his seat. One of the ladies in the choir stand began to fan him.

"Deacon William Harris, I am your son. I am your oldest son with Cynthia Mae Joseph. My father did nothing wrong. This was before his present marriage. He was forced to leave the town of

Vidor, Texas. My mother is white, and her parents would not allow my parents to marry. They forbade my mother to tell him about her pregnancy. My mother told me the truth about my father and this is why I am here today."

Deacon Harris embraced his son. "I am so sorry. You never told me the details. I haven't heard that name for over 25 years. Welcome home, son"

The church exploded with applause as Deacon Harris' family looked on in shock.

"As a result, Sister Finley and her family never really embraced Ray Sr. and his family. He relocated to Southlake. He and his wife became active members at New Light," stated Deacon Jenkins.

"New Light has an interesting history. Everyone is related in some way, if not by blood or kinship, then by strong emotional bonds," I said.

"I worry about this," Jenkins said.

"What?"

"Church members are more concerned about their personal relationships in the church, than they are about their relationship to Christ, that is when the church is in danger of behaving like a social club or even a cult."

"What do you mean?" I asked.

"Church members value their friendships in the church more than they value Christ. People treat each other rudely and they take sides over issues that are not salvation based issues. The mission of the church is lost or forgotten."

I was so engrossed in our conversation that the waitress had to snap me back into reality.

"Here is your lunch, Sister Stevens and Deacon Jenkins," she said, setting our main lunch entrees down.

"We must pray for our church. I feel a storm coming," Deacon Jenkins said.

"I will pray, Deacon. I sure will," I said as the knots in my stomach churned with an all too familiar uneasiness.

Chapter Sixteen

Anonymous Letters

I came home after having lunch with Deacon Jenkins and walked into my bedroom to retrieve my journal that I placed in one of my secret places of my home. I wrote:

Dear First Lady,

Today, I had a great afternoon with Deacon Jenkins at Thelma's Diner. He is a really smart man and I think Vivian has a crush on him. They would make an attractive couple. Mr. Jenkins told me he wasn't dating right now, because he is still grieving over his late wife, even if five years has passed since her death. This is something I will pray that he finds: a female Christian companion.

I pray, Lord, that you deliver Brother Ray Joseph from vanity and the love of his own image. Turn him back to you. Help us show him unconditional love for we know that nothing can separate us from your love.

Tonight is Junior's game, and I hope Lance is going to arrive home in time to come to his game. I learned so much about the history of Southlake and New Light from Deacon Jenkins. That man is a walking encyclopedia. I pray our church will not turn into a "cult mentality" where their personal friendships outweigh their relationship with Christ.

Deacon Jenkins told me about his 40-year marriage to his deceased wife and their travels. They were not able to have any children because of his infertility. The fact that he wouldn't have a son to carry on his name is something that had haunted him most of his adult life. I asked him why he didn't adopt any children and he said that he and his beloved wife, Doris, were so busy giving and tending to the children of New Light, that they were like the children they never had. He told me his sister, Betty Jean Pepperdine, can't conceive either. This was the bond they shared together, so they helped other people raise their kids and had a special relationship with the children of New Light. The selfish side of me wanted to remind him that Betty Jean Pepperdine was overheard by my son talking about our family. Lance Junior may never view Betty Jean as a friend or supporter as a result. I respect Deacon Jenkins too much to inflict something negative to him about his sister. He knows her better than I did. Some things are better off not being said at all.

I know Sister Pepperdine is loyal to Sister Finley since they grew up together. I long for friendship in my life outside of my family. I am praying for a friend in Southlake who loves me for me and not because I am Pastor Stevens's wife. I haven't found that kind of companion here.

The ministers' wives in the Southlake metropolis area are standoffish and not too friendly. Some of them talk too much for my taste, and I am generally afraid to trust them. For example, just last month, one of the pastor's wives in McKinney actually got up in the congregation during a banquet held in honor of First Lady McDonald and shared how she and Sister McDonald, a bishop's wife, talked on the phone about their husbands' infidelities. Yeah, First Lady she really said that! She said, "My husband may love the Lord, but he also loves the skirts and the butts, isn't that right, Sister McDonald?"

Poor Sister McDonald ran out of the banquet hall crying. Just imagine, if I had shared some intimate things with her and she told an entire church family. So, I have determined to be discreet and try not to bring shame to my husband's ministry. As a result, it can be a lonely life. I am not active with anything at the church yet. It is by choice, but Lance is not encouraging my involvement in anything in the church except Victorious Workers, which is outside of the church in another location. At his other churches, I sang in the choir, worked with the youth, mission groups, and played an active part in the Pastor's aide. But it was during the times of my great involvement that I faced my greatest dilemmas with his members. They used me for their own personal agendas and tried to pick and set me up to achieve their own goals.

It was at times very confusing and caused me to not trust anyone within the church. It was also a source of great bitterness for me. Now, at New Light, Lance was encouraging me to take it slow and take my time to discover my purpose. Lance thought I needed time to allow the members to get used to me first. I enjoyed singing and sometimes I missed singing in the choir and leading songs. I love giving praise to God. Last week, our new musician, Brother Marcus Graves invited me to participate in the new Praise and Worship Team he was starting. I told him that I would have to speak with my husband about it first. I hadn't bothered to ask Lance, fearing that he would tell me, "No, not now, it's too soon." I guess I will ask him sooner or later. Perhaps I will wait until after the one-year Pastor's Appreciation service in six weeks.

I saw a draft of the printed program in Lance's administrative assistant office and it read, "Pastor Appreciation Day" and no one has bothered to say anything about his family. I guess I don't mind. Every church does it differently. Typically at the other churches my husband pastored, they would always include the children and me with a poem or something as a token of respect. And the programs usually included a picture of the pas-

tor's family. I know it was probably Sister Finley's idea to exclude the pastor's family from the appreciation service programs. The church's new administrative assistant is her distant cousin and I am sure Sister Finley had her to change the programs to delete the pastor's family. I know that Sister Finley does not care too much for me, but she tries to be respectful. I can tell that it is killing her to even speak to me on Sunday mornings.

Every Sunday, she looks me up and down from head to toe and never says a "You look nice" or anything. She takes a full view and walks away. I feel like I am being inspected when I am in her presence. I am praying for her, because she doesn't realize she won't see Jesus if she doesn't learn to love me. I need to go by the church and get a church membership record for Victorious Workers. So, First Lady, I will talk to you soon and please keep praying for me . . .

Love,
Jackie Stevens

I closed my journal and placed it under my bed mattress. One of the secret places I kept it so that I could get to it quickly when I needed it. I found this journal to be very therapeutic. I took a class in psychology while attending the University of Texas and I learned life is full of curves and pitfalls. It doesn't get any easier, but you have got to find better methods of coping with life's pitfalls . Destructive coping habits can lead to death and bitterness. I learned this early in my journey as a minister's wife.

I met a pastor's wife years ago who used alcohol to deal with the pressures of being married to a prominent pastor. She was home alone, while he covered the country preaching revivals. She had two children who kept her company, but she told me she often felt like a single woman as she cared for and nurtured them. They owned a 5,000-square-foot home in a prosperous section of Los Angeles, California. They drove luxury cars and she was unfulfilled. She loved Jesus, but she allowed alcohol to fill her void. She was a raving alcoholic at the age of forty. I will always remember her testimony at a Minister's Wives Conference of drying out at an Alcoholic Anonymous Retreat Center and getting her Christian and family life back on track. Her husband was so busy trying to save other souls, he didn't realize his own wife lost fellowship with God and him. I knew alcohol and other numbing drugs can be a real problem for those who are constantly under the limelight or living in a fishbowl. I attend self-help conferences and seminars that cater to clergy wives or women in leadership just to help me stay encouraged. I remember learning from one of the Ministry Wives Conferences I attended about the anonymous letter that is common among clergy wives.

Lance was pastoring at Little Mt. Zion. We were there four years when my first anonymous letter came in the mail. This letter said Lance was having an affair with his church secretary at Little Mt. Zion, Sister Sharon Dancey, who was a thirty-two year old college student who was single with two kids. She became a great friend to us and babysat our kids while we traveled during Lance's ministry engagements. The letter was typed and it said this:

Dear First Lady, or in the words of your husband, I'll call you Goldie.

I know you are wondering why I am writing you, but you have a right to know that Sister Dancey is not your friend. I saw your husband pick her up and take her to a local motel in town at least three different times around 2p.m. That's right, Goldie, your precious man is cheating on you and right in your face. I thought you should know everyone smiling in your face is not who you think they are. So beware and remember to trust in the Lord. Of course, I cannot leave my name, but my prayers are with you. Handle your business and set that woman straight. Remember, boys will be boys so don't be so hard on the pastor.

Signed
Anonymous

I remember thinking that I was officially in the sisterhood of the First Ladies Sorority now. Lance was furious someone would disrespect our house and his wife by having the audacity to send an anonymous letter. He wanted to go to the pulpit on Sunday morning and expose everything and dare anyone to send anything else to our house. I told him that we would not give Satan any time or energy during a service dedicated to worshipping God. Who ever sent that letter wanted attention and wanted to start some friction, and I wouldn't dishonor my integrity by getting on their level.

I told my husband I loved and trusted him, and a letter could not take that away. Now, if there were problems going on and I had a question about Lance's whereabouts, then the letter may have caused me to cringe. Lance was a good father and a respectful, predictable husband, and at 2:00 p.m. he was picking up his three-year-old from school every day. Nevertheless, we shared the letter with his secretary, who was implicated in the letter. Sister Sharon Dancey broke into tears, and quit her position as secretary and left Little Mt. Zion one month later. She couldn't deal with the drama that came along with being a secretary to a pastor. Lord knows church secretaries have to deal with as much drama as clergy wives.

Lance and I grew together after that episode and we were determined to stay together in spite of vices within and outside of the church that had tried to separate us. We never discovered the writer of the anonymous letter, and neither did we try to find out, but I will tell you I put a prayer on that person that Jesus would take them down like David slew Goliath. I am a firm believer in asking God to fight our battles. And believe me, none of my enemies have ever won against my God. He is my strong deliverer and redeemer. About four months after that, I received another anonymous letter which simply said,

Dear Goldie,

I guess you have more class that I thought you did. You need to start taking better care of your man before I do. I know what he needs and what he deserves. I should be his Goldie. Are you wondering, how I know his name for you? You can keep wondering on that one. It may have slipped out one night when he was with me.

I can give him what you are apparently refusing, of late, to give him. I saw you at the conference walking around in your big silver hat like a rooster crowing. Let this be a warning, your man is up for grabs and his heart is lonely and his eyes are beginning to wander. You think your man is super spiritual, but I know that he is just a man; a man that can be broken. Remember, to say that you are the first lady, implies that there is a second lady. A lady, you are not. Even your hats can't cover that fact. I am what the Pastor needs; A lady of distinction and respect. And you might want to learn to cook better because he loves my sweet potato pies and fried green tomatoes. There is more than one way to a man's heart, and his heart is leading straight to me.

Signed
You Know Who, Anonymous

Soon after this second anonymous letter came, Lance began to check and scan all mail coming to our home. He was furious someone could be so cruel to disrespect our family. I laughed it off, and wondered what conference this person saw me at. I attend two or three major conferences a year, and I can't remember where I wore a silver hat. Anyhow, I said a fast and furious prayer that God would bring justice and mercy to the writer of that letter. I knew my God protected me from many other situations that would seek to destroy and hurt me so I trusted in Him completely to guide me and hold me in times of great frustration.

Apparently, the anonymous sender was frustrated by the lack of our visible response and they soon changed their plan. Letters were sent to the church full of pornography, and my name was on the front of them. Now, they were disrespecting the house of God. Lance dealt with the matter during the next church worship service at Little Bethel.

"I pray the wrath of God on the lives of the persons who want to dishonor the house of God and discredit the man of God," he had said. *The church was shocked to hear their preacher speak with such force and apparent anger. "This is the Lord's house. It's not my house, it's not your house. This house was consecrated to belong to the most High God,"* Lance said to the congregation.

After Lance stood up to the demons that tried to take our focus, we never received another anonymous letter. Members of the church began to respect us in a different way. As a result, a new prayer warrior team was started at Little Zion, that met on Sunday mornings at 8 a.m. specifically to pray for the pastor, his family and the unity of the church.

I knew Satan wanted to sway the church from our first love, which is bringing souls to Christ. I prayed I would not get distracted from my focus on God, my family, and my community. In 39 years, I learned that life is a journey. It is a process. It is a seasonal experience. As King Solomon said in Ecclesiastes 3:1, "There is a time for everything, a season for every activity under heaven." I learned that every experience should be a learning experience and the experience came because God either caused it or allowed it. God is omnipotent and omnipresent, all at the same time. I learned to trust Him and put my complete faith in Him. I needed to get my praise on before bitterness would start to call my name again and beckon me to her bosom.

I walked to the music system in our bedroom and turned on gospel artist, Natalie Wilson and SOP's gospel song, "He's Working It Out for You." I loved that song. I lay on my bed and meditated about God and the things He has done for me. I listened as Natalie Wilson sang the song about how God is working everything out in our lives. I said a silent prayer that Lance would get home safely from Austin. I thanked God for His blessings in my life. I changed the CD and turned on one of my favorite gospel artists, Chester D. T. Baldwin, and listened to his song, "A God of Another Chance." Tears of triumph flowed as I recalled God's grace during those times where I wanted to give up and walk away from the church. And how God gave me another chance to see Him work in my life and let me see the vision and purpose that He has for my life.

I am learning to surrender my all to God on a daily basis so that His will, will be accomplished in my life. I felt God embrace me as I lay on my bed of meditation and His glory filled my empty space of loneliness. It seemed like I had cried for hours until I opened my eyes from resting to see my husband leaning on one knee, kneeling by my bedside.

"Hello, Goldie," Lance said, kissing me on the cheek.

"Hi, sweetheart. You made it home safely. Praise God!" I said through tear stained eyes.

"Are you okay? It looks like you have been crying. Your eyes are red and puffy," Lance questioned. "Did the light bill get paid? Is the gas out? Did the deacons look after you while I was gone?" he quizzed with a look of worry over his face.

Reaching for the Kleenex beside my bed, I lightly sat up on the bed and dabbed my eyes. "So many questions; the church treated us fine while you were gone and yes the bills were paid timely this past month. I was rejoicing and thanking God for all that He has done for us. You know I remember the parsonage that we lived in when you first pastored a church. Remember how the parsonage was leaking all the time? We had to keep moving Connie's crib around the house so that she wouldn't get wet because we had so many leaks."

"Do I remember?" Lance said, rolling his eyes in the back of his head.

"I remember the financial struggles, the small love offerings that we lived by, and the church drama God delivered us from. I was overwhelmed by His divine protection and awesomeness. It has been a year now at New Light, and God is still blessing us and keeping our family. We don't have everything we want right now, but God has delivered on His promise to provide for our needs," I said.

We reminiscenced while Chester D.T. Baldwin's gospel hit song, "God is Good," played in the background. Lance began to sing with the lyrics, "My God is good all the time. When I woke up early this morning, I thank the Lord for a brand new day!"

I watched my husband as he changed his travel clothes, removed his suitcase clothes from the suitcase and placed them in the laundry basket to be washed. I settled comfortably on the bed and thanked God for a man who seemed to care so much for ministry work. I remembered that this was the man I once ran from because I was afraid of being a minister's wife. I didn't want the title or the pressure that came with it. I looked at Lance, and I knew God put us together. I prayed nothing would ever separate us. I knew if I was to stay connected to God, that I must stay connected to God's Word. I grabbed my Bible, and read from the Psalms. I read Psalm 100 out loud:

"Shout with joy to the LORD, O earth!
Worship the LORD with gladness.
Come before him, singing with joy. Acknowledge that
    the LORD is God!
He made us, and we are his.
We are his people, the sheep of his pasture.
Enter his gates with thanksgiving;

go into his courts with praise.
Give thanks to him and bless his name.
For the LORD is good.
His unfailing love continues forever,
and his faithfulness continues to each generation."

As I read this passage out loud, Lance mocked me like a Southern Baptist proclaimer, "Say it again. Can I get a witness? Isn't the Lord good? Yes sah! He is good! I know He's all right!"

We looked at each other with adoration as we celebrated this moment of God's Word and His wonders! I continued in Lamentations 3:22-25, reading out loud with enthusiasm:

"The unfailing love of the LORD never ends! By his mercies we have been kept from complete destruction. Great is his faithfulness; his mercies begin afresh each day. I say to myself, "The LORD is my inheritance; therefore, I will hope in him!" The LORD is wonderfully good to those who wait for him and seek him."

All the while Lance sang Baldwin's song, "God is Good," with high energy and he slid across our wooden floors as if he was preaching with a pretend microphone in his hand. I loved hearing Lance sing. He was blessed with a beautiful voice. His natural vibrato and ability to sing scants and runs could bring any church congregation to their feet. He came to the bed and scooped me in his arms and kissed me passionately. The kids would not be home for another hour, so we knew we had the house to ourselves. The phone rang, which interrupted the mood.

I looked at him and his eyes said "Don't worry about it, I won't answer it." He held me tighter and kissed me deeper. The phone kept ringing. I broke away from him with a hint of disappointment and answered the phone. I checked the caller I. D. The number read Southlake Medical and I handed it to him. He reluctantly took the phone, upset that our precious time together was being interrupted yet again.

"Hello, this is Pastor Stevens," Lance said, straightening up his clothes as if the speaker could see him through the phone.

I patiently waited as I smelled his cologne upon my face from his passionate kiss. I knew that our time together was over and I glanced at the drawer that held my new lingerie and wondered if we would find the time or the energy to enjoy some time together.

"Yes, ma'am. I wasn't aware that your son was in the hospital. I will be there in about an hour. I am sorry, and we will be praying for you. Yes, I promise you I will be there today."

I motioned to him about Junior's basketball game tonight and how he needed to go. I motioned like I was shooting a basketball hoping to remind him about his obligation to his children.

Lance looked up and shook his head and said into the phone. "Yes, ma'am, I will be there. Don't cry, sister. God knows what is best. Let's pray right now, okay? Lance closed his eyes. "Lord, watch over this sister and protect her child. We know that you know what is best for us."

As Lance prayed for this sister on the phone, I got from under his embrace and got out of the bed and walked to the restroom because I knew I would be going to another game alone. I freshened up my makeup and went to the kitchen to prepare dinner for my family. I walked by him as he was still praying for this woman and her son. He opened his eyes, when he felt my presence walking by. I winked at him to let him know I enjoyed our little moment together.

Later, Lance finished his phone call, cleaned and washed his car, showered and headed over to Southlake Medical. I watched him leave as I wrapped his plate of fried chicken, mustard greens, corn, sweet potatoes, and peach cobbler. I placed it in the refrigerator. I fed my children and ironed Junior's uniform. On our way out of the door, Junior asked, "Mom is Dad going to be there tonight?"

I looked at my fourteen-year-old who absolutely adored his daddy and I said, "A member's son was critically injured in an accident today, and he is with the family. I think he will be there if time allows."

Junior just looked at me and gave a small smile and said "I will pray for that family that Dad is trying to help." I knew he was disappointed his father may not be attending another one of his basketball games, but he had developed a sense that his father was a hero who helped to rescue people. At the age of ten, Junior drew a picture of a superhero with his father's face on it as a show and tell project in the fifth grade. Now, I prayed his hero would never disappoint him or let him down.

Chapter Seventeen

The Game

We arrived at the gym to find it packed with parents, fans, and spectators. Junior's game would not begin for another thirty minutes. I watched as the Southlake cheerleaders performed their pre-game dance routine to pump up the crowd for the game. I spotted Deacon Jenkins in the stands, and we walked over and sat by him. My girls, Connie and Jaylyn, gave their customary hellos to Deacon Jenkins and lightly pecked him on each of his cheeks. It was times like this that I missed my father the most. My children did not have a maternal grandfather and Lance's father lives in Oakland, California, but we rarely communicate with him.

"How are my precious angels doing today? How was school?" Deacon Jenkins asked Connie and Jaylyn.

"Fine!" They both responded simultaneously as they both sat down beside him.

"Deacon Jenkins, I made an A on my math test today!" Connie excitedly told him.

"I made an A+ on my science project," said Jaylyn trying not to be outdone by her older sister.

"That is absolutely fantastic! I am so proud of you both!" said Deacon Jenkins.

"Deacon Jenkins, when I grow up, I want to be a college professor just like you," said Connie.

"One day you will teach at a college campus. I can feel it in my bones," Deacon Jenkins said while juggling his body from side to side. Connie and Jaylyn both laughed hysterically.

"Look, there is Daddy!" exclaimed Connie as she pointed across the gym. Lance was shaking a man's hand as he walked into the gym. He scanned the crowd while we waved our hands to get his attention. He spotted us and coolly made his way over to us. His lean stride and confident gait let others around him know he must be an important man. Lance greeted a few people in the stands, and even stopped to talk to a young couple he gave his card to. We waited patiently for him to sit with us in the stands before the game started.

"When is Daddy going to come and sit down with us? It's two minutes until game time," said Jaylyn. I watched my son practice and warm-up with his team. Lance missed so many of Junior's games this season, that Junior rarely scanned the crowd anymore looking for his dad. I caught Junior's eye as he warmed up, and I pointed in the direction of his father, who was now shaking hands with Southlake's mayor, whose son also played on the eighth grade basketball team. Junior saw Lance and nodded his head to acknowledge he had spotted him. I breathed a sigh of relief that Lance had made it to Junior's playoff game in time.

About ten minutes into Junior's basketball game, Lance finally made his way to us.

"Man, I am beat from all that talking and politicking," Lance said as he plopped on a seat next to me, giving me a light kiss on the forehead. I politely looked away as if to say 'the king has arrived.'

"How is the Morris boy doing at Southlake Medical?" I asked Lance.

"He is going to be just fine. He broke his wrist and has some scratches and bruises. But, it is a miracle he is doing well after being hit by that car," Lance said. "Can you send them a card or bake them a cake of encouragement?" Lance asked.

"Yes, I'll make sure they get it by Tuesday. How are his parents doing?" I asked.

"They are both calm knowing their boy will be alright. Mr. Morris said he was going to visit our church this Sunday," Lance said to Deacon Jenkins and me. "Mrs. Morris has been at New Light for six months, but her husband hasn't been in church for over five years. Let's pray that this experience will bring him closer to God and the church.

"Deacon Jenkins, thanks for taking care of my family while I was away," said Lance, giving Deacon Jenkins a firm handshake.

"Pastor, you know how I love you and your family, and we want to make sure you all are well taken care of, especially when the preacher is away," Deacon Jenkins, said giving me a slight wink.

I felt a little uncomfortable and blushed. Lance looked at Deacon Jenkins and me and laughed. "Why Deacon Jenkins, if I didn't say so, I think you might be flirting with my wife."

"Pastor, your wife could be my daughter and that is how I look at her. So as her father, I'm saying, you betta treat this gal right!" said Deacon Jenkins, hitting Lance on the back with a playful left hook.

"Seriously, Deacon, I appreciate the way you always look out for us and the way you look after my family. I've never had a chairman of deacons that cared for my family and me as you have. You are a blessed man, Jenkins," said Lance.

I looked at Deacon Jenkins and said, "Pastor is right, Deacon, We have never had a chairman that cared for us as much and we are both very grateful." I hugged Lance around his waist and gave him a kiss on the cheek. "And Deacon Jenkins is right, Lance, you betta treat this woman right."

We watched the game. Junior scored twenty-one points, with six assists and five steals. Junior's team, the Southlake Cougars, beat the Fort Worth Tors, 62 to 59. It was a close game and Junior, who played point guard, made the three point winning basket that put the Cougars on top! The fans went crazy at that last second three point shot! Junior was destined to be on the varsity basketball team by the time he reached his high school sophomore year.

We celebrated by going out to eat at Thelma's Diner after the game. It was Junior's request. I was uncomfortable, because I just ate at Thelma's today for lunch. I didn't tell Lance this. God knows I hadn't done anything wrong, and surely had nothing to hide. I learned, as a pastor's wife, that the "appearance" of things is very important. Any peculiar or odd moment can get a person in trouble.

"Deacon Jenkins, won't you join us for a celebration dinner at Thelma's Diner tonight? My boy is the man tonight, and you are like family. Come celebrate with us," said Lance.

"You young folks go on, and I'll see you at church on Sunday. Besides, I had enough of Thelma's for one day. Her apple pie just tore up my stomach for lunch today, so I better settle for my sister Betty Jean's cooking tonight," said Deacon Jenkins. He quickly looked at me and I diverted my eyes.

"We will see you Sunday. You have a blessed weekend, and tell Sister Betty I said hello. I am looking forward to eating one of her peach cobblers this Sunday after church," said Lance.

"I'll let her know that you hinted that you would like her to fix one of her cobbler dessert dishes" said Deacon Jenkins. "You have a nice celebration dinner." He gave Junior a nice high five in the air.

"Thanks for coming to the game, Deacon Jenkins," said Junior

"Sure, son. You are a star in the making," Deacon Jenkins replied.

He walked past us, out through the gymnasium side doors.

"Thanks for coming dad. I know you must be tired from your revival. I am glad you are here," said Junior as he walked up to his dad to give him a hug.

Lance hugged him and replied, "I try my best to be here for you. I'm not too tired to be here for my boy! You played an awesome game. I am proud of you. You are representing the Stevens men well. And one day, you will grace the pulpit like the three previous Stevens men, your great grandfather, grandfather and your father before you and proclaim the good news of Jesus Christ.

Junior looked at his daddy, and replied his customary response that I had coached him to say whenever his father tried to push my son in the pulpit, "Whatever God wills me to do, Dad, I will do it," Junior responded.

Junior was growing up with much wisdom. He knew it was better to give Lance a response that was neutral. Since the age of four, church women with their white gloves, would come by and pinch Junior's face as they passed by the communion table, and tell Junior, "Boy, you are going to be a preacher one day, just like your daddy."

Little Junior would just grin and say, "Whatever God wills." Those church women just loved his response and they would just chuckle and keep on walking as they shook hands with the other parishioners passing the communion table.

Later that night, we all went to Thelma's Diner. Lance was in a great mood. He was so excited that his son won a premier basketball game. As soon I walked in to Thelma's Diner, I noticed Vivian Daniels was also at her cousin's restaurant for dinner eating with one of her beauty salon operators. She looked at me, politely smiled, and waved. I nervously waved back and sat Connie and Jaylyn down next to me at the table.

"Hey, babe, isn't that your beautician, Vivian Daniels, over there?" Lance questioned.

"Yes, it is," I replied.

"Isn't she the one you said you had been trying to get to come and visit New Light for the last year? I hear she can really make an organ talk and that she is really talented. Maybe I should go over and introduce myself and personally invite her to New Light," Lance said.

"Sweetheart, we are here for Junior's game celebration. Can we just concentrate on him winning the game?" I said as the children nervously looked at their father and me.

"I'm sure you will have another time to talk to her about New Light. She is always in her cousin's diner, and she is trying to enjoy her meal. It's 9:30 at night, and I can guarantee Vivian has had a long, hard day, working at her salon," I said.

As soon as I sputtered out the words, Vivian made an exit toward the door. However, before exiting, she made her way to our table. "Hello everyone. This must be Pastor Lance Mc-Clain Stevens," she said as she greeted Lance with an elegant handshake.

"Hi, I am Vivian Daniels. Welcome to Southlake, Pastor," Vivian said with an outstretched French manicured hand.

Lance shook her hand. "Thank you, my sister. It is nice to finally meet you. I love the French rolls you routinely give my wife. I love to see her hair like that. You are mighty talented. I hope you would be able to visit us one Sunday morning at the New Light Church. I also hear you are a great musician," said Lance.

"Why, yes, Pastor. I enjoyed playing in the church for many years, and I told your wife that I will try to make it to your first Pastoral appreciation service at New Light," said Vivian.

"Would you bless us with a solo at our appreciation 11:00 a.m. morning service? We have two special appreciation services planned in the month of June. I would love if you sang for our culmination service the last Sunday in June? I hear you can blow the roof off of a church with your eight octave range, and your range is so that your voice never developed a falsetto. Is this true?"

I wondered how Lance knew so much about Vivian. I knew she was a former musician, but I didn't know she could sing as well. I started to think it was his idea to get Vivian back into the church by telling me about her hair salon when we first moved to Southlake. I told him only once that I had been trying to invite her to church. That is my Lance, always trying to get someone closer to Jesus.

"Pastor Stevens, you have heard a lot about me. Yes, I do love to sing and God has blessed both my sister Thelma and me with gifted voices and a gift of cooking. I will check my schedule, and get back to you on that invitation to sing. It has been quite some time since I have sung or played in a church. But, after seeing Deacon Jenkins today at lunch with your first lady, it might be time to visit New Light. That Deacon Jenkins doesn't look a day over fifty years old," Vivian said with a gleam in her eye.

Lance immediately looked at me, and raised his eyebrows as if to say, "Oh, really," Lance cleared his throat. "I will let Deacon Jenkins know that you asked about him," he added while he pulled his business card out of his wallet. "And here is my card, feel free to contact me to let me know if you will be willing to sing. We will confirm the final program agenda by May 15th, so if you can please call me by that date, I would appreciate it," Lance said.

"Yes, Pastor Stevens, I will do that. You enjoy your meal. Thelma's special tonight is fried catfish, collard greens, potato salad, baked beans, apple pie, and iced tea for only $4.99. It is absolutely delicious. Enjoy, y'all, have a nice night," Vivian said as she strutted out of the door.

"You sure know a lot about Ms. Vivian," I said looking at Lance directly in his eye.

"And you know a lot about Thelma's Diner. Why didn't you tell me you had lunch with Deacon Jenkins today?" Lance quizzed.

The waitress suddenly arrived to take our orders. We ordered our food and I then carefully responded. "I didn't schedule a lunch date with anyone today, Lance. I came here today for lunch, and he was already here so we ate together. Remember," I said, leaning over to him, "I planned a romantic evening with my husband who didn't make our date, so I did enjoy some company over lunch," I responded.

"You have to be careful. We are still new to Southlake and you need to be mindful of appearances," he said.

"Yes, dear. I have been a preacher's wife for over fifteen years, so I am well aware of appearances. I was hungry, I came for lunch, Deacon Jenkins was here alone, and we ate together. You know that man is old enough to be my daddy, so why are you making a fuss about it?" I responded.

"Well, the look he gave you at the game tonight, it seems like Deacon wants to be your daddy alright" Lance said, looking away.

I smiled. "Is the great Lance Stevens jealous?" I asked.

He smiled at me and said, "Yes, I don't want anyone messing with my Goldie."

"Oh gosh, Mom and Dad," said Junior. "Please, not at the table."

I think we forgot the children were within earshot.

"Mommy," said Connie with her big light brown eyes and long eyelashes. "Why does Daddy call you his Goldie?"

Lance and I looked at each other and laughed.

"Sweetheart, Goldie is Mommy and Daddy's little secret. Now, eat your food," I said.

"I notice that sometimes Daddy, you call Mommy, Jackie, and then sometimes when you get that weird look in your eye, you call her Goldie," observed our curious eight-year-old.

Lance put his arm around my chair and said, "Yep, she is my Goldie," and gently kissed me on the check. "Go ahead little Connie, finish eating your food."

Lance ordered sparkling ginger ale to celebrate the win for Junior, and the waitress filled all of our glasses for a toast. He began with a toast and said, "Did not Paul say that some wine is good for the stomach?"

Connie and Jaylyn giggled as they raised their glasses in the air and said, "To Junior!"

"Daddy, this is gingerale, not wine, "quipped Junior as he raised his glass in the air. "Come on, Dad, stop joking."

I prayed that no one from New Light entered, at that moment, to see their pastor making a toast in Thelma's Diner. I know we had a discussion about appearances and here we are drinking ginger ale in wine glasses in public. I raised my glass in the air. So much for appearances, I guess.

Later that night I wrote in my journal:

Dear First Lady,

Today was an eventful day. My romantic morning with Lance was postponed. I had a nice lunch with Deacon Jenkins at Thelma's and I think Ms. Vivian Daniels has an eye on him. Junior won his game and he was great tonight. I am so proud of him. We still have yet to talk to his dad about all of his extracurricular activities. I pray that Lance will listen to him.

Our appreciation service is now less than two months away and I am getting nervous. Tomorrow, Lance is going to meet with dealers to purchase a sixty passenger bus for the church. He wants to start allowing his members to travel with him on his revivals. I need to schedule something productive to do while he is away. I will probably take the girls to the park or something.

I was supposed to go to a mission meeting at the church tomorrow, but I think I am going to skip out on it. I have been at that church at least six times this week, and I need a break from it. Maybe I will take Connie and Jaylyn to the movies as well. I just don't want to be stuck at the house doing housework all day, because I know I will start snacking and eating too much. I learned today from Lance that the new member Marilyn Steele will start assisting the financial team at the church.

She is rising up pretty fast in the church. I hear she is quite good with finance books and she will be conducting internal audits on church finance and inventory records. She also sings in the choir and serves in the Women Ministry. She has been at New Light for only six months and she is already in positions of leadership. She even directed the youth choir last Sunday.

She finally stopped wearing the color red every Sunday. Lately she wears a white flower in her hair every Sunday. That girl, must be obsessive about clothes or something. I have noticed that she is quite friendly with Lance and some of the other men in the church. Sister Graves told me that Sister Steele has been calling Brother Graves a lot lately just for counsel and advice. I suggested to Juanita that she pray over the situation before jumping to any conclusions. Juanita mentioned that Sister Steele is not close to any of the sisters in the church and is not looking for any type of womanly companionship. She still avoids me for some reason as well. I prayed with Juanita on the phone and I shared with her a scripture in James, chapter 1, verse 2: "Consider it pure joy, my brothers, whenever you face trials of many kinds." I told her to keep praying for God's protection over their household and that this was a test of her faith. I am praying that I will have a discerning spirit to pray for others when they need it. Today was a good day and I am grateful to God for His blessings.

Goodnight, First Lady . . .

Chapter Eighteen

A Turn of the Tides

It was a beautiful Sunday summer morning in Southlake, Texas. Lance was driving us to church and talking on his cell phone. "Good morning, Sister Steele, can you please bring a copy of last Sunday's financial records? I need to make a copy for our new trustee who has joined the staff." Lance paused for a few moments and then he said, "Yes, ma'am, I did enjoy the chitlins you made last week, and your seven-up cake was to die for. Thanks for sending it to Houston. There is nothing like a home cooked meal, when you are traveling on a revival. Thanks again. We'll see you at church. Bye now."

I looked over at Lance and raised my eyebrows.

"Some of the mission sisters sent up a plate of food to Houston for my last revival. I forgot to tell you," Lance said as he slightly tugged on his tie.

"You know those mission sisters never check on the kids and me, but they manage to send a gift to you during one of your revival trips. Did Sister Steele personally deliver the meal herself?" I asked with a tinge of anger.

"No, Jackie. Brother Jamison brought it to the hotel, because he had a work related conference in Houston during the same week. The missionary sisters asked him to bring it to me," Lance stated.

"There is something strange, yet familiar about that Marilyn Steele lady. It's like I know her from somewhere. Yet, she avoids me every Sunday. Every time I attempt to speak to her, she purposefully walks away and she avoids direct eye contact with me," I said.

Lance looked uncomfortable, and a few beads of sweat were appearing on his forehead. He raised the air conditioner in the car up to the highest level to bring in some more cool air. "You need to give her a chance. She has not been in church very long, and she is adjusting," Lance said.

"I know she has not been in church very long, but she has propelled pretty fast at New Light. She directs the youth choir, serves as one of the financial secretaries, works for the mission Women's Ministry and the list goes on. She is learning how to work in the church," I said. "Did you know that she has been spending a lot of time talking to your musician, Brother Graves? So much so, that his wife called me last week and shared her personal concerns about it. She feels it doesn't seem right that Sister Steele spends so much time talking to her husband on the phone, and she refuses to even acknowledge Juanita."

I knew Lance didn't like to talk about church gossip or mess on Sundays before he had to preach. So, I knew he probably would not respond to my comments, which he didn't. . We rode silently for the rest of the way to the church. New Light was approximately fifteen minutes from our house, so it wasn't long before we were parking in Lance's parking space. We parked our Navigator next to Sister Finley's pink Cadillac. It was 8:15 a.m. and we knew that the early bird saints had been at church since before 7:00 a.m. There was talk about starting an early morning service since the 11:00 a.m. worship hour was packed now every Sunday. Later on this week, Lance was scheduled to meet with his board, elders and trustees about adding an additional worship time.

This Sunday kicked off our appreciation special services with the culmination services in two weeks at the Sunday 11:00 a.m. worship hour. We had a special guest preacher this morning coming from Chicago, Illinois. His name was Pastor Theodore Roosevelt. He and Lance met while attending seminary school. Pastor Roosevelt was now a senior pastor of a 2,000 member church right outside of Chicago. Deacon Jenkins went to pick him up from the airport at 8:00 this morning. Sister Finley and Sister Pepperdine were in charge of feeding the guest evangelist and the pastoral family. When we walked in the fellowship hall, Sister Finley was in the kitchen giving her customary orders to her committee and working with Sister Pepperdine to make sure the food tasted just right.

"Good morning, Mary and Martha," Lance said jokingly to Sister Finley and Sister Pepperdine.

"How are you doing, Pastor. Good morning Sister Stevens. Why, I like that yellow suit and hat you got on this morning. You look like the Queen of New Light!" said Sister Pepperdine.

"Thank you, Sister Pepperdine," I said.

Sister Finley walked out of the kitchen to give me a quick inspection. She looked me up and down and did not say a word but returned to the kitchen.

Lance noticed the awkward moment and quickly said, "Sister Finley, you and your team have done it again. These are some beautiful decorations. You all have done a superb job on creating an atmosphere of celebration."

What I loved about my husband was that he knew how to encourage church folks and get the ball rolling on a positive note. I decided this was a perfect time to make an exit to the pastor's study. I put my key into Lance's study, and noticed that my key no longer worked on his door. Lance gave me a key to his office ,when we first arrived at New Light due to his important life insurance papers. He liked me to clean it up the way he preferred it. I took my key out of the key hole, and Sister Steele suddenly walked down the hallway and said, "Good morning First Lady. Having trouble opening that door? Here let me open it for you." I stood back and was astonished to see that her key opened up my husband's office.

"There you go, First Lady. Your husband ordered all of the locks changed in the church two weeks ago, because so many members had access to the church and you know they updated the security system and only certain individuals now have access to church keys and the access code to the alarm system," she said as she straightened the white flower to perfection in her mid-length, bone straight now auburn blond streaked hair.

She was wearing a pink pantsuit. Her jacket flared around her hips. Her three-inch white pointed shoes gave her a model type look that would make any man look twice at her. The pink in her outfit brought out her light brown skin and hazel green eyes. Sister Peterson had resorted to calling Sister Steele, "that yella' heifer with the green eyes." Sister Steele was indeed a beautiful woman, and she could easily use her beauty to gain influence and power wherever she went.

"I will make you another key to Pastor's office if you'd like," she said with a smirk on her face. "I'll let Pastor know that you are waiting for him in his office." Then she walked away.

Okay, what is she now, his personal secretary or what? This woman was rising up way too fast within New Light. I walked into the office and felt a pang of fear grip my body. Something was not right, and my spirit was telling me to open up my eyes. How could this woman have a key to the pastor's office?

I walked into Lance's office, and noticed that his entire office had been rearranged. The old burgundy plaid sofa had been replaced with a new leather full sofa, which apparently had a full size bed underneath. A new burgundy recliner was in the corner of his office, and a new 52-inch flat screen plasma

HDTV laid fastened to his side wall. A new Apple iPhone was on his desk, placed with a bow on it and a small card attached. There was also a new mahogany five-level bookcase where all of his books were placed and stored under lock and key. His computer niche was now upgraded with a new computer and a 32-inch monitor. On the second shelf was a mobile Dell laptop and IPod. His new office appeared to be a home away from home. Two tall black file cabinets now stood in the corner. I walked over to the file cabinet, and opened it up.

The file cabinet contained individual folders for all the families at New Light. It was very well organized and alphabetized. Just last month, Lance's file system was in total disarray. Someone had to have helped him with this.

I noticed his closet door was partially opened. I gently opened the door and peeked inside. His entire closet was clean and aroma fresh. I saw a new black and red pastoral robe and man's full vested Steve Harvey suit hanging in the closet. The tags were still on the clothes. I gasped! The robe was $500.00 and the suit was $700.00.

I thought back to my conversation with Deacon Jenkins and what he had told me about Betty Jean and Sister Finley's planned "make over" of the pastor's office. But surely, they couldn't have done all of this? I prayed the church purchased this new material, because we didn't have any extra money to spend on this type of new furniture. After we pulled out of almost having to file for bankruptcy about five years ago, Lance allowed me to help him in managing our financial accounts and we promised never to purchase any major items unless we communicated about it first.

I suddenly remembered the Apple I Phone on his desk with the card. I walked over and opened it up. It read, "A gift to myself—Job well done." What? Was this a set up or did Lance purchase all of these items?

I was in pure amazement! Why didn't Lance tell me that he changed his office around? Why didn't he tell me he bought a new suit and robe? It was so expensive. In the past, he always allowed me to help him rearrange his office or help him to get organized. He loved for me to go shopping with him when he was purchasing a new suit.

I walked over to Lance's bathroom, and twisted my church hat back to perfection. I applied more lipstick, because my mouth had gone dry when Sister Steele opened up my husband's office. I assumed she had something to do with rearranging his office as well. Who else could have done that? Sister Finley and Betty Jean couldn't have moved all of this furniture by themselves. How would they know all of the latest electronic technology? Sister Finley discovered a posse that could help her with her schemes: Sister Betty Jean Pepperdine and Sister Marilyn Steele.

I heard Lance enter his office talking to Deacon Jenkins on his cell phone. He walked in his office and exclaimed, "What the . . .? Oh, excuse me, Deacon, but my office . . . someone has been in my office!" he said. Lance shook his head and continued, "Deacon, Pastor Roosevelt is about six feet tall, he is a dark skinned brother, with a gap between his teeth. You won't be able to miss him. If you still can't find him, have someone to page him in the airport. He didn't call to say he missed his flight or that he wasn't coming, so I know he is there at the airport somewhere. Just try and look again. Thanks Deacon Jenkins. I will check the church's voice mail as well," Lance said as he sat down at his desk.

Sister Steele entered the office and went to the flat screen TV and turned it on.

"This is a surprise for you, Pastor" she said. She looked at me, smiled and walked her little curvy tight pink pants suit out of his office.

Lance and I both gazed at the TV screen, which had a perfect picture of New Light's sanctuary. Apparently a new in-house TV security camera system had been installed as well. Lance was now able to view the sanctuary from his office. We watched as members came in and out of the sanctuary. I looked at Lance and he quickly looked away.

"Since when did you change the lock on your study? And when did Ms. Thang, excuse me, Sister Steele, get a key to your office. Did she also redecorate your office as well? Did she help you organize your files?" I carefully asked with a whole lot of sarcasm in my voice.

"Sweetie, can we talk about that later? I need to check my voice mail," Lance said. "I have an emergency going on right now. Deacon Jenkins cannot locate Pastor Roosevelt and his plane came in over an hour ago. I need to see if something came up with him." Lance shuffled papers on his desk that I noticed was unusually very organized this morning; most of the time he had papers scattered all over his desk.

"Who organized your desk? Did your new assistant finally get around to helping you with your office?" I asked.

"What, uh no," said Lance hastily, apparently looking for Pastor Roosevelt's cell phone number. "I let her go before I left for Houston, because she just wasn't working out. So, Sister Steele is helping me out for a couple of weeks until we can hire a new church secretary."

"Doesn't she already have a full time job serving as a corporate engineer at Verizon or something like that? How can she find time to be the church financial secretary and the church administrative assistant?" I said. "Did she buy your suit and new robe too that's hanging in your closet?" I boldly asked.

"What? Look, Jacqueline!" Lance said pointing his finger at me. "Can we talk about this at a later time!" He looked me squarely in the eye with a hint of rage in his voice. "I have a dilemma going on right now and I need to focus, sweetie. Please, let's discuss this matter later on tonight."

Lance stood up and walked around to the front of his new mahogany desk. "Honey, would you please allow me to handle church business and give me some alone time right now?" Lance said. "I am at work."

It was more of a command than a question. I looked at him, grabbed my purse and Bible and calmly walked out of his office. Out of the corner of my eye, I noticed Sister Steele leaning against the wall with her arms folded and a smirk on her face. Apparently, she must have heard our entire conversation. I really didn't care what she had heard. I still wanted to know why that "yella' heifer with the green eyes" had a key to my husband's office, and if she was behind redecorating his office. Something just wasn't right.

I revisited the conversation with Deacon Jenkins about Sister Pepperdine and Sister Finley. Was this the surprise Junior overheard them talking about as well? Surely, those women did not pull this off. Would they stoop this low? Perhaps they were trying to bless the man of God. Who would spend over $5,000.00 just to hurt a pastor? Only time would tell. Lance was too busy to talk to me; I was too busy to share this pertinent information with him. I silently prayed, *Lord, please let me know if I need to share that conversation with Lance. Please show me the motivations behind this surprise.* I calmly walked into the worship service as my thoughts raced into a "What if" syndrome.

Chapter Nineteen

Fruitful Frustration

Pastor Roosevelt walked into the pulpit at exactly 12:00 p.m. I could tell Lance was furious he was late to worship service. Of course, he gave his collegiate seminary buddy a grand introduction. Pastor Roosevelt preached on "Raise up his Arms," how Aaron and Hur raised Moses' arms found in the Bible in Exodus 17:12 which says: When Moses' hands grew tired, they took a stone and put it under him and he sat on it. Aaron and Hur held his hands up—one on one side, one on the other—so that his hands remained steady till sunset.

Pastor Roosevelt preached so hard that spit was coming out of his mouth, strands of sweat fell from his face, and he began to sing-song the celebration part of his sermon. Brother Graves got on the organ, and tuned up Pastor Roosevelt.

"And Aaron and Hur knew how to help the man of God. Can I get a witness? Tell me children, do you know how to help the man of God? Don't you know that when you bless the man of God, God will bless you! Don't you know that the Lawd is al—-right! I—know he's alright! Yeesss He is! Can you say Yeah?" He leaned back until it seemed his head would touch the floor. "Can you say Yeah?"

I watched the church roar in celebration. Sisters were passing out on the floor. Sister Finley had thrown her hat off so far that it slung into one of the church's side windows. Sister Pepperdine was dancing so hard in the middle aisle, she lost both of her high-heeled shoes. Sister Marilyn Steele had completely passed out on the floor, and a ton of male ushers rushed to her aid. I could hear her saying, before she fell out, of course, "Yes, Lord, I will help the man of God!" Sister Peterson who was sitting behind me in the pew, leaned forward and said, "Now, do you hear that mess! She needs to quit that. You betta watch that lady, she means us no good here at New Light."

I quickly told Sister Peterson to be quiet.

By this time, the church was on its feet and over ten people had joined the church as Pastor Roosevelt invited people to turn to Jesus. He sang the song, "I Won't Complain," made famous by the late Houston, Texas, Pastor, Paul Jones, while people made their way to the front of the church for prayer and restoration.

Everyone noticed that Sister Steele had miraculously come to herself, and was now taking the information from the new members who accepted the invitation to accept Christ and become a member of New Light. Two or three women in the pews looked at me to say, "What is going on here?" I looked at them and smiled as if I knew exactly what was going on. I learned to never let church folks see me sweat. Not that Sister Steele was causing me to sweat any, but I was a little alarmed by her uncanny ability to be everywhere at the same time.

I couldn't help but notice how good Marilyn Steele looked standing next to my husband as he welcomed each new member to New Light. In fact, they made an attractive couple. They looked like the kind of ministry couple that you see on *TBN* or those other religious network stations. And to top it off, there seemed to be a certain chemistry between them that made me a little uncomfortable.

After church, Lance, Deacon Jenkins, and Pastor Roosevelt

went to lunch while the kids and I went home for lunch. We were scheduled to return to church at 4:00 p.m. for the pre-appreciation service with guest church Pastor Wiley and the Mt. Olivet Church Family. After lunch, Junior begged me to stay home, so that he could finish his science project that was due on Monday.

"Junior, why do you wait to the last minute to do everything?" I questioned. "You knew that we were having church today at 4 p.m. So I'm sorry son, you have to learn to prioritize. Your daddy is expecting you to play the drums for the youth choir when they sing this afternoon. Now, this is his special day. It wouldn't look right if you were not there."

"Yeah, you are right, this is his day," said Junior under his breath.

"What did you say, young man?" I said, stepping closer to him so that I was right under him. Junior had recently grown to at least 5'9" tall, and with my frame of 5'5", I had to look up to him now.

"I said you are right, it is Daddy's day. Did you see the program? New Light didn't even recognize us. Did you know that no one is on program to even talk about you? They have completely blotted you and the rest of us out, like Daddy is the only one they truly care about. They don't even have any reference to us, Mom. And I know Daddy sat quietly by and allowed them to do it. Doesn't he have the final say to what is on the program? Don't we sacrifice too, because we are in his family also? I may not be a preacher, but I know many times Daddy has chosen his church work over me. Last Friday, for example, was the first game my daddy has been to in at least a month, and he never gets there on time!" Junior said as tears of frustration rolled down his face.

"I said I am not going to church. I'm working on my science project, so you can tell my daddy that now I have more important priorities!" Junior ran to his room and shut the door.

Connie and Jaylyn ran from their rooms to see what the

commotion was. "Mama, what is wrong with Junior? Why did he slam his door like that?" Connie asked.

"Junior just needs some time to be alone," I said.

"I bet if Daddy were here, he wouldn't be slamming any doors," said Jaylyn with her hands on her little hips.

"Alright girls, go ahead and get dressed for service. Your dresses are ironed and are hanging up in your closets," I said.

"Is Junior going to church?" Jaylyn asked. "Because if he isn't going, I'm not going either," she said with her arms folded against her chest.

"Listen, missy, you go to that room and put those clothes on or I am not going to spare the rod on you," I told her as I inched closer to her with every word.

"Yes, ma'am" Jaylyn replied. "I don't want to go to that stupid church anyway!" she stomped off. I later heard her screaming at the top of her lungs the lyrics of the song called "Me" by R&B singer Tamia. "And her name is me. And she loves me more than you'll ever know!" Jaylyn sang and yelled at the same time.

Lord have mercy with me and my children today. I grabbed the phone to call Lance and let him know what was going on with his son. I could handle screaming Jaylyn but Lance needed his daddy's reprimand to get him to act right. I dialed Lance's cell phone.

"This is Pastor Stevens," he answered.

"Lance, we have a problem. Junior won't come out of his room. He doesn't want to go to church today at 4 p.m., because of his science project that is due tomorrow. What do you suggest?"

"Jackie, can't you handle that? I am trying to finalize some things for this afternoon program. Look, go put him on the phone."

"Lance, did you not hear me? He won't even open up his door and he is not coming out," I said with anxiety in my voice. "For years I have handled this family, and there comes a point in life when a boy needs his father. Now, you need to get over here and talk to your child!" I screamed.

"I said I am busy and I need for you to take care of it," Lance said. "Hold on, Jacqueline."

I knew that when he called me by my full name Jacqueline and not his customary Jackie, it meant that he was not pleased with my actions. It was going to be a long night.

"Yes. Thank you, Sister Steele. These programs look great. I like the picture that you have of me on the front," I heard Lance say.

"Well, Pastor, this is *your* special day and you deserve that and much more," responded Marilyn Steele, "Is there anything else I can do for you today?" she coolly asked.

At this point, I was boiling as I sat on the phone listening to everything.

"No, no you have done a fine job. Do you know who redecorated my office? I really like the new furniture and especially the new flat screen TV. Are you behind this?" I heard Lance ask. There was silence, and I imagined Marilyn giving him her trademark smile. But there was no answer. "Okay, I have Sister Stevens on hold, and I need to complete this call. Thank you very much, my sister," Lance said.

"Jackie, thanks for holding. Okay, listen I have some other business to attend to but let Junior know that if he is not here by 3:45 p.m. I will personally see to it that he won't play in his next basketball game," Lance said.

"Lance, you and I both know that is not fair," I said.

"You heard what I said, and I mean what I say. I'll see you all later on. Don't be late, Jacqueline, because you have to all sit together in the front pew," Lance said and then hung up the phone without saying good-bye.

Now at that very moment, I felt like taking off my clothes, putting on some Texas summer clothes and taking my kids to the amusement park, Six Flags, in Dallas. But, I knew that wasn't the right thing to do. I walked to the breakfast area, and nestled down at the prayer nook and began to talk to God.

"Dear God, I thank you for another day. I praise you for your awesome wonders. I magnify your name. Lord, create in me a clean heart. I confess any impure thoughts, actions or feelings within my heart. Lord give me the spirit of David found in Psalm 51, for I know that is true biblical repentance. I stand on that Psalm right now, Jesus. Forgive me of my sins.

"Lord, I pray for my child, Junior. Lord, you know this child better than I do. Give him what he needs to serve and worship you. Help him to learn to balance his school work and church life. Lord, help him to realize that he needs to be a good example for his little sisters.

"God, watch over my husband. Teach him how to prioritize his time with the church and the family. Help him to be a better father and watch over his children and be there for them even more. Lord, I thank you for my husband and my family. Help me to hold my tongue and give me what I need to be to my children when their father cannot be there. If it is your will, God bless us with prosperity, both spiritually, physically and in some ways materialistically. I stand on your Word where you say, "You have not because you ask not." And Lord, right now I am requesting peace in my home.

"Anoint my husband, give him joy to serve you even more. Bind the enemy from tempting my husband in any shape, form or fashion. Hold him in your palm of obedience. Lord, keep your Holy Ghost power around him. Father, help me to hold my tongue and to only speak of your praises. Lord, give me an unconditional love toward my husband even when I want to hit him on the head with an old black frying pan. Help me to be an example of holiness so that others will see your light in me.

"I need you right now, Jesus. Expose and reveal to me my enemies. I know we wrestle not against flesh and blood, but against principalities. Help me to realize that this battle will take much prayer and your power. Give me the strength to always assume the position of prayer, on my knees, and to truly make it through this test and not try to do it on my own, without your guidance and protection. I stand on your Word in second Corinthians 12:9 where you said, 'My grace is sufficient for you, for my strength is made perfect in weakness.' Help me, Lord. Bless this program today. Let your Word be magnified in all we do. I love you, Lord. In Jesus name, let your will be done in our lives. I do pray this prayer, Amen."

I got off my knees, went to Junior's bedroom, and told him his father's threat about not playing in the next basketball. As soon as I turned around, Junior came out, dressed in his Sunday suit and he made his way to the car. Connie and Jaylyn soon followed in their pink and green matching dresses with matching hat and gloves. They looked like little darlings. Their granny, Eva Montgomery, had those dresses mailed to them last week for this pre-appreciation service. I am really looking forward to seeing all of our relatives in two weeks who will be in town to help us celebrate our one year appreciation here at New Light. I really need their presence and encouragement right now.

Chapter Twenty

The Pre-Appreciation Service

The ushers led us to our front row pew when we entered the church. It was 4:10 p.m. and the service had not started. The church was packed with New Light and Mount Olivet members who were greeting and hugging one another. The deacons finally came out and started devotion, followed by Brother Marcus Graves and Genesis, his new Praise and Worship eight-member team, who ushered in a celebratory atmosphere of worship into the sanctuary. The choir did their processional to the choir stand, followed by the processional of church officers, preachers and pastors.

Little eight-year-old Connie, nudged my side when she saw her daddy walk by during the processional, "Why didn't we walk with Daddy down the aisle this year?"

"Because it was not necessary this time," I said.

"Daddy, doesn't love us anymore? Is that why he didn't want us to walk with him?" she continued to ask.

"No, it's because New Light doesn't like us anymore. We are just part of Daddy's package that's all," Jaylyn said.

I turned around and told both of them to behave and be quiet. It bothered me that Jaylyn would say something like that to her little sister. Since when did she think we were a package? That girl must have been watching too much television again or overhearing the conversations of adults. I prayed daily that my children were not emotionally disturbed by some of the comments that they may have overheard in the church.

I noticed that Marilyn Steele followed in after the pastors down the middle aisle behind them. I couldn't tell if this was planned or if she just happened to be walking behind them.

She marched up to the choir stand, but she wasn't wearing a choir robe. She wore an elegant beaded off-white knee length dress with matching hat, shoes and purse. It accentuated her ample backside and small waist.

The congregation sat down after the processional and the ministers conducted pulpit devotion. I noticed Mt. Olivet's first lady, Sister Patricia Wiley sitting over in the fourth pew with a red pearl beaded hat and a red and white suit. She looked absolutely beautiful. I wondered why the ushers did not seat her next to me. I specifically asked all of the ushers to sit any visiting minister's wife on a pew with me. I remembered Lance had to have a protocol session with the ushers to share with them his seating preferences, and the type of drinks that he needed for his throat along with air conditioning concerns over the pulpit. All New Light's and visiting ministers' wives or deacons' wives were to be escorted to the first two pews on the right. At that moment, Sister Wiley caught my gaze, I mouthed "hello" and she quickly looked away without even speaking to me in response.

Okay, I thought to myself. What is up with her?

Our new and improved fifty-two member choir brought the house down by singing Israel and New Breed's single, "We Worship You," and the Luke Mercer Jr. & Chosen title cut, "My New Life." The church was on fire! Brother Marcus Graves and his wife Juanita led a duet together singing a melody of hymns, which included, "Blessed Assurance," "He

Looked beyond My Faults," "Oh Sweet Jesus" and "I Must Tell Jesus." It was awesome! Juanita belted out her customary first soprano and brought the church to tears as she sang while playing the piano and Brother Graves worked his magic on the organ. They ended their song service with national gospel artist Houstonian Kathy Taylor's song, "Come Let's Worship the Lamb of God."

Afterward, Deacon Finley was listed on the program to talk about his pastor as a leader. But instead of Deacon Finley getting up to speak, Sister Marilyn Steele took the podium.

She straightened out her pearl beaded white dress, which was, by the way, the same color dress that I had on, and cleared her throat.

"As you can see, I am not Deacon Finley," she said as the congregation chuckled. "But it was determined at the last minute, with the pastor's permission of course, that a man and a woman should speak about our great pastor."

"Amen," said some of the people in the pews. "Alright . . . say that."

"Giving praise to God, in respect to the pulpit, to our honoree, and my brothers and sisters in Christ, Pastor Lance Mc-Clain Stevens is an awesome man of God. I have only been a member of this great fellowship for the last six months. Within those months, I have seen this church grow tremendously. We average about ten people joining our church per month. We purchased a new church fifty-seven passenger charter bus on yesterday. So, get ready New Light. We will be on the road in our new bus traveling with our pastor as he preaches on the road," Marilyn said.

"The choir has new robes, and a great musician in Brother Graves," she said with a huge smile on her face and nodding to Brother Graves on the organ. Everyone noticed how Sister Steele ignored Juanita Graves or forgot to mention her name as part of the musical team. I looked at Juanita who was sitting on the piano. She kept her chin up looking at Marilyn Steele.

Marilyn continued with much confidence. "Pastor Stevens is an astute business man who knows how to conduct the Lord's business with professionalism and accuracy. He established a 501c3 Community Development Corporation, which created Victorious Workers, a Christian Temporary Agency. He also created at least four new ministries in his first year tenure at New Light. As a matter of fact, he has just appointed me Women Ministry Coordinator here at New Light by the recommendation of Deaconess Sarah Finley, who will be stepping down as Coordinator at the end of the year," Marilyn said with a smile to Sister Finley.

I noticed Sister Sarah Finley out of the side of my peripheral vision look straight at me with a smile on her face as if to say, "I finally got you!"

I wished I could have knocked that purple hat off of her head right at that moment. I definitely needed to go home and meditate on Psalm Chapters 55 through 57 concerning my enemies. I needed to call out Sister Finley by name when I read those scriptures.

"Pastor is taking our church to a new level in Kingdom Building!" Marilyn exclaimed, her voice rising with each new sentence. "He is a community builder serving on two Ad-Hoc committees in Southlake. His sermons are clear, plain, and yet thorough. He teaches us to understand the scriptures, not only for content, but for context and historical purposes as well. He averages at least fifty people a week in his Bible study classes. And, our church school has grown to over one hundred class enrollees! Lance, . . . uh, oops, excuse me; Pastor Stevens is a great friend, confidante, counselor and father to his children. When I joined New Light, I was desperate for deliverance, in more ways than one. Pastor Stevens delivered me toward the light of Jesus! And, I am going to follow him for the rest of my life!"

I looked over at Lance, who was sitting on the side of the pulpit in a kingly chair that was purposefully decorated in pur-

ple and gold. He shifted in his seat as Sister Steele continued
to talk. He was looking at her with this weird expression on his
face like he was somewhat confused. Lance returned my gaze,
and I slyly rolled my eyes away from him as if to communicate
to him, "Whatever!"

"I have known Pastor Stevens since the age of eight when I
would visit my grandmother in Houston, Texas," Sister Steele
continued with a dreamy expression upon her face like an ob-
sessed woman. "We all knew in Houston's third ward neighborhood that he would become a great man of God. When I
was a little girl, he would say to me, 'God made His prettiest
angel when He created you.' Little did we know that one day,
we would be together again ,and I would be blessed to work
with him in ministry, side by side," she said as she smiled at
Lance.

"And I must say, he has turned into a great man and fine
pastor. I am very proud of you, Pastor Lance McClain Stevens.
I always knew that you would make me, I mean us proud. I
love you, Lance, . . . oops . . . uh . . . forgive me, Pastor Stevens.
Let's give it up for our pastor!" she said as she began to clap
her hands.

Sister Steele walked down from the podium and proceeded
to walk over to Lance and gave him a quick kiss on his lips and
a big bear hug. Lance looked at her quite awestruck, and obvi-
ously hoped no one had seen her quick brush across his lips as
she hugged him. But, she positioned herself to where only the
first three rows of people on her right could see it. I saw it all,
and so did dear old Sister Peterson and Juanita Graves. Marilyn Steele turned, looked at me, smiled and took her seat behind the pulpit in the choir stand.

As the people were clapping for their beloved pastor and
Sister Steele's sincere expressions, Sister Peterson threw up
her hat from her head across the church where it landed in the
center aisle and screamed, "Oh Lord!" and she passed out on
the pew behind me. I turned around and motioned for the

ushers to escort her out. When she came to herself after about ten seconds, she hollered "Why, Jesus, Why?" as the ushered carried her out. She began to sing.

"I don't know what Jesus is to you. But I hope He is to you what He is to me."

I could tell that some people were uncomfortable with Sister Steele's familiarity with the pastor. She called him by his first name twice. They knew I didn't even call him by his first name at church. I displayed respect for him, his position, and called him Pastor around his members. I rarely kissed him on the lips at the church in front of parishioners. This woman was bold, and she didn't seem to care who knew about her affection for her pastor.

Lord have mercy! Well I couldn't clap in jubilee. I was stunned. Lance already knew this woman, yet he never told me that he knew her! Now, that was something that needed to be investigated further. I could tell that there were some people who were looking a little concerned as well. Sister Steele didn't use a Bible verse in her talk about her pastor, and then she had the nerve to say, 'I love you, Lance.'

Okay, calm down, Jackie or else you may find yourself on the front steps of this church fighting Lance, Sister Steele, and probably Sister Finley, too. I imagined myself getting my Bible, slapping him, knocking Sister Steele out with the back side of my Bible, and karate kicking Sister Finley with a round away right foot kick, all in the name of Jesus of course.

I wanted to let them all know that Jacqueline Renee Stevens is not to be played with. First Sister Steele disrespected me by avoiding me every Sunday, then she sarcastically opened the door for me to my husband's office when she knew I didn't have a key. She snickered by his office upon hearing our slight discussion, and finally she let me know publicly she had known my husband longer than I had, and they had a history together which I knew nothing about. I assumed Sister Finley cleverly deleted the pastoral family from the appreciation service, and she is probably the culprit who convinced Sister Steele to have a speaking part on the program. Deacon & Sister Finley were the chairpersons of the Appreciation Ministry Celebration. Yet, wasn't my husband, the pastor, and didn't he have to approve all of this? Upon this realization, my heart sank and I wiped away a small tear that crawled its way out of the corner of my eye.

Deacon Finley took to the podium to talk about his pastor as a shepherd, but I was in a daze and I couldn't even tell you what he said about Lance. I wanted to grab my purse and get out of that church, but I decided to be the regal queen that I was expected to be and I stayed glued to my seat with a plastered smile on my face. I watched the festivities continue. Everyone raved about their new fresh pastor who had a vision for the people of New Light and the community of Southlake.

Pastor Wiley preached a sermon on learning to be content in whatever state we are in. His wife, Sister Patricia Wiley, who was now only singing gospel songs and not her customary R&B lyrics that some folks would hear at Southlake's The Back Door Club, sang a song by Yolanda Adams called, "In the Midst of it All." She sang it during the invitational period when Pastor Wiley was calling for sinners to be saved and saints restored.

Now, Sister Wiley may have talked a lot, but she sure could sing. There was something in her eyes when she sang that let me know she was battling something deep within. She wasn't able to finish her song, because of her tears. A Mount Olivet usher led her outside of the sanctuary to the women's restroom. I thought this might be a good time to talk to her. I followed them to the women's restroom.

"Sister Wiley, are you okay?" I asked giving her a hug.

"Yes. I am," she said, dabbing her eyes with a Kleenex. Her eyes were red and she removed her hat. "Sister Stevens, I want to thank you for the advice you shared with me about my tongue. You were so right. I am having a horrible time adjusting to being a pastor's wife. I am so unhappy. I'm still learning how to be a good wife and then with the addition of having the scrutiny of being a pastor's wife, it's a bit much.

"Everything I do is under a microscope. It's like I am supposed to be superhuman or something. I know I need Jesus. I wasn't going to church like I needed to when I met Pastor Wiley. I finally figured out that everything I shared at Heavenly Hands Beauty Salon, Vivian Daniels and her crew went around town telling everyone what I told them. Now, I do my own hair and I am looking for a new beautician," said Sister Wiley as I held her in my arms.

"And, Wiley seems to give all of our money to the church. A member needs a bill paid or a child has an emergency and they come to us. I'm tired of giving all of my money away to his members and they treat me so cruel. We tithe and give offerings, shouldn't that be enough? The church let Wiley's health insurance lapse by mistake, and now we have to pay a $2,000 medical bill of his from last month. I am sick of it all. I feel God played a trick on me or something. I thought being a pastor's wife was a glamorous life. I loved the way I would see preachers' wives strut in their suits and hats with a joyful smiles on their faces. But, how can you be joyful on this journey? All of these expectations. Go to Sunday School every week, Bible study, choir rehearsals, youth meetings. The next thing they are going to want me to do is to be a janitor or an usher. I can't serve the Lord with gladness if I am always trying to please these folks," she cried.

"Stop trying to please those folks and learn to please God and realize that in your serving God you will offend some people. But still count it all joy! You have got to be delivered from being a people pleaser," I told her as I hugged her. "In order to have joy in this life, you must concentrate on Jesus. The J in joy stands for Jesus! The minute you take out the J in the word joy, then all you have left is the OY. Then you will find out that you have the Oh Why Me Syndrome. Why is this happening to me, Lord? Why are the members treating me so bad? What have I done? You must focus on Jesus to have real joy," I ministered to her.

I looked her straight in her eye. "Get into the Word of God and study His Word. Your songs will take on new meaning when you have the Word of God in your heart. This life doesn't get any easier, but you have got to find positive ways to cope with the pain. Pray more, run to exercise off some steam, take a walk around the block; but being in a pity party will only lead you into the throngs of a deep depression. You have to find positive methods of coping in this life. Paul said that in whatever state he was in, he learned to be content. You've got to seek holiness in this life to truly be happy. Focus on being the best Christian you can be and everything else will fall into place," I assured her. "Pain is inevitable, but misery is optional. You are wasting time feeling sorry for yourself. There are people in the world who need to be saved; who need Jesus.

"Girl, you are not fighting people, you are fighting evil spirits and principalities," I continued. "Don't you know the demons rose up the minute you walked into that church? They recognize the gifts and the purpose that God has for you and they are determined to cause you to stumble and cripple your Christian walk. You have got to put on the whole armor of God if you are to survive in this life. Stop looking with your physical eyes but see the Christian fight with your spiritual eyes," I urged her .

Sister Wiley leaned against me and cried, and for a moment, I forgot about my own troubles and the hurt I was feeling.

We rocked together on the sofa in the ladies' bathroom. I had locked the door, forcing other parishioners to use the women's restroom in the front of the church. We prayed together, and I helped her readjust her makeup. I helped her with her hat, and noticed that her short bob was actually a weave that needed some attention. I told her to reconsider about not going back to Heavenly Hands and learn not to allow Ms. Vivian or her patrons to pick her for information anymore. If she couldn't resist talking about her issues, then perhaps she needed to go to a salon out of town. By the looks of her weave, she needed to go to somebody's salon and quick!

We promised to keep in touch, and become prayer partners. We waited until the benediction was over, and the church members were dismissed, and then we returned to the sanctuary. I noticed Marilyn Steele was standing by my husband and greeting visitors and members as if she was the pastor's wife. When she saw me walking toward them, she politely excused herself and walked away. She walked by me and didn't even say hello. Well, I didn't bother to speak either, so the feeling was mutual. I did see her trademark smirk upon her face as she passed by me, and I raised my chin higher as I walked toward my husband and Pastor Wiley.

"Sister Stevens," said Marilyn Steele.

I turned around to face the woman who refused to acknowledge me in the past.

"Yes,"

She calmly walked up to me and whispered so only I could hear her, "My last name is not Steele for nothing . . . you better watch your back. And by the way, Pastor was so good last night." She laughed and walked away.

I sat there totally stunned, furious and confused at the same time until something came over me. As Marilyn turned around to strut away, I gently tapped her on her shoulder, looked that green eyed monster in her face and coolly replied, "Well, you better learn how to stop using your tricks. You see, sister, I don't fight with my hands, I fight with my knees. I pray on weak sisters like you, who don't know how to wait for God to bless them with a man, or better yet purpose for their own life. So y'all get a 'Jezebel spirit' and mess up the plan and discredit the blessings of others. But I still love you with Jesus' love and I'll start warring in the spirit for you tonight. You might be

Sister Steele, but I am Sister Fired Up. Like the prophet Elijah, I am fired up for the Lord and He will prevail. The Lord will hear my prayers and answer. You are still my husband's sheep and my job is to lift you up in prayer and you can believe I will do that," I said with a smile as I twisted my hips around so that she could watch the sway of my Christian confidence.

I don't know why some women in the church think that pastors' wives are supposed to be doormats. Jesus was not a punk and neither am I. Sister Steele had the nerve to act a fool in the Lord's house. I know some pastors' wives would have dragged her by her long hair and proceeded to whoop her down real good. I could just see Sister Peterson now. . . .

"Whoop up on her, Sister Stevens. That gal wearing red need a good beat down. Let her know that some preachers' wives are from the Slapahoe tribe. We will slap a . . . tear her up, Sister Stevens!"

I would hit Marilyn with my Bible, and take out my nail cutter (my unofficial razor) and get to tearing her apart! By the time I finished with her, she'd be in the mental ward and I'd be declared the winner. But what would that prove? Sister Steele just wanted what I had. Why would I physically fight her over something that was already mine? Oh, well, but it was fun thinking about beating her down. But Jesus would not get the glory in that.

I walked up to stand beside Lance, and Sister Wiley gave Pastor Wiley a hug for a great sermon. I heard him tell her that she blew the roof off with her song. I could tell that they both really cared for each other.

"Hey, Goldie. You are looking mighty fine in that white dress. Is that the one I bought you from Neiman Marcus from the Houston Galleria?" Lance asked me.

"No, it isn't," I calmly replied. "This is the one you bought me from Kmart," I said loud enough so Pastor and Sister Wiley could hear me. They both looked at me and lowered their eyes.

"Girl, you are such a jokester," Lance said, looking at me uncomfortably. I looked at him as if to say, "Yeah, Negro, you got some explaining to do."

"Pastor Wiley, please follow me to my study, and we will give you your love offering and then have dinner in our fellowship hall," Lance said.

"Pastor Wiley and Sister Wiley, thank you so much for coming today. I will talk to you soon," I told them.

I walked coolly away, retrieved all of my children, then I got in my car and went home. I didn't want to fellowship with anyone, and I knew my absence in the fellowship hall for dinner might cause some eyebrows to raise. But, at that moment, I really didn't care what anyone thought. I would not allow Lance to take this family for granted. So he would see how it felt when we were absent. It would cause him to look a little shady, or not as perfect as he tried to make us all look for appearance's sake.

I am sure they had a nice fellowship dinner. My children were happy to be home early, and it allowed Junior enough time to work on his science project before bed. I took off my Neiman Marcus dress, put on my familiar cotton pajamas, and retrieved a Snicker's Ice Cream Bar from the freezer I snuggled down to watch a good chick flick on *Lifetime Channel for Women*.

As I waited for Lance to come home, in the midst of all of the drama, the Lord put a song in my heart. I quickly wrote in my journal as the words flowed from the spiritual realm.

Remember the Cross
Today my heart is not the same
The hurt, the bitterness is to blame
I try to serve you Lord
To worship you with liberty
Yet my enemies they unfold
—so that my story will not be told

Yet Lord, my soul speaks of your goodness
And all that you've done for me
I stand on your word where you said
You'll never forsake or leave me

Help me to remember your cross
The pain, the suffering
Help me to remember your cross
So I can serve with joy again

Chorous:
Remember the cross
The pain, the suffering
Remember the Cross
The lies, the whips, chains
Remember the Cross
How you died to set me free
Oh' remember the cross

Sometimes I feel like giving up
My work doesn't seem enough
At times, I feel I can't go on
But your Spirit tells me to Fight On

And then I remember the cross
And it reminds me that I am not lost
The battle is not mine to fight
For at the cross Jesus made it alright

When I remember the cross I have hope
Cause' I know you got up and
And one day you're coming back for me
Until then I will wait, I have hope
When I remember the cross

I know
In the end, we will win . . . .
Remember the cross

I closed my journal and prayed that God would show me His will and His way for my life. I had a feeling that the drama was just beginning to unfold.

Chapter Twenty-One

Why Church?

I awoke to the ringing of my phone and quickly grabbed it as I noticed that it was dark outside and the side of my bed where my husband usually laid was empty.

"Hello."

"I'm sorry to call so late, Lady Stevens, but I really need to talk to someone," a familiar voice said.

"Pastor Stevens is not in right now," I said, because I truly didn't want to talk to anyone right now. I needed to be ready when Lance came home so that I could deal with what happened at church today.

"That's okay, I would rather speak with you. This is Sister Tammy Benjamin. I joined New Light about five months ago. I serve on the Greeter and Hospitality Ministry," she said.

I remembered Sister Benjamin. She joined New Light fresh out of graduate school, and had a vital and charming personality. When she joined, she came to every one of the New Member Survival Classes and completed them and faithfully served as a New Light Greeter. But in the last couple of Sundays, I hadn't seen her warming smile in the foyer.

"Oh, yes, Sister Benjamin. I have seeing you in worship and your welcoming presence. How are you doing?" I asked.

"I must be honest. I am quite discouraged by what I see going on in our church," she said.

An alarm went on in my head. *Careful Jackie, don't get caught in a snare. Just listen and don't be quick to respond,* I thought as I cradled the phone against my ear and sat up against the headboard of the bed.

"Okay," I carefully responded.

"Sister Stevens, five years ago I left all signs of organized religion. I was tired of the church dramas, the constant conflicts, the positioning of power controlled church officials, and money hungry preachers. So, I left the church. I read self-help books to bring me closer to God. I even invested in a life coach who I later found out was a New Ager, who believe that we are gods, and that kind of freaked me out. I started tithing to online and television Christian shows and watching televangelists, but still there was a void in my life. I rationalized I was closer to God than I had ever been and that I didn't need organized religion. I was comfortable. It was just Jesus and me in my home. I didn't have to share Him with anyone. I thought He was satisfied with me and I was satisfied with my "at home, jack-in-the-box , private Jesus" who only came out when I really needed Him. But then I was asked to attend a small home Bible study group and I loved it. I loved the fellowship of the saints. This small group of believers challenged my faith to grow and held me accountable. I began to feel a great need to worship Jesus in His sanctuary. One day, while reading the paper I saw a clipping about New Light and I decided to visit and I kept coming back," Tammy said with excitement.

"I didn't realize how much I missed corporate worship. It was empowering and uplifting to be in a place totally consecrated to God; a place where His children can freely worship Him." Tammy paused. "But now I feel some of the things that

I am hearing at church, it is driving me away again. Sister Stevens I don't like gossip and conflict in God's house; it totally turns me off. I don't believe in putting down the pastor and his family because we don't necessarily agree with a decision or the antics of another."

I thought that it was not necessary to ask her what she has been hearing, but to let that comment go. This woman may have pure intentions. She may not have been trying to bring me mess, just stick to the Word of God in your response.

"Some people of the church are hypocrites. Some of the worst hurt in my life has been by so called Christians," Tammy continued. "I used to think church wasn't important because I can worship God anywhere, even while I am shopping." Tammy laughed. "I justified my absence from church from one excuse to another. I don't go to church because I don't like traditional churches, I can't wear pants to church, or this church wouldn't let me wear make-up. I let it keep me from going to the house of the Lord. I was watching the Chapel Tube every morning in my bed, and I loved it because I didn't have to even dress up."

"First, let me say, that we are grateful to God that He led you to New Light," I said. "You are an encouragement to me every Sunday morning when I enter those doors and see your beautiful smile. Let me ask you a question? Is that okay?" I asked.

"Sure," Tammy responded.

"Why do *you* go to church?"

"I attend church first off to have my needs met," she said with confidence.

"Our first priority should be to worship. Do you have a Bible with you, Sister Benjamin?"

"Yes, let me get it."

I needed the Lord to give me the strength to minister to this saint and to show me where to lead her in His word. I silently prayed. I grabbed my Bible that I kept inside my bed foot board.

"Okay, Sister Stevens I have my Bible."

"The Bible says in 1 John 1:3 that we enter a fellowship that goes two ways: with God and with other Christians. When you became a Christian, you were called into a relationship with God that is found in First Corinthians 1:9."

"Yes, I am reading that," Tammy responded.

"Sister, we go to church first to worship God. It is an extension of our faith and an outward expression of our love for God. We go to church to exercise our faith and strengthen our walk. The Bible says in Romans 10:14b 'how can they hear without a preacher.' We need the message of God to help us and to make us accountable to our spoken faith. Remember, faith without works is dead. And then Hebrews warns us in chapter 10 verse 25 that we are not to forsake the assembly of ourselves," I carefully said, trying my best to give her God's Word and not my personal opinion.

"Going to church, for those of us who are physically able, is an act of our obedience to God. It honors the Lord's Day, and is a celebration or memorial to the death, burial and resurrection of Jesus. We attend church to use our spiritual gifts for the Body of Christ. First Corinthians chapter 12 and 1 Peter 4:10 talk to us about using our spiritual gifts for the common good and to help each other," I noted. "Regular contacts with other Christians can keep us sharp. When believers come together, it combines our spiritual strength in prayer as found in Leviticus 26:8 'Five of you shall chase a hundred, and a hundred of you shall put ten thousand to flight; your enemies shall fall by the sword before you.' There is power when the believer comes together for purpose, praise and prayer!"

I was getting overjoyed just thinking about the power of Christians totally committed to serving and preserving God's house and building up His Kingdom.

"Now, Sister Benjamin, when you became a Christian, you stepped into the heat of an age old battle. You have a three fold enemy at work: the world, the flesh, and the devil. And sister, you have got to be prepared to deal with all three." I said from experience. "Stop focusing on the negative, you are always going to have to go to church with unhappy people who don't know the joy of Jesus. You are always going to have to go to church with those that judge others before they inspect themselves. The wheat and the tares, or the roses and the weeds have to grow together. Don't you let the enemy "weed" you out of the Christian fold. You are doing a superb job in the Hospitality Ministry. Now, what I need you to do is when you hear hurting comments, just learn to pray and then ask God to show you how to respond appropriately where the Gospel will not be shamed. There are some things that we just need to ignore. Remember, we fight against our flesh and it can roar up and make us remember our wounds and how we were hurt by others. But, that is just another way that the flesh is trying to defeat you from your purpose in Christ. And lastly, we come to church to give. I have heard some people say that tithing is the last frontier. It is the final area to be conquered or surrendered unto the Lord. When we stay away from the church, we also tend to stop giving to his church as well. Sister Benjamin, we must be surrendered servants," I said as I awaited her response to all I had said. Lord, I needed some water. I don't see how Lance could do this every day all day. Whew!

"Sister Stevens, you are so right. I am sitting right now looking at my empty tithing envelope because I didn't attend church last week. I wrote down every scripture you mentioned and I am going to meditate on them. That was a mighty word, First Lady! You ought to be a preacher with your husband!" Tammy exclaimed.

I smiled and let that last statement go. Be careful, Jackie.

"Sister Benjamin, preaching is the death, burial, and resurrection of Jesus Christ according to the ministry of the Apostle Paul. What I just shared with you were scriptures of encouragement and life; there is a difference."

I thought about all the people who were "called" into the

preaching ministry, yet you never heard them preach Jesus. They seemed to "preach" inspirational messages or self-help strategies, but if the Apostle Paul were here in our times, he would be alarmed at the preachers of our day. Paul said in First Corinthians 1:18 "that the message of the cross is foolish to those who are headed for destruction! But for those of us who are saved know it is the very power of God."

"Can I pray with you before we end this call, Sister Benjamin?" I asked.

"Yes."

I got on my knees on the side of my bed and held the phone to pray. We prayed together and I encouraged her to focus on the Word and not be distracted by her distrators.

I hung up the phone, and rested on the side of the bed and just exhaled. I knew that the phone lines of New Light would be hot as word about Sister Steele's speech would travel among the membership. Lord, just give me the strength to deal with whatever comes our way. Then, the telephone rang. I knew my phone might be hot the rest of the night. I breathed in deeply and calmly answered the phone.

Chapter Twenty-Two

Good Gossip

"Hello, this is Sister Stevens," I said as I laid outstretched on my king sized wooden canopy bed.

"Sister Stevens, this is Deacon Jenkins, I was calling to check on you and make sure you are okay. Are you okay, First Lady?"

"I am fine, Deacon, thanks so much for calling, I am sure the church is a buzz right now about the scene that played out in church today," I said.

"We need to really start praying for our church. I see the enemy trying to press his way into the fold. I just left Sister Finley's house and of course the conversation I overheard over there, well, you know. Sarah Finley, the good Lord will have to deal with her because Abraham is not running his house over there. She calls the shots.

I waited to see if Deacon Jenkins would continue.

"Betty Jean and I went over to the Finley's house for dinner tonight and I was watching the baseball game with Deacon Finley and overheard Kayla, Sister Finley, and Betty Jean carrying on in the kitchen. Believe me when I say, First Lady, we need to pray. Their conversation went something like this," said Deacon Jenkins.

"*Did you see that woman kiss Pastor Stevens on the lips?*" asked Kayla, Sister Finley's niece.

"*Naw, girl, I guess from where I was sitting I didn't see it. It must have been quick,*" said Sister Pepperdine. They were both enjoying a Monday brunch in the home of Sister Finley.

"*Auntie Sarah, what do you think about what happened at church today?*" Kayla asked her aunt.

Sister Finley brought their coffee to the table and sat down. "*I think the young woman really cares for our pastor, and she wants to do whatever she can to help our great church.*"

"*Sarah, I can't believe that you are not going to lead the mission group or Women's Ministry anymore. You led that ministry for over twenty years,*" Sister Pepperdine said.

"*I think it's time for new leadership within our church and I am not getting any younger, just better,*" snickered Sister Finley. "*Besides, Marilyn Steele and Pastor Stevens look good together. They are a strong power couple, and the look for leadership to represent New Light,*" said Sister Finley.

"*But Auntie, Pastor Stevens has a wife and so,*" Kayla said carefully.

"*And so?*" responded Sister Finley, cutting her off.

"*And you shouldn't try to put someone between a man and his wife,*" said Kayla. "*Auntie, that is a sin against God and I know that Jacqueline Stevens is a praying woman. You go around meddling with her, and find yourself sick or something.*"

"*Oh, please. I have been around New Light long enough to see many things, and the handwriting is on the wall that this Marilyn Steele is going to be the next Mrs. Lance McClain Stevens. Our preacher is not strong enough to stop the advances of a beautiful woman like that. Hey, I keep reminding Abraham from looking at the woman too hard on Sundays and I for one wasn't so happy when she became the deacon's financial secretary. However, I have formed an allegiance with her and so now we are friends.*"

"*Do you really think that she may be the next Mrs. Stevens?*"

Sister Pepperdine asked as she leaned against the table. "Well, Sarah you said that about our last pastor too and you were right."

"What? I just heard that happened with our last pastor and I didn't think it was true. These preachers today need to stop judging others so hard and start living the life of a saint. If it is not money that tempts them, it is another woman," said Kayla shaking her head.

"And in some circles, it's little boys too!" hollered Sister Pepperdine as they all leaned back in their chairs with laughter.

"Satan is just having a field day with men of the cloth. Auntie, is it really true that our last pastor at New Light, had two children with a woman that was not his wife? Is that true? Is she from Southlake?" asked Kayla.

"I don't think you know her, Kayla. She was from Houston or something like that," said Sister Finley with a sudden look of disinterest on her face.

"Yes, I heard in the beauty shop a couple of months ago that her name is Mona, LaMonica, uh . . . Monique Howard or something like that. Yes, that's her name, Monique Howard," said Sister Pepperdine looking up into the air trying to recall the name she had heard in the beauty salon. "And she isn't from Houston Sarah, she is from Dallas." She continued looking at Sarah strangely, who was now shaking her head and lowering her eyes to the floor so that Kayla couldn't see her expression.

Kayla looked at her Aunt Sarah and knew that something wasn't quite right. "That's funny," Kayla said. "We have a cousin named Monique Howard who lives in Dallas. She used to stay in Abilene, Texas. Hmnn. That's odd. I just saw her about three weeks ago at the mall, and she told me she was eight months pregnant. Somebody is sure enough taking care of her, because she was sporting a huge ring on her finger."

"Do you all need some more coffee?" Sister Finley interjected quite oddly. "I just bought this imported coffee last week and it is absolutely delicious."

"Wait a minute, Auntie, is this our distant cousin? Our third cousin, Monique Howard from South Oakcliff? Our own cousin had *those two babies by our last pastor? Monique Howard with the Coca-Cola bottle shape, and booty for days that can make any strong man weak? Monique, with the naturally curly jet-black hair that falls to her shoulders? Everyone knows that Monique and her mama, Janie Sue, are convention and revival whores. Just natural born gold diggers! Their reputation is known from Galveston to El Paso, Texas within the church circuit!" Kayla said, looking at her favorite aunt like she was stone crazy.*

"Auntie!" exclaimed Kayla rising up from her seat. "Did you have anything to do with helping to break up that man's marriage? I remember how you couldn't stand Pastor Stewart."

"What?" said Sister Finley with a look of guilt all over her face. "I didn't break up anybody's marriage. Their marriage was already broken when they first came to New Light. Monique just needed a place to live, because her mama would always bring different men in the house. I helped her relocate to Abilene. I couldn't have anyone in Southlake knowing that we were kinfolk. Her mama was too busy chasing this married minister to do anything to help her own child. So, I had to help Monique. That girl's reputation and her mama's past would ruin my good reputation in Southlake. Pastor Stewart was doing a revival in Abilene, and I asked him to stop by and pray with her because she was in a strange place with no family members near by. She was only twenty-five years old at the time and she needed some guidance, and I for one was tired of always coming to her rescue and giving her money every other month."

"You knew that Monique would freely give her body to any man who was a preacher or a blue collar $80,000 a year plant man. All she sees is money, power and prestige. Monique is a wounded soul who is looking for love in all the wrong places. How could you, Aunt Sarah?" Kayla accused with tears in her eyes.

"Did I put a gun to his head to sleep with that woman? Did I tell him to go and have two babies with that woman?" replied her Aunt Sarah with anger in her voice.

"He should have known to take a deacon or another witness with him to go see her. So don't go blaming me for Pastor Stewart's weak-

nesses," responded Sister Finley with her arms folded against her chest and her chin up in the air. "Monique did call me for some money and counsel, so I sent Pastor Stewart by there to drop off some money and to pray with her when he was in Abilene for a revival. How was I to know that fool was going to fall for her tricks?"

"No, you didn't put a gun to his head, Auntie. You did however set him up to meet a very aggressive man hungry, beautiful young girl who you knew was poison and used goods. And you probably didn't warn him about her either. You won't even let your own husband step within two feet of Monique or Janie Sue. You know that Monique has had issues ever since she was date raped at the age of fifteen and you paid for her abortion. You pretty much excommunicated them from the family after that. Yeah, you didn't know I knew about the abortion, but she told me. Janie Sue had a field day telling some of the family members at our last family reunion that 'if you were such a Christian, then why did you pay to have her grandbaby killed?' She also said that we shouldn't judge her for just spending time with her preacher friends, when you are out committing murder and setting up evil traps for preachers," Kayla said with her arms outstretched in the air.

"I thought Janie Sue was out of her mind or perhaps just extremely jealous of you. How could you, Auntie? You are not a Christian, but just an example of "church folk" who do not know Christ, but only want power and control for themselves and use the church as a game or a tool for their own agenda and vain glory," said Kayla.

Sister Finley sat straight up in her chair and looked over at Kayla squarely in her eye, "Now you listen to me, nobody is going to set foot in my house and disrespect me; especially not some twenty-five-year-old young girl like you, who I practically raised and sent you to college because your poor mama and daddy couldn't do it. So, you hush your mouth right now and stop all this foolishness. You don't know what I have had to do to protect the dignity of New Light and our good family name. Monique and her mama, Janie, Sue had always used me to get them out of trouble.

Kayla looked at her aunt and quietly sat down at the table. The silence that followed was deafening.

Sister Pepperdine looked at her lifelong friend, Sarah Finley, and shook her head.

"Don't you look at me like that, Betty Jean Pepperdine!" shouted Sister Finley

"Don't you sit there and judge me. You sat with me and talked about Pastor Stewart and his wife like a dog as well. Nodding your head and laughing with me. And silence is agreement, isn't it Betty Jean?"

"Sarah, if I laughed, it was because of all the information you were telling me about them. I didn't think it was true. But, you purposefully set up a good man, a man of God. That man's marriage was destroyed. Well, that is going too far. Even I know the Bible says, 'Touch not my anointed.' It's a wonder you haven't ended up sick or worse. You can't play with the man of God. You have let the enemy use you in a mighty way. And you paid for a teenager to have an abortion? You helped to kill a child! Sarah, you are supposed to be a Christian woman. You are supposed to believe that nothing is too hard for God," said Betty Jean as she looked at her friend in a new light. "You always told me that you were a pro-lifer, but I guess when faced with the abortion question, when it hit your family, God wasn't big enough to solve that problem, huh? May God forgive you, Sarah."

"Kayla grabbed her purse and silently walked out of the kitchen back door," said Deacon Jenkins. "I sat there listening in from the den with a view of everything that was being said and done. Sarah Ann was all Kayla had. For all of Sarah faults, she was completely loyal to her family, and would bail them out with money or promises of money in order to fulfill her own goals. Even I knew that more than half of her kinfolk in Texas were in Sarah's pocket for one reason or another.

"I watched Kayla burn rubber as she raced out of the oval driveway in her white pearl Chrysler 300. That car was a present given to her by Sarah, when she completed her first two crucial college years at Southern Methodist University. Kayla was in her Aunt Sarah's pocket too and she knew it," continued Deacon Jenkins.

"I watched Betty Jean pick up the dishes left on the table, and silently placed them in the sink. As she looked out the window, her face seemed to show all the times she had prayed to bear a child and the many times she had confided to Sarah about her frustrations about being unable to bear a child. With her back turned to Sister Finley she said, "*Sarah, you knew how badly I wanted a child. I could have raised Monique's baby.*" She turned around to see her friend with both elbows on the table and her head in her hands.

"*But I know that Monique's baby would have been a constant reminder to you of your family's shame and your lack of control over the situation. You know, you think you truly know a person and then they do something that knocks you off your feet. For years I looked up to you as a person who loved God and would do anything to protect the Kingdom of Christian believers. I've seen you up at the crack of dawn cleaning the church, visiting the sick, helping members with their bills. You would do anything you could to make sure that New Light had a good name in the community. Now, I know you truly could not get over the fact that Pastor Stewart did not make your husband the chairman of the deacon board like he promised under the table during one of your meetings,*" continued Betty Jean as she walked over to the table.

"*I know you didn't know that I knew that piece of information did you? I guess you thought that since my brother, Jenkins, had lost his wife, he would be too grieved to lead the church. But I prayed for you and I forgave you, and God looked after my brother and gave him strength. I love you, Sarah. We have been friends for more than fifty years, but I was wrong not to let you know when you were doing wrong. I haven't been a good friend to you because I felt I couldn't stop you anyway, so I let you go on and do your damage. I didn't even try to minister to you because I wanted to stay in your good graces. I have seen you talk about people like garbage, and then try to get those same folks to do your dirty work," continued Betty Jean as she grabbed her pocketbook and sunglasses from the table.*

"But today, you have been exposed. Your true heart, motives and deeds have been revealed to your best friend and to your favorite niece." Putting her sunshades on, Betty Jean made her way to the back door, and on her way out, she looked back at her friend and said, "I have a hair appointment today at Heavenly Hands, so I will try to check on you later. I pray that you pray for forgiveness and I know the good Lord will help you. Come on Jenkins, I'm ready to go home."

"I walked in that kitchen and shook my head as I walked past Sarah Ann. I saw her tremble in tears as she sat at the table. Yet, I bet her heart remained unchanged as she probably had a few other tricks up her sleeves so that she can discredit our current pastor in order to gain control. I am really praying she doesn't do anything stupid during the final appreciation service in two weeks. First Lady, I don't understand why people like Sarah Ann attend church in the first place. I am praying to God to show me how to deal with this as a leader in the church. I couldn't do anything but shake my head and walk out the door. I was speechless," said Jenkins.

"I will definitely start praying for you and how to respond to what you saw and overheard," I said. *Lord, Jesus. Please protect us from the enemy, Satan.* I thought to myself. I knew this information was not for me to pass on to Lance, but for Deacon Jenkins to share with his pastor. I had learned that second hand information from anyone, including me, could be incorrect or misquoted. I had learned to carry my burdens and take them to the Lord in prayer. There are some things even a pastor cannot fix. I deeply inhaled and exhaled. It was all too much to hear and experience for one day and I needed some emotional rest.

I hung up the phone, and waited for my husband's return to deal with *our* situation, until my eyelids became a curtain and rest called my name.

Chapter Twenty-Three

The Confrontation

I awoke to a sound at the foot of my bed. I opened my eyes to see my husband pulling off his shoes at the edge of the bed. I looked at the alarm clock and it read 11:30 p.m. I wondered to myself where had he been for the last few hours. I exhaled to let him know that I was up and it was time to talk about today's events. I leaned up on one elbow and said, "When were you going to let me know that you personally knew Sister Marilyn Steele? How does she get a new key to your office before me? Why did she walk down the middle aisle with the preachers? When did she get so comfortable with you that she can kiss you on your lips? Is she your whore now? What is going on, Lance? It doesn't look right! And the Spirit of the Lord is telling me that something is not right."

By this time, I was standing up on the side of the bed with my hands on my hips and my French roll purple wrap on my head. I wanted to know what was going on, and I wanted to know right then.

"I am tired right now, and I don't want to talk about it. Yes, babe, I know it looked odd. I'm trying to figure it all out too. I am just exhausted right now," Lance said.

I could see the exhaustion in his face, but I didn't care. It was time to communicate and I wouldn't wait until he was ready.

"You come home at 11:30 p.m., don't even call to say that you are going to be late, and then you stroll up and say you don't want to talk about it? Did you come home late on purpose so you wouldn't have to talk about it?" I screamed.

"If you must know, I have been at the hospital with one of our new members, Justin Brown, who is suffering from a diabetic coma. The boy is nineteen years old, and I've been at the hospital with the family for the last two hours, praying and ministering to them," Lance said. "Sweetie, I am tired right now. I know we need to talk, but please, I am too tired to talk tonight. I was hoping that I could fall asleep in your arms, but I guess that is out too," he said.

"Yes, you guessed right because Goldie is out of commission until you and I communicate," I quipped and folded my arms across my chest.

"You know the Bible says in First Corinthians 7: 5, that you cannot withhold from me unless we both consent for a time," Lance said, using one of his favorite Bible quotations to hook me in.

"Your coming home after 11 p.m. without a phone call is enough consent, so since you can't respect Goldie, you can't have Goldie," I said. "Matter of fact, you can't even sleep with Goldie. So I advise you to sleep in the guest room until you are ready to communicate," I said without backing down.

"Are you serious? Jackie, please," Lance begged. "Well, this is my house, my bed, and I am going to sleep in it tonight," said Lance.

"No, Lance! First of all, this is not your house. It is New Light's house. Remember that. We don't own a home. I am tired of you taking me for granted, and I am always playing by your rules. This time I need to talk to you, share some pertinent information, and ask some questions. I don't want to wait until tomorrow," I said.

I was totally ticked off, because he didn't even ask me why we didn't come to the fellowship hall to have dinner with him. He seemed so unconcerned about us, that I wondered if he even noticed that we weren't there. This time he was going to talk to me or face the consequences.

"Lance, talk to me!" I screamed. "Why won't you talk to me? I want to talk about what happened today right here, right now!" I said with my hands on my hips and my neck seemed to be doing loops. As soon as I said that, I felt so childish. Now at thirty-nine years old, I felt like I was acting like a twenty-two-year-old newlywed. "Okay, fine. Fine Lance, you win. We can talk about this tomorrow or whenever you are ready," I reluctantly relented. "I am going out to take a walk. I just need some air."

As I turned to walk away I said, "But just remember, preacher man, the Word of God says in First Peter 3:7—'In the same way, your husband must give honor to your wives. Treat your wife with understanding as you live together. She may be weaker than you are, but she is your equal partner in God's gift of new life. Treat her as you should so your prayers will not be hindered.' So just in case your prayers for your precious New Light can't get answered," I said sarcastically, "check out how you are treating me!"

I put on my gym shorts, tennis shoes and a light shirt and headed downstairs. I needed to walk or else I would eat and I knew that was a bad habit that wouldn't help me to cope well with this dilemma.

"Honey, wait, it's too late at night to be walking by yourself," Lance said as he rolled the covers over his head.

"Then come with me," I said knowing that he was too lazy and tired to follow after me.

"What? Didn't you hear me say that I was tired? If I don't want to talk, then I definitely don't want to walk. Come to bed, Jackie, it's too late for you to be going outside," Lance said sitting up in the bed.

"If you love me, Lance, then you will come with me," I said trying to get him to move. "You know, Lance, those church folks down there at New Light, that you love so much, might be the same ones that cut you," I said thinking about Sarah Ann Finley's surprise. "They can call you anytime, day or night, and you are ready to talk to them. I want to talk now. Ain't I a member too? So come walk with me so that we can talk," I said.

"It's late. Be careful, Jackie. I don't want to hear any church gossip right now. My head is already beginning to hurt from the pressures of the day. I'm going to bed," Lance said pulling the bed covers over his head.

I turned around in a huff and jogged downstairs. I needed some air and quick. Dealing with Lance and now this revelation about Sister Finley's conniving schemes had me on edge. At this point, she could plant a bomb in his office next Sunday. I didn't care anymore.

On my way out, the refrigerator called my name and the ice cream inside beckoned me. I quickly walked out the door. I thought to myself: *Do positive things to deal with my anger.* Walking would definitely do the trick and settle my nerves.

I walked and then power walked some more around our neighborhood. I felt much better afterwards and it allowed me to think and calm down. I knew I might be a little tired at work, the next day but I needed to relieve my stress. I truly enjoyed walking because it also allowed me to talk to God. I prayed that God would help me deal with my anger issues and to reveal to me the truth about this Marilyn Steele woman and Sister Finley's surprise. As I walked, I prayed for protection over my husband, that he would not fall into temptation. I was, in fact, prayer walking over my situation. I wanted to make sure that Satan would not penetrate into my marriage or into my spirit. I truly believe that it is through praise and worship

that we can receive our breakthrough. While I walked I re-
cited Psalm 91, a passage that I had memorized over time to
speak strength into my spirit.

Psalm 91:

> He who dwells in the shelter of the Most High
> will rest in the shadow of the Almighty
> I will say of the LORD, "He is my refuge and my
>   fortress,
> my God, in whom I trust."
> Surely he will save you from the fowler's snare
> and from the deadly pestilence.
> He will cover you with his feathers,
> and under his wings you will find refuge;
> his faithfulness will be your shield and rampart.
> You will not fear the terror of night,
> nor the arrow that flies by day,
> Nor the pestilence that stalks in the darkness,
> nor the plague that destroys at midday.
> A thousand may fall at your side,
> ten thousand at your right hand,
> but it will not come near you.
> You will only observe with your eyes
> and see the punishment of the wicked.
> If you make the Most High your dwelling—
> even the LORD, who is my refuge—
> Then no harm will befall you,
> no disaster will come near your tent.
> For he will command his angels concerning you
> to guard you in all your ways;
> They will lift you up in their hands,
> so that you will not strike your foot against a stone.
> You will tread upon the lion and the cobra;
> you will trample the great lion and the serpent.

"Because he loves me," says the LORD, "I will rescue
     him;
I will protect him, for he acknowledges my name.
     He will call upon me, and I will answer him;
I will be with him in trouble,
I will deliver him and honor him.
     With long life will I satisfy him
and show him my salvation."

It took me about four years to memorize the entire passage
of Psalm 91, but I determined that I would hide God's Word
in my heart that I would not sin against God. I knew that my
flesh is weak and naturally contrite. I needed to get this scripture in my spirit to know that the battle is truly not mine, but
it is the Lord's! I learned a few years ago by reading Cindy
Trimm's novel, *The Rules of Engagement* that I am to position
myself to war in prayer to cover over the situations in my life
that try to separate me from God. I remember a time when I
would get all up in Lance's face with my concerns, and demand that he communicate. I had learned over time that huff-
ing and puffing in anger only tired me out. So, I began to cool
my steam by prayer walking. Lance knew that if I was out
walking this late, then I was praying over our family and our
current situations. He would often tease me and say, "Man, I
couldn't get away with anything if I wanted to. My wife has me
covered in so much prayer, that I'm afraid if I even thought of
something lewd, the Holy Ghost would knock me out."

I knew I couldn't change any man, but I serve a God that
can change any person, thing, creature or law, and that is my
Jehovah God who has all power in His hands. I nurtured a
personal relationship with God about five years ago. I was
brought up in the church all of my life and had long since accepted Jesus in my heart. But it wasn't until about the age of
thirty-two that I really began to know the person of God.

Jesus became my best friend. He truly began to talk to me in ways that I had never heard before, but it was only after I truly began to read His Word, fast and meditate upon it. I still try to fast at least once a week so that I can effectively hear from God.

My feet were beginning to get sore as they pounded upon the pavement. In my haste, I forgot to put my socks on with my tennis shoes. Beads of sweat began to form around my forehead. I kept walking and I kept walking until I felt a blister pop under my foot. I knew I had probably power walked for about four miles, because it was now 1:15 in the morning. I continued until I reached our home, and I stood on the front lawn and looked up into the sky to feel the radiance of the moonlight upon my face.

"Oh, God, you are my refuge and my strength," I said out loud. "Now, Lord, my head says to wake up that man in there and give him a piece of my mind, because he needs to talk to me. But I need you, Lord, to calm my spirit. I want to be a woman who builds up my house and not one who tears it down. I am still angry, because that fool let me walk out here by myself and it's past 1:00 in the morning. Lord, doesn't he care for my safety?"

A small gentle wind passed over my face and I heard a still small voice within my spirit say, "You chose to go walking at this time of morning, and so you compromised your own safety. You can't blame him for your own choices."

I silently laughed to myself. My God has a sense of humor, and I knew that it was His voice that I had heard. I quickly walked into the house, silently went upstairs to our bathroom, showered, and returned to my husband's side underneath our covers of safety and warmth.

Lance turned over and put his arm around me and I snuggled under his embrace. I exhaled and prayed that a new day would bring new mercies as I fell asleep in my husband's arms.

Chapter Twenty-Four

A New Day

I awoke in my husband's arms and gently kissed him on the lips.

"Good morning, sleepy head," I said.

"Good morning, Goldie," Lance said with a wanting look. So, I encouraged him to pass through my Golden Gates.

An hour later, we both showered and had a quiet breakfast together while the kids were still asleep. I decided I wouldn't say a word about yesterday. But, I would wait until he was ready to talk. I informed Lance that my family would be in town on next Friday for the Pastoral & Family appreciation celebration, and that I had a housekeeper scheduled to come in to clean the parsonage on next Thursday. I reminded him we had a barbeque planned on Saturday at the community park center for all of our guests and family that would be in town that weekend to help us celebrate our first year at New Light. Lance's family would be in next Thursday, and they would be staying at the local Hilton Hotel in Southlake. Most of my family was coming into town on next Friday, and for many of them, this would be their first time setting foot at the

New Light Church. We both scheduled our palm pilots for the next two weeks personal and church events.

"After the final appreciation service, I am going to take at two Sundays off, and we are going to have some family time together. I know this past year has been quite busy for all of us, and we haven't had any time to really travel or vacation anywhere. I talked to Deacon Jenkins last night, and he agreed that I needed some time away with my family. Would you like to go down to Galveston for one of those weekends?" Lance asked.

"Sure, honey, that would be great!" I said as I entered those promised weekend dates in my palm pilot. "I just hope that nobody dies or anything and we would be forced to change our plans. It just seems like every time we plan something to do as a family, the church came calling for us to rearrange everything. Somebody dies or somebody's second cousin dies and the family requests that you preach. It always seems to be something. Remember how we saved all that money to take the kids to Disney World four years ago for a two week vacation and on the way on the road, we got word that one of your deacons died at that church and we had to turn around and drive back home? The kids were so upset and they seemed to cry all the way back home. We still haven't taken them to Disney World. It is just so hard to get excited about anything because there have been so many disappointments in the past," I said, lowering my eyes to the table.

"I know, baby. You all have been so supportive of me and my ministry," Lance said walking over to me and planting a kiss on my forehead. "I will make it up to you and the kids. I promise. We are going to take that trip to Disney World next year, no matter what. I think I need to spend some quality time with just Junior and me. That boy is fourteen years old and time is going so fast. I am going to try to take him fishing or something and bond with him."

"Fishing? Lance, do you even know how to fish?" I said with a smile on my face.

"Nope, but Deacon Jenkins said that he is going to show me so that I can show Junior," Lance said.

"That is great, sweetheart. I am sure that Junior would enjoy that. I'm going into work early today. Can you make sure that the girls brush their hair? I put a wrap on their hair last night so they should be set to go. Their clothes are ironed in their closet and they know what shoes to wear to school. Make sure that Junior doesn't try to wear his pants sagging to the floor to school today. Connie and Jaylyn have dance practice right after school at four. Can you please have them there on time? And make sure that they all complete their chores and finish their homework before they even think about turning on a TV, playing a video game or talking on the phone. If you need me, just call me at work or on my cell phone. Don't forget to make sure that our bills are paid for this week on the parsonage," I said as I gathered my materials together to take to Victorious Workers.

"Yes, honey. It's Monday and it's my day off, but it sure seems like I still have a 24/7 job here at the house. I'll make sure the kids look nice, and don't I always ensure that they get to their practices and clean up their rooms?" Lance said with a hint of sarcasm.

"Yes, right, Lance. I love you, have a good day," I said as I left out of the back door.

I got into our Navigator, put my hands on the steering wheel and calmly exhaled. "Thank you, Lord," I said to myself. "Thank you for helping me hold my tongue, make passionate love to my man, and keep peace in my home. Now, Lord, I need you to work on him to communicate to me in his own time. Give me patience, in Jesus name, Amen."

I drove to work and arrived about 7:00 a.m. The office was quiet. I put on some coffee and checked my messages from last

Friday when I was off. Our voice mail stated that I had three
messages. Two of the messages were from potential workers
who wanted to fill out an application. Another message was
from Deacon Sable who called on Sunday evening at seven
and said that he needed to speak to me immediately upon my
return to the office.

Deacon Sable was a member of the board of Victorious
Workers and a respected deacon of New Light. He was in
charge of employee concerns and ethics. Deacon Sable was
known for having a bad understanding. It would take a person
telling him something three or four times before he received a
proper understanding of the issue. However, he was a good
man, just a little mentally slow. He was a faithful member and
deacon to New Light and a distant cousin of Deacon Finley.

I wrote a note to myself to call Deacon Sable after 9:00 a.m.
today. My assistant, Julie Jones arrived at 7:30am. The one
thing I loved about Julie was that she was always thirty minutes early to work every day. She called it her cool time and
preparation time to get ready for the day. We had over ten potential workers coming in for interviews this morning and five
people being assigned for temporary work. In the last two
months, Victorious Workers had successfully placed at least
six people into permanent jobs from their temporary assign-
ments.

Every Thursday, we held seminars that helped workers
learn how to dress for success and how to talk professionally
on interviews. We advised them on filling out job applications
and providing day care information for families. Our reputation as a reputable temporary agency was quickly growing in
Southlake. I had two meetings with area commissioners slated
for Tuesday and a luncheon with the Southlake Chamber of
Commerce. I worked between twenty-five to thirty-five hours
a week at Victorious Workers, however I was only paid for
twenty hours of work a week because we were still waiting to

hear if we were awarded for our second funding grant. We would know by the end of July.

I hope that perhaps Deacon Sable was calling with the news that we had passed the first hurdle to get additional funding that would support me working thirty hours at least a week and Julie working full time. She desperately needed more hours. Lance didn't like me to work more than twenty hours a week, but we were trying to save money to send our children to college and perhaps buy our own home so I felt it was necessary for me to help bring in some more income.

I was so nervous that if anything happened to Lance that I would be out in the cold. I had known many pastors' wives that when their husbands died, their churches refused to bury their husbands, or gave them tacky funerals and absolutely refused to help out the widow.

Upon coming to New Light, part of Lance's package was a life, health, and funeral insurance policy for him and his family, and within ten years, closing costs to help purchase our own home. At the other churches that Lance pastored, he didn't have any type of benefit package. Once our children were on Medicaid while Lance attended seminary. I used to have nightmares that Lance would die in a car wreck and I would be flat broke with no money to bury him. We put our whole lives into the church and trusted church folks to take care of us. Yet, God gives you common sense as well.

Just two years ago, one of Lance's close preacher friends, Reverend Chad Morris, died at the age of thirty-eight of an apparent heart attack. His widow was left financially with nothing and her husband's church abandoned her and her five kids. Several local politicians, Lance and a few other pastors went in together to help cover the funeral expenses for this young preacher. Two weeks after burying her husband, the church forced Sister Morris and her children to move out of the church parsonage. Today, she lives in one of the Dallas public housing properties with her five young children. Reverend Morris was not financially prepared to die and he entrusted his family's care to the church where he had pastored full-time for ten years. He had not bothered to invest in any health or life insurance for his family. When Reverend Morris died, he left his family financially insecure.

Lance promised that would not happen to his family and he made the necessary requests to the deacon board at his last church and when they refused to honor his requests for benefits, he prayed and the Lord moved us to New Light with a full health and life benefit package for the entire family. I inhaled as I thought about those years where God's divine providence took care of us and finally God granted my husband wisdom to take care of his family. The ringing of the phone interrupted my memories . . .

"Good morning, Victorious Workers. How can I help you?" Julie said. "Good morning Deacon Sable, yes, Mrs. Stevens is here today. I'll put you through to her."

"Good morning Deacon Sable," I said. "What can I do for you?"

"Hello, Sister Stevens. I would like to talk to you in person rather than over the phone. Can I meet you at about 9:00 this morning?" Deacon Sable asked.

"I do have an appointment at 9:00 this morning, but perhaps I can fit you in at 9:30. Is that okay?"

"Sure, that will be fine. I will see you at 9:30."

He hung up and I wondered what he wanted to talk to me about? I advised Julie about my new appointment and asked her to have some coffee and donuts ready for him when he arrived. I cleaned up the office and prepared for my first client.

At 9:25 a.m., Deacon Sable walked in the door looking quite pensive. I politely greeted him at the front office. Victorious Workers was a small edifice with three offices, one bathroom and a break room. I walked Deacon Sable back to my office, which had a side picturesque view of the adjacent

Southlake Mall. A picture of Lance, the children and me were on my desk, along with my nameplate. My college degree from the University of Texas hung on my left wall, my online seminary degree in church administration from College of Biblical Studies, my certificate for interior design and my MBA from the University of Phoenix degree hung on the right wall. A picture of our Victorious Workers logo that displayed a man and woman with outstretched arms hung behind my mahogany desk. I motioned for Deacon Sable to have a seat. I walked behind my desk and calmly sat down.

Deacon Sable began speaking first.

"Sister Stevens this is quite awkward for me but I must talk to you about this. Who did you notify concerning closing Victorious Workers early on Friday? I sent my cousin down here to apply for a job last Friday and no one was here to take his application," he said. "Now if this office is going to be closed, it is proper protocol to let the board members know, don't you think so?" he said.

"I did inform Deacon Jenkins, in writing, a month ago, that I would be out of the office on that day and that Julie was leaving at 12 p.m.," I said.

"When did you let him know and did you ask him? I recall that employees are supposed to request a day off, not inform that they are just taking off," Deacon Sable said with his arm folded against his chest.

"I requested the day off and reminded Deacon Jenkins last Monday, who is the president of the Victorious Workers 501c3 board, and he reiterated that it would be okay. He also knew that Julie would be here until 12 p.m.," I said.

"I thought that you are supposed to contact all of the board members when you are going to be out," said Deacon Sable.

"Our policy states that I am supposed to notify the chairman of our board. And I did that, Deacon Sable," I delicately said.

"How is this Julie Jones working out for you? Some of the

members of New Light have reported that she is always on the phone making personal phone calls. By the way, did you ever interview Kayla?" Deacon Sable asked.

"First of all, we do receive a lot of calls from persons looking for employment and I haven't noticed that Ms. Jones is making any personal phone calls but I will look into that matter and no, I didn't get a chance to interview with Kayla because I had already hired Ms. Jones." I stood up from my desk. "Can I get you some more coffee?" I asked.

"No, sister, that is okay. I was just concerned that this office was closed and I didn't know why. At any rate, how are you doing after what happened yesterday at the church?" asked Deacon Sable.

I shifted nervously from one leg to another. "What happened yesterday at church, Deacon?"

"Well, you know, with uh, Sister Marilyn Steele calling the pastor by his first name. We found out he appointed her temporary financial secretary and he did not receive a quorum from the deacon board to approve it. And your husband bought all that new furniture in his office and didn't get approval to purchase those materials with church funds. There are a lot of things happening within our church and it's happening too fast if you ask me. So, when I found out that this here office was closed Friday and I didn't know about it, I decided to investigate. Sarah, told me that she stopped by and saw this office closed and then she told me to look in the pastor's office to see his new furniture, and for the life of me, I couldn't understand how our pastor could afford such expensive furniture and—"

I interjected, "Sarah, uh, Sister Sarah Finley stopped by on Friday?"

"Yes, ma'am, she called me early Sunday morning, about 5:30 a.m., and told me. She felt that it was proper that all the board persons be notified when a church business was closed on a normal business day and that she didn't think it was right for the pastor to purchase items in excess of $5,000 without deacon approval. She has been pushing for us to put Pastor on a worker's contract since he first came to New Light. Well, if he continues to break policy, we need to at least suspend him. I know Sister Finley has been hot at me because I am against putting a preacher on a contract. If this is true, maybe we should put Pastor on a contract after all," said Deacon Sable as he looked at the floor.

I sat down at my desk and my spirit began to discern that there was something evil at work and Deacon Sable was being used in the game. An all too familiar uneasiness crept into my gut.

"If you don't mind me asking Sister Stevens, but is everything okay at the house? Are you and Pastor getting along? Some of the members are beginning to talk about how Sister Steele is always in Pastor's face all the time. Pastor has really started to place her in some powerful leadership positions and she has only been at New Light for six months."

Okay, by this time I was getting a little angry that this man was trying to talk about my husband and insinuate that he was not being faithful. In essence, he was disrespecting both my husband and me. I hate it when church members tried to pry into our personal lives. Furthermore, it was improper for him to discuss my husband's employment with me or anyone else that was not on the deacon board. I said a silent prayer for the Lord to help me keep my cool.

"Deacon Sable, Pastor and I are fine. I know you know that Pastor is great at helping members to find their place within the church. Sister Steele is an old friend of Pastor and I can assure you that they are only friends. Let's not let the rumor mill of New Light get the best of us," I said as I walked around my desk, motioning toward the door.

"We have a great church and a great pastor. You must excuse me Deacon Sable, but I do have another appointment, but if you have any concerns about office closures, please be sure to check with Deacon Jenkins. I am very good about following Victorious Workers personnel policies and protocol," I said.

Deacon Sable stood up from his chair and began to walk out of the door. "Thanks for straightening that out for me. Your office really looks nice and I am glad to hear that you and Pastor are doing fine. Now maybe Sarah Ann Finley would leave me alone with all her concerns. You know how demanding she can be. I don't know how Abraham Finley has put up with her for all these years," he said.

I looked at him and smiled without saying a word. I have learned that sometimes it is better to be silent, and besides, I didn't want him to carry anything I said inappropriately back to Sister Finley. "You have a good day, Deacon," I said.

I walked him to the front door and said goodbye. My 9:45 am appointment was seated waiting for me to conduct his interview. I went into the bathroom and checked myself over. A small quick tear fell from my eye. It had secretly escaped. I exhaled, cleared the black trail of mascara that the watery tear had formed, and returned to my duties as supervisor of Victorious Workers Temporary Agency.

Chapter Twenty-Five

Mahogany Soirée

After all the latest drama and gossip at the church, I decided I needed to relax and escape from it all by purchasing a good book to read. I overheard a sister at the church talking about this new African-American owned bookstore that opened up within the last month named "Mahogany Soirée."

After I dropped the kids off at church for their weekly Youth Bible study group, I drove to Mahogany Soireé looking forward to picking up Victoria Christopher Murray's latest book. As I entered the store, my brown skirt got caught on the front door. As I struggled to get my skirt from the rigors of this iron prison, a handsome chocolate brother appeared out of the air to rescue me. He gently tugged at my skirt to set me free from the door.

"There you go, madame. I hope it didn't bother your skirt too much" he said with a thick New Orleans accent.

I straightened my skirt only to get a strong whiff of his Vera Wang cologne. It was one of my favorite masculine colognes. I inhaled his strong scent.

"Oh, thank you so much. It doesn't look like anything was

torn," I said not looking him in the eyes, which I noticed were a light brownish gray.

"Welcome to Mahogany Soire, the best little bookstore in Southlake, formerly the best bookstore in New Orleans," he said.

"So you are a Katrina evacuee?" I asked.

"I'll like to say that I am Dorothy and this is my Oz," he said.

"Welcome to Texas, Mr . . . , I'm sorry, I don't know your name," I stuttered.

"Gerald Vaither. Please call me Gerald and you are the lovely."

With that lovely statement I instantly blushed. "Sister, I mean, you can call me Jackie," For some reason, I didn't want to give him my formal name.

"Jackie, this is my little idea of paradise. Can I give you a tour?" he said with his arm outstretched to walk me around his piece of heaven.

"Sure."

I noticed the store was not very full, only a cashier and two customers strolled the six aisles of book shelves and paintings.

Gerald walked me around his store, which was decorated in brown and neutral colors. We walked down the aisle, our shoes clicking against the shiny oak wood floors. We walked through the small internet café to the right of the store where patrons could hook up to their laptop and drink a frappinchino.

"I decided that Starbucks shouldn't hold a monopoly on coffee, so I call this section of my store Moonlight Blue Internet Café. It is a real hit with the fifty and under crowd."

I noticed a microphone and small stage where a small band or a spoken word artist could showcase their skills. The young woman behind the counter made a complimentary New Orleans style coffee with a tinge of caramel and cinnamon for me. I gently brought the cup to my lips as I saw Gerald's eyes

travel up and down my body. I knew he thought I wasn't looking, because I was so into this new taste of coffee, but a woman
can sense when a man's eyes are devouring her.

"Would you like to see some of my original paintings?" he
asked, taking me out of my coffee dreamland. Good Lawd'
that New Orleans coffee was the bomb!

He gently intertwined his arm around mine as he walked
around the store like a king and handled me with care like I
was his queen. I prayed that no one from New Light would
walk in the store to basically see a fine, attractive man, who
wasn't my husband, escorting me.

He showed me his original paintings, ten of which were for
sale. We walked into his personal office. It contained a black
lacquer desk and chair, a computer station, a couch, and two
sitting chairs.

I instantly noticed that Gerald had a modern deco flair that
really illustrated his sense of style. Perhaps he was one of those
metrosexual type males that you hear about in *Vibe Magazine*.
He was truly elegant in his tan sweater that was snug enough
to show his rounded biceps and even toned muscular chest.
His brown courdaroy Sean Jean pants and brown Stacy Adams
loafers completed his professional but Euro style. Gerald was
completely bald with a nicely shaven black and gray peppered
goatee, which accentuated his dark chocolate face. He had
deep dimples which peeked around his goatee and perfect set
of white teeth which glittered when he smiled. I imagined him
to be about 6'0 on a good day and about 190 pounds. I knew
then that I must have been staring too long.

"So you like Moeshe?"

"Uh, excuse me?"

"My Moeshe sweater?" He said pointing at his chest. "I
bought this online, and it was delivered last week. Do you like
it?"

"Yes," I said feeling completely busted for staring at him. I
needed to change the subject and quick.

"So how do you like Southlake?" I asked.

"I like it. I like the newness of the city and that there are so many successful African-Americans here. I miss New Orleans though. There is no place like home. But, I guess it was divine fate I would end up in Southlake, Texas. Business has been awesome so far. What can I do for you today?"

I was memorized by his conversation, that I completely forgot why I had come into the store in the first place.

"Oh, I am looking for the latest Victoria Christopher Murray book. I love her books," I said.

"She is one of my favorite authors. She is scheduled to visit our store later this year. Fill out a customer card before you leave, so we can contact you when she comes to town. The Christian fiction section is right this way, and if you need any more additional assistance with anything else, please let me know."

With that, he was gone. His masculine scent still lingered, and I silently exhaled. But, be ye holy, said the Lord. I purchased Victoria's book, *The Ex Files*, and left the store before my eyes betrayed me. On the way, home I reflected on this man's chemistry and the way he strolled with me in his store, because he did not know who I was. Why didn't I tell him I was a pastor's wife? Now, that's a good question.

I found myself going back to the Mahogany Soire the next four days for coffee, and conversation with Gerald. We talked about current events and the world around us without ever getting too personal. Our conversation would last no longer than thirty minutes as he returned to work and mingle with his customers. I found him easy to talk to and I looked forward to our morning caramel macchiato and New Orleans style coffee before I went to work. He paid attention to me as a person, Jacqueline Renee Stevens, and not as the pastor's wife who wasn't supposed to be intelligent but appear dumb, ignorant and silent partner of the ministry.

One particular morning, I noticed that Gerald seemed to be brooding over something.

"Gerald, is everything okay?" I cautiously asked.

We were sitting at the small coffee table and Gerald was staring out of the window and a tear fell down his cheek.

"You know, it's mornings like these that I miss New Orleans; the flavor of its people, and our unique culture. Most of all, I miss my family and my spiritual family back home. My family is scattered all over Texas and California now," he said as he looked at me and smiled.

"But you know who I miss the most? I miss my church family. We only had about 150 members in our church, but we were on fire for Jesus and we loved each other. I was tighter with my church brothers and sisters than I was with my own family. I miss our old deacon that seemed to cough his way through the entire service right up until the sermon. I miss our other deacon, Deacon Bunker, who talked back to our pastor so much during the sermon that it was hard to figure out who was preaching, him or Deacon Bunker. He was always trying to finish up or try to figure out what our pastor was going to say next," Gerald said, shaking his head.

"And then, Jackie, we had an old mother of the church named Mother Lydia who would stand by the offering and look to see what the other members were putting in the church offering tables, and if she thought you were robbing God, should would send you a note that said, 'Church Police: You have been given a citation for robbing the Lord, pay up or stay out.' We all thought she was crazy, but our church treasury was never broke. Over 70% of our church members were tithers."

"It sounds like you were very active in your church," I said.

"I was a doorkeeper. I served as an usher at my church. I loved my job, greeting the people every Sunday. I was saved five years ago. I grew up in the church, but I was just a church attendee. I didn't have a relationship with Jesus. I didn't know Him, but He knew me. The Lord saved me from myself. I was using every excuse for not being active in church and seeking a relationship with Christ. I had grown tired of the same old kind of religion. I stopped going to church and started having church on TV. I thought if I just prayed and read my Bible daily that it would be enough. But as I grew by reading God's Word, I found myself longing for His sanctuary," Gerald said. "And so God led me to this small fellowship of Christian believers," he continued.

"What was the name of the fellowship?" I asked.

"God's Chosen Vessels Fellowship: Where everybody is somebody! Our pastor was Revered Devereau, but we affectionately called him Pastor Hoop because he had a hoop when he preached, you could hear him within two blocks of our church. Pastor Hoop . . . he was our gift . . . He perished in Hurricane Katrina. They said he refused to evacuate until he knew that all of his members had safely made it out of the city. They found him in his pastor's study with the phone in his hand and a Bible on his lap."

"What happened to him?"

"He died of a heart attack. He was seventy-five years old. Pastor Hoop's wife passed away years earlier and his children all lived up state. So we were his family, the church.

"Wow, I miss that old man. I would give anything to hear his hoop right now. You know, some people complain about their churches and some of the sin sick people that go to their churches; but I would give anything to have one last service with my church members. We are all scattered across the United States now and we lost our church when the levees broke. Only about twenty of our members have returned to New Orleans."

I felt a tinge of guilt as I thought about my feelings toward the people of New Light. I thought about the young people who were eager to learn about Christ. I felt sympathy toward dear Sister Finley and even Marilyn Steele. I thought about new members of our church who were excited to do something for God. I realized God, in His divine mighty power and will, could take it away in a second. What if I woke up one morning and it was all gone? The church gone, and my employment gone, my family forced to move unexpectedly. *Oh, Lord. I have taken so much for granted*, I thought to myself.

"I'm sorry, Jackie to let you in on my pity party. I try not to think about it," Gerald said. "I try to think about positive things and what's happening right now in my life. Yet every now and then something will remind me of home."

"How is your relationship with Christ today?" I asked him.

"At first I was real bitter. I lost my home and business in one day. I had over four close friends die in the flooding of New Orleans. Two of my other friends, they are living, but they suffer from post traumatic stress. They will never be the same," Gerald's voice cracked a bit. "I received an email last night. One of my old neighbors in New Orleans committed suicide last week. He was seventy years old and he lost everything he had in the storm. He hung himself in his home. He relocated to Houston, but he returned home to die last week. So how is my relationship with Christ, you ask? Well, I haven't been active in church since Hurricane Katrina. I tithe to a local church here in Southlake, but I have yet to walk through those doors. I believe the church is called New Light or New Bethel something like that," he said. "I plan on making my way there. Yet so much of a church will remind me of home."

I shifted in my seat uncomfortable all of a sudden. I felt beads of sweat began to form on my forehead. I looked around to see if anyone walked into the café that I knew.

"One of my customers, Kayla Barnes, told me about her church, and so I thought I would give my tithes and offering to this church. I think they have a new pastor or something like that. Kayla is a regular customer, and she is always trying to introduce me to the ways of Southlake. I think her family was one of the first African-American families to reside in the area. She is very proud of her ancestry in Southlake and her church," he said.

I finished my coffee and grabbed my purse and got up from the table to leave.

"Jackie, you are leaving so soon? I'm sorry if I sound sad this morning, um, please stay for a few more moments. I look forward to your company every morning. I know it's only been a week, but I guess it seems that you are really listening to what I have to say."

"I have an early appointment this morning for a potential worker and I need to get the office ready." I hoped the Lord would forgive me because I just told a lie.

"I do need to be going, Gerald. I am so sorry for your loss and my prayers are with you." He stood up and gently grabbed my hand. "Jackie, did I say something to offend you? If I did, I am so sorry. I didn't mean to sound so depressing. I hope you will stop by tomorrow morning," Gerald said.

"You did not offend me and it's not you or anything you said. It's me. I will see you tomorrow morning," I said as I turned to walk away. I realized that it would be a long time, before I walked through the doors of Mahogany Soire again. It was yet another reminder that I was, Jacqueline Stevens, the pastor's wife of New Light. Once Gerald became aware of that, our unique friendship, our unbiased talks and his ability to see me, the real me, would be over. I walked to the door and looked back to see Gerald oddly looking out of the window of the café with a strange look of loss. I totally identified with that loss of identity and innocence. I exhaled and turned to walk through the door and that's when I saw him.

Brother Ray Joseph, our fired former musician stood in the aisle with his arms folded and a huge grin across his face. I didn't bother to speak. As I walked out, I heard him say, "Yes, First Lady Stevens, I guess we all do have something to overcome. And hello to you too."

Chapter Twenty-Six

A Wonderful and Meaningful Experience

The week leading up to celebrating our one year tenure at New Light was finally here. It was Monday and I had six days to try to lose two more pounds.

I looked forward to my family coming in to town on this Friday for the appreciation service. It was one of the few things I liked about the appreciation service celebrations. Our family would come down to encourage us and spend some time with us. We scheduled fun activities for the children on that Saturday. Lance had ordered a moonwalk for the children to jump in, and the brotherhood of New Light volunteered to provide the barbeque. I sat at my desk after a long day and looked over my palm pilot for my schedule. Connie, Jaylyn, and I had a hair appointment on Thursday. I was going to pick up my dress with matching hat, shoes, and accessories I had ordered out of a catalog at one of the boutiques in Southlake on Friday. I didn't want to wear anything that any of the women in Southlake had been seen in, so I special ordered my dress for the appreciation service.

Lance took Junior, about a month ago, to purchase a new suit with matching Stacy Adams shoes. I prayed he could still fit those clothes. He was growing like a weed. My mother purchased Connie and Jaylyn's dresses, matching bows, and shoes for Sunday and she was bringing them with her. Lance decided to just have an 11:00 a.m. appreciation service because a lot of the members could not find time to attend any of the 3:30 p.m. afternoon services.

After his first three months at New Light, Lance had began to cut back on afternoon services and completely eliminated the 6 p.m. Sunday evening service for lack of support. This angered Sister Finley because it was a New Light tradition to have an evening service. She let it be known she was very upset about this change and surveyed the deacon board with the question "How would New Light survive without the offerings and the occasional chicken sale dinners held at the evening services?" Lance told me that he called her in for a meeting to dispel her ramblings, and told her that the Bible encouraged that the church be maintained through tithes and offerings. Sister Finley was upset, because Lance put a stop to her mission group's annual chicken dinner sale that netted her group over five hundred dollars per sale event. "These folks are not going to give money up for free, and Pastor Stevens you will see that for yourself."

Instead, the tithers in New Light, grew from twenty-five percent to a whopping forty-two percent within the church because Lance put a stop to weekly and monthly dues within ministries, bake sales, and chicken sales. The only ministry that was allowed to raise funds outside of the evangelistic CD, video and audio ministry, was the Youth ministry, and that was limited to car washes, T-shirt sales and donations. Most of the children did not work so Lance compromised on events that warranted more money for the children to be exposed to other things outside of Southlake.

I closed the office at 5:30 p.m., and proceeded to go home. I knew that Lance would have the children's dinner on. I went to pick up Connie and Jaylyn from dance practice. I was exhausted from a mentally draining day, and I was having a hard time focusing on my work. I received some good news that another one of our temporary workers we placed at a local law firm had been asked to stay on permanently. I loved my job and I loved hearing good news, especially on days when I needed to hear it.

I picked the girls from dance practice and drove home. They told me about school and dance practice. They were so excited that Big Mama Thompson and Granny Eva would be coming into town and they couldn't wait to see their new dresses. I drove into our driveway and I was alarmed to find the house eerily dark. I walked into the kitchen and turned on the light switch, but there was no light. Connie tried to turn on the TV, but there was not any power.

"Mommy," she said, "the TV won't come on and where are all the lights?"

Our lights were out. Memories of past experiences in church parsonages where someone forgot to pay the bill or Lance forgot to give it to the finance team began to numb my brain. Fear ran up my spine sending a small chill. I told the girls to get back in the car and we would eat out tonight.

I felt an uneasy knot in my stomach. I thought about Gerald and then the devilish grin of Brother Ray Joseph's face as I left Mahogany Soire bookstore. Was I being punished now? Why didn't Lance call me on my cell phone to let me know the electric had been cut off? I would have never come home with the girls if the lights were out. I hated trying to explain to them what was going on. When they were smaller, I used to tell them that we were having dinner by candlelight and that it was a special night for mothers and their children. Lance would be out trying to find the nearest deacon or the person who forgot to pay the bill. I was slightly confused. New Light was doing very well financially and it didn't make sense for the parsonage lights to be turned off.

I backed the car out of the driveway and we made our way

to the nearest McDonald's. I called Lance's cell phone number and I noticed he tried to call me at least three times, but I guess I turned my ringer off by mistake. I wondered why he didn't try to call me at work. I dialed Lance's office phone.

"Hello?" Lance answered on the second ring.

"Hey, babe, the lights are not working at the house. What is going on?" I asked, trying to remain calm.

"I am not sure, but I am at the church and I am trying to contact the light company's after hours number to see if someone can come out and restore our lights. If they won't come out, then I will call the mayor of Southlake if I have to. I am trying to find out how this happened, but no one on the deacon board is taking responsibility, and I can't locate Marilyn anywhere. Somebody dropped the ball and I will get to the bottom of it."

"Have you and Junior eaten yet? I am taking the girls to McDonald's for dinner. Is Junior with you?" I asked.

"Yes, I picked him up from school and we were both at home when the lights went out, and no, I don't have much of an appetite right now. I took Junior by Jack-N-the-Box to grab a burger. Look, I'm sorry, baby. I'll get to the bottom of this," Lance said.

"Okay, we should be at the church after we eat. I love you, Lance," I said.

"I love you, too, Jackie."

Later on that night, the electrician came out to our home and our power was restored by 10:30 p.m. While we were out, the gas company came and disconnected the gas and our land phone was disconnected. It was as if someone had purposefully called all of our utility companies and told them we were moving or something.

Lance was tired and confused. We dressed for bed and he held me in his arms.

"I promised you that you wouldn't have to ever deal with this sort of stuff again. And here we are with no gas, no phone and I don't know what I did or why this has happened. Deacon Jenkins assured me he would investigate," Lance said.

"It's okay, sweetie. As long as I have you and the kids, that is all that matters right now," I said. I thanked God He is my strength, because I remember a time I might have called all of those deacons, and given them a piece of my mind.

"I promised your daddy I would take care of you. Sometimes, you know I doubt my ministry, and I want to throw in the towel. I know I could do right by my family if I worked in Corporate America, and made big bucks. Yet, the Lord won't allow me to quit this preaching business. I'm like Jeremiah, 'God's Word is like fire, shut up in my bones!'" said Lance in his preaching voice. He held me tighter. "Are you are going to be okay when you have to take a cold shower tomorrow morning?" he asked

"I don't want to think about that right now. We'll deal with that in the morning. I am glad that the phones are not ringing off the hook though. Remind me that if our gas is not on by the morning, I need to go and purchase the Morris family a cake for their son who was injured. I've been so pre-occupied, I haven't had a chance to do that yet. Is he still in the hospital?" I asked Lance.

"Yeah, baby, their son is still in the hospital. What would I do without you? Here we are with no phone or gas service and you are still sweet enough to remember that I asked you to bake a cake for the Morris family. If you are too tired or busy, don't worry about it," Lance said.

"No, I don't want to let that family down. It won't be a problem, Lance. I know how I would feel if Junior was in the hospital right now. I may not have a phone or gas, but I do have my family all together and that is a blessing. I just hope we get this thing situated before our family gets in town. That would sure be very embarrassing. They are looking forward to coming to meet our new church family," I said.

"Did you catch up with Sister Marilyn?" I asked trying to

see if Lance was ready to talk about the situation that happened at church two Sundays ago. I stroked his arm as my head lay within his bosom.

"Not yet. Deacon Jenkins said her phone number has been changed and the new one is unlisted now. He called her office, and her boss said that she took a sixty day medical leave of absence.

"That Sunday, I was so embarrassed by what she said about me. She caught me totally by surprise with her hug and quick kiss. I think she was the one who personally bought me all of the new furniture in my office. I am still not sure who had access to my office. I knew Deacon Finley was creating new key locks, but he never informed me when he was going to do it until he contacted me in Houston while preaching out of town. Apparently, he gave Marilyn a key to my office. I let him know I wanted my office re-keyed next week, and only certain people would have access to my pastor's study. I told him I didn't want any of my female staff to have my office key, because of the potential turmoil it could cause. He agreed with me wholeheartedly.

"Like she shared, I knew Marilyn since she was eight years old. Her family is from Houston and she would come there every summer to visit her grandparents. We weren't close growing up, because I was six years older than her. I ran into her at a Florida Christian convention. She told me that she would be relocating to Texas, and she would look me up when she returned to live here," Lance said, stroking my hair, ever so gently.

"When she showed up in Southlake and joined New Light two months after seeing her in Florida, I was shocked and uncomfortable with her presence. I knew she had been baptized before because I saw my Uncle Rupert baptize her when she was ten years old at our home church in Houston. But she told me that she wanted *me* to baptize her. She then showed me a picture of her new fiancé who was back in Florida. She said he was going to move to Texas within the year. I thought perhaps I judged her wrong. She always talked about her wedding plans and how she was going to get married. She was planning for her wedding to be two times as spiritual as Juanita Bynum's 2002 wedding. Somehow, I think that young lady was not planning to get married. Sister Finley suggested we appoint her as the new temporary administrative assistant and allow her to lead the Women's Ministry at the church. I informed Sister Finley that Marilyn had a full time job, and would not be able to keep any church hours. And then the very next day, Marilyn shows up to work in the secretary's office," Lance said. "It was rather strange."

I sat up and looked into his eyes. "You know I love you, and I trust you. But whatever you decide to do to expose this woman, make sure you have a witness in the room with you, because she can turn this around on you. I know most preachers may go through a circumstance where their character and integrity will be scrutinized," I said. "But I must tell you, my female radar tells me that something is not right with this woman and my spirit tells me that Sister Finley may have set this whole thing up. Sister Finley's name comes up too often, when there are negative issues within the church," I said. I thought about all of Deacon Jenkins' previous conversations concerning Sister Sarah Ann Finley and I shivered.

I wondered if I should tell him about Deacon Sable's visit to my office last week and what he tried to insinuate about Lance and Marilyn. I decided to wait to share that information, as the day had already been a trying one for him.

"Let's get some rest, sweetheart. Don't forget to get on your knees and say your prayers," I said.

"I can say my prayers lying in this bed," he said.

"Come on Lance, let's get on our knees," I knelt beside our bed. "This is a position of worship and humbleness. Now, if

Muslims can get on their knees five times a day and pray toward Mecca to Muhammad, I know we can get on our knees
once a day and pray to the Almighty God," I coaxed Lance.

He rolled over and knelt on the floor beside me. I realized it
had been at least a year since Lance and I had prayed together on
our knees in private. He looked at me and said, "Okay, you pray."
Even though my husband was the great preacher pastor in public,
I often found that I was the spiritual prayer warrior at home. I
closed my eyes and began to talk out loud to God in prayer:

"Lord, Jesus. How we love Thy name. For you are holy,
holy, holy, worthy is the Lamb of God. You are awesome and
your wonders are marvelous to behold. Thank you, Lord for
your daily mercies. Tonight, God we confess our sins to you
and we pray for your forgiveness. We decree your blessings,
oh Lord, in the lives of our family. We stand in faith and bind
every enemy that has been set in place to hinder and thwart
the purposes that you have for our lives. We pray in the name
of Jesus that our spiritual enemies are exposed and that their
works be uprooted and destroyed this very moment. We pray
in Jesus' name that angels be released to defend the well-being
of our family, the well-being of God's Kingdom in our lives together and that the principalities at work in our lives be devoured by the swords of the angels of the Lord.

"We pray the enemy be confused and confounded, and that
they be entangled in the plans, traps, and snares that they have
set for us. We decree peace! We decree, Oh God, your perfect
order in our lives! We decree that your plan and purposes be
fulfilled this day at this very moment. We bind the ruling
forces over our church, New Light . . . the forces seated in the
highest ruling places . . . that their plans come to ruin . . . in
Jesus' name," I declared in a loud voice.

"And it is in Jesus' name that we decree that nothing that
you have in store for us be held up in the realm of the spirit,
that everything you, oh Lord, desire for us during this season
it shall be . . . that it is so . . . that it be released unto us and

our family. None of God's favor from us shall be withheld. None of God's finances from us shall be withheld. None of God's miracles from us shall be withheld. In Jesus' name.

"And finally, we decree that we are able to rightly discern the times and seasons and to pray accordingly. In Jesus' name, we lift up this prayer to you, Oh God! Let your will be done in our lives, Amen."

I looked over at Lance and he was crying. I reached over and grabbed him. I held Lance in my arms and we wept together. I knew my husband was probably enduring more than he cared to share with me. I understood there are some things men had to bear alone with just Jesus. I am learning to not always pester him with questions, but just be there for him to lean on and provide emotional support. I wondered if Deacon Sable had stopped by the house or called him last week as well. I knew that though our journey had been tough, we learned to make it together with Jesus. This journey was a wonderful and meaningful experience because it taught us to trust in God and lean not unto our own understanding. We both understood that we don't fight against people, but we fight against our great adversary, Satan, who tries to use every trick in his book to keep us from our God given purpose.

Lance and I returned underneath our bedcovers. He grabbed his Bible and began silently reading Hebrews 6:10, a scripture that Lance would read and reread when he needed encouragement. It reads as such: "God is not unjust; he will not forget your work and the love you have shown him as you have helped his people and continue to help them." I watched his lips move as he spoke the scripture silently and meditated on its promise.

I picked up my journal and wrote:

Dear First Lady,
   Well, it seems to be happening again that our lights were turned off, the gas and the phone service all in one day. I

prayed that New Light would be different from the other churches Lance pastored but I guess all churches are alike in some ways. It seems that someone dropped the ball on paying the parsonage bills and I guess that someone must be upset with the Lance about something. I know that Lance has something on his mind but he is not really talking about it right now. He did let me know that he knew Marilyn Steele casually from Houston, Texas, but he still did not share why he didn't communicate that to me when she joined New Light. But, First Lady, you would have been proud of me. I kept my cool and held my tongue to a limit and didn't lose my temper and I even prayed with him without starting an argument about who would pray.

I am growing. God is giving me new strength everyday. I am still praying that he removes some of my evil thoughts that I have toward Sister Finley. I know if I don't deal with this anger, I might actually go off and hit that old sister. But I must remember the words of my mother and I quote, "this life was meant to be a wonderful and meaningful experience." Though situations in my life have served as the thorn in my flesh, I know that my thorns shape me for better service in God's army.

This Sunday, we will celebrate one year of service at New Light. The Lord has brought us through this year. Our relatives will be in town on Friday and I am praying that everything will be nice this weekend. I am now looking forward to this celebration to see what God is going to do. The kids and I have a surprise to give to Lance on his big day. I can't wait until he sees it! He is really going to like it. Good night, First Lady. I will talk to you soon.

Love,
Jackie

Chapter Twenty-Seven

A Family Reunion

At twelve noon sharp, Friday afternoon, my Big Mama Thompson and my mother Eva Montgomery turned their big Escalade Cadillac SUV into my driveway. It had been eleven months since I had traveled to Richmond to see my family, so I was eager to see them. My two sisters were planning on coming to town on Saturday. I ran out of the front door to greet them. A tall, lean man with a black Kango hat opened the front door and proceeded to open the rear back seat car door.

"For you, my lady," I heard him say.

My mother got out of the backseat and carefully placed her perfectly French manicured toenails on the concrete. "Thank you, Mr. Bentley. Can you please hand me my white sandals? Where will you be staying for the weekend?" she quizzed.

"I will be at the local Hilton Hotel if you all need me. I'll get your luggage and place it in the house." Mr. Bentley retrieved their luggage from the car and placed it within the parsonage.

"Hi, baby" my mother said to me with outstretched arms. She gave me her trademark kiss on both cheeks. "Ooh, your house is lovely." I knew it could never compare with her mini mansion back at home, but this was the best parsonage Lance and I had ever lived in since he began pastoring. My Big Mama Thompson creaked her way out of the Cadillac and strolled over to me with her new walker ensemble.

"Big Mama T when did you start walking on a walker?" I questioned. "Nobody told me that you were walking on a walker now!"

"Well, if you weren't so busy with your husband's church and all, you would know that I started walking on a walker about two months ago," Big Mama said.

"Gul', you know I am just playin' with you," she said in her classic Texas country drawl. "This here is Mr. Woods' old walker, he's just letting me use it just in case I need it if we get a ticket, cuz' you know how those laws like to stop us colored folk on the road. So, I told Bentley that if any of those cops stopped us, to tell them that I had a mini stroke, so that we could get a warning or something," Big Mama said as she reared back and laughed her customary contagious laugh that caused her entire body to shake. "Gul', get over here and give your Big Mama T a hug."

I walked over to Big Mama and gave her the tightest hug and kiss on her cheek. At eighty-three, my Big Mama T was still a wise cracker and could still wear a pair of three-inch heels any day. My mother developed her sense of style and got her lean, long legs from my Big Mama. I instantly thought that Sister Peterson and Big Mama T would probably hit it off great this weekend. I only hoped that Sister Peterson wouldn't try to spread her poison to Big Mama T about what is going on in our church.

I walked them into the parsonage and I was so glad that the maid service had sent extra help to clean the house. My house was sparkling clean and it smelled absolutely divine. I seated them both in the living room.

"Now where are those grandbabies of mine? I can't wait to see them," my mother said.

"The kids are still at school," I told her.

"Where is that fine, hunk of a preachaman that you married? Where is my grandson-in-law, Lance?" Big Mama T asked.

"He is at the church right now, but he is coming home for lunch. He should be here any minute," I said.

I was grateful that my lights were on, the gas was back on, and the phone service was reconnected. The housecleaner came and did a superb job with the house. The girls went to the beauty salon, and we received a gorgeous spiral roller set from Ms. Vivian, who let me know she had notified Lance she was willing to give a solo on our appreciation day. I looked forward to hearing her sing. Upon hearing the news that she would be singing and playing the organ on Sunday, several of her customers within the salon remarked that they would be in attendance to hear Vivian Daniels return to the church and sing again.

I gave my mama and Big Mama T a tour of the parsonage. They both loved the prayer nook and remarked how New Light must really care for their pastoral family. I didn't let them know that Lance and I had personally paid for the upgrades within the house.

"Now, baby," my mother began, "when are you and Lance going to finally purchase your own home? Because you know when that man closes his eyes in death, those church folks are going to want you out of their property. So you make sure that you and Lance make plans for that. Mama, didn't raise a fool and I didn't send you to college so that you could land flat on your behind," she said as she smoothed out her ivory linen Capri pantsuit.

"I know, Mama. We are working on that as we speak," I said.

"Good!" she exclaimed, giving me another hug. "This is the best looking parsonage you and Lance have ever lived in."

"Okay, Eva Montgomery, stop being so judgmental and let's

go to our room to unpack. Jackie, you know your Big Mama T had to go through Elgin and get my baby some sausage. I got it in my luggage just for you," Big Mama T said.

"Oh, Big Mama T, I am staying away from pork right now. It's only chicken and fish for me now. I am trying to lose these 15 pounds I gained since we have moved to Southlake," I said.

"Yeah, I noticed that you picked up some weight," my mother said as she inspected me from top to bottom. "You know you are an emotional eater. Is everything all right? The last time you picked up a lot of weight was when you and Lance were at that God forsaken church in the country. What was the name of that church? Bethel or Little Zion? I thought those folks were going to cause my baby to have a nervous breakdown. You gained over 20 pounds in six months," my mother said as she held me tight.

"Mama, I am doing fine and we are blessed to be at New Light. I haven't been jogging or walking as much as I used to. I have lost some weight within the last three weeks, though. So I know the weight will fall off," I said, shifting nervously from one foot to the other.

"Well, who's going to eat all this sausage?" Big Mama T asked.

"Big Mama T, you got a fourteen-year-old great-grandson who can eat all of that pork in one sitting. So, don't worry about it. Your food will not go to waste," I said, reaching out to grab her within our sister to sister circle hug. "I miss you all so much. Why can't Richmond be right around the corner?" I asked.

Just then Lance entered the back door. "Will you look at this? Y'all are already cuddled up next to each other. Hello, Mama Eva and Big Mama T! It is so good to see you!" Lance gave them each a hug.

"My, my," my mother said, "don't you look prosperous and very handsome? You must have found a good church this time.

You look great, Lance! Are you taking good care of my Jackie like her daddy told you to? Because you know I think that man will rise up from the grave if any man abused any of his daughters," Mama said, sarcastically with a smile on her face.

"Yes, ma'am, I am. And I am trying my best to spoil her," Lance said, giving me a peck on the cheek.

"Y'all are so cute together," Big Mama T said. "Now after we eat, I want to see your office place, Jackie. What is it called again?"

"Victorious Workers," I said.

"I still can't believe those chu'ch folks even allowed the preacha's wife to run their business. Now I know that times are a changin'. In my day, they were to sit pretty, wear those tall chu'ch hats and they bet not dare say a word in the Lawd's house. Today, preacha's wives are helpin' to run the chu'ch businesses and even obtaining seminary degrees too. What you say? I know the Lawd is on His way back!" Big Mama T said.

We all laughed at her antics. I went into the kitchen and prepared our lunch. We all sat down and ate together. I noticed that Lance seemed to have a forced smile upon his face during our lunch. Afterward as we prepared to drive Mama and Big Mama T over to the Victorious Workers office, I cornered Lance and asked, "Sweetie, is everything okay? You look a little pensive," I gently placed my hand on the side of his face.

"Yes, it's just that Deacon Sable came to visit me this morning in my office and he told me about all of these rumors that are floating around town about me," Lance said.

"What rumors?" I asked

"I am going to need you to come to a Deacon's meeting with me tonight at seven at the church," Lance said.

"Why do I have to attend a meeting? You know I don't like going to a witch-hunt session. I've gone through that before.

Why can't you speak for me? Aren't you my husband? You promised, me Lance, that you wouldn't allow another church to gang up on me," I said as tears began forming in my eyes.

"Baby, wait, just listen," Lance said, as he held my arms on both sides. "They are trying to say I slept with Marilyn Steele. They are saying I made a romantic pass at our last musician, Brother Joseph, and that's why he quit. And, they are saying that you are refusing to notify the Victorious Workers board about your missed days at work. Now, we know that this is not true. However, we still have to deal with these allegations and face them."

"What does Deacon Jenkins have to say about all of this?" I asked

"He is very upset about it and believes Sister Finley is behind all of it: our lights, gas and phone being terminated, our secretary quitting last week, my redecorated office, and the mysterious disappearance of Marilyn Steele," Lance said.

"Who brought allegations against you and me?" I asked.

"Deacon Sable came into my office this morning with over fifty signatures of New Light parishioners who have requested a formal review of me, due to these rumors," Lance said looking at the floor.

"Can they do that?" I asked

"We are not sure yet. Deacon Jenkins is at our attorney's office right now going over our church bylaws, procedures and policies. I have asked our area bishop to come to the meeting tonight to mediate," Lance said.

"Oh, Lance, I am so sorry. How can they do this the week of your appreciation service?" I said, as I put my arms around his neck and hugged him tight. "I'm so sorry. You know I love you and I will stand with you tonight. I'll tell Mama and Big Mama T that something came up and I'll ask Sister Peterson to come over and keep them company while we are out," I gave him a kiss on both his cheeks.

"I am going to stand in the Lord. I know that this is a

process where God will weed out and reveal my enemies. Thank you for your prayer the other night. It really strengthened me," Lance said. "You have always stood by me through it all. You have a way of smiling through all of our tests and trials. I know you are my gift from God. None of these rumors are true. I have been faithful to you. I have never compromised our marriage through a physical or emotional affair. I am not perfect, but that is one sin I know I haven't committed in our marriage."

"I know, sweetheart. I know. God has not revealed to me that you have been with anyone outside of our marriage. I will testify to this fact tonight. I can't believe that Brother Joseph is trying to say that you made a romantic pass at him. Everyone knows that he is just ticked off because you fired him. Why would they give credence to a suspect character like him? I just feel like whooping up on Sister Finley, but I know that wouldn't be the Christian thing to do. And I am praying that the thought of revenge flee from my spirit," I said as my body tightened up at the very thought of Sarah Finley.

"Vengeance is mine, said the Lord. Let's allow Him to work this out for us. I need you at the church by 6:00 p.m. Deacon Jenkins and I are meeting early for prayer and I want you to join us," said Lance.

"Okay. I will be there. Now, we better get downstairs before those old women think we are doing something else besides talking," I joked.

We took my mama and Big Mama T to the office building of Victorious Workers. They marveled at the professionalism of the office and the biblical scripture decals posted on each wall. There were information brochures about New Light and its ministries in the front office. Each office was equipped with a Dell Flat Screen Computer and both Julie and I had our own personal Dell laptops in storage for home use. I introduced them to my assistant, Julie, and told them that she was a member of New Light. I explained to them about our Wall of Fame of temporary workers who had been placed in permanent positions from their temporary assignment. As of today, eight Victorious Workers had been placed in permanent positions, their names, pictures and new positions aligned our Wall of Blessings.

"Baby, I am so proud of you and Lance. This is a wonderful way to bless the Kingdom of God. You are instructing and providing a quality workforce," my mama said. "This is what I knew you could do besides sitting down in church every Sunday in your church hat. I'm glad that your daddy's good money and my networks are beginning to pay off," she said, as she stroked her hair.

"Yeah. This here is a nice office. Your Big Mama T is proud of you too!" said Big Mama.

My cell phone rang. I answered and it was my college friend, and Lance's cousin, Amanda Deshay, on the line. "Hello?" I said.

"Hey, girl, this is Amanda. I just arrived at the Hilton Hotel. I just wanted you to know that I am in town for you and Lance's big day. His parents should be here some time tonight. Is the big barbeque still planned for tomorrow? Even though I live in Los Angeles, I still miss that good ole' East Texas Barbeque!" she said with a huge laugh. "Has Big Mama T and Mama Eva arrived yet?"

"Yeah, girl, they arrived around noon today. I really miss you and I can't wait to see you."

"Where is that cousin of mine?" Amanda asked.

"Lance? He is at the church. Give him a call. I'm sure he would love to hear your voice right now."

"Hey, I'll do that. But first, I am going to go down to the hot tub downstairs and relax," Amanda said.

I walked around the corner where my mama and Big Mama T would not be able to hear me.

"Listen, Lance and I have a meeting at 6 p.m. tonight at the church. Do you think you can come over to the parsonage and keep my mama and Big Mama T company?"

"A meeting? Isn't this supposed to be the week that you guys relax? Is everything okay? Do I need to go over there and do a spiritual drive-by and blow it up?" she playfully asked.

"Everything is fine. I will share with you about it later," I said.

"Sure, I'll come over to your house about 5:30 p.m. Girl, you are in my prayers," she said.

"Don't just say that you are going to pray for me. I need you to intercede for us around seven tonight," I requested.

"Sure. I will lift the both of you up in prayer around 7pm, tonight. Done! Now you know if you need me to bring a prayer and a shotgun I will!" she said with a hearty laugh.

"Girl, you are so crazy. I'll talk to you later on tonight. Good-bye," I said.

I calmly exhaled. I was glad that God had sent my best friend to Texas to help me shoulder this burden. Amanda was an enthusiastic prayer warrior and she was accustomed to interceding for Lance and me over the years. I needed a Barnabus' touch at this moment and Amanda was my Barnabus. She was my shoulder to lean on and cry to; I've never known her to break our confidentiality with one another. She lived in Los Angeles, California, yet her friendship and her love for Lance and me closed the gap on the miles that separated us. In essence, she was Lance's cousin, but she was my one true friend. Thank God for her.

Chapter Twenty-Eight

The Meeting

I drove my white pearl Lincoln Navigator into the church parking lot at ten minutes to six. I walked into the church and pulled the olive oil from my purse. I walked around the church and anointed the pews, praying at the same time. I anointed the pulpit, the piano, the organ, the deacon pews, and I finally walked into the boardroom where our meeting would be held and I anointed the doors of the room, the table, and the seats. I prayed earnestly that God would honor this symbol of faith. I knew the power was not in the oil, but in the power of God. I prayed that His will be done in this meeting.

As I finished this prayer, Lance and Deacon Jenkins walked in. I slipped the bottle of oil in my purse and the three of us joined hands in prayer. We each took turns praying for this situation. Deacon Jenkins began to cry as he prayed about the history of New Light and the previous turmoil that took a great man of God away from this church. He interceded for a church that he had invested his entire life in. I knew and understood Deacon Jenkins loved this church dearly and for the right reasons. His love for his church did not have to do with family loyalty, legacy or obligation; it had to do exclusively with his love of God and His sanctuary of worship.

At 6:55 p.m., the other eight deacons of New Light began to show up for the meeting. Deacon Sable showed up at 7:15 p.m. with his notebook of paperwork. Bishop Needly of Greater Praise Church in Dallas arrived at seven sharp to serve as mediator. He finally opened the meeting.

"We are gathered here today to discuss the request for a formal review of Pastor Lance McClain Stevens concerning allegations of adultery, homosexuality, and misuse of church funds," said Bishop Needly.

My heart sank as I listened to these allegations. I gripped the sides of my chair and held on tight. Lance was seated to my right and Deacon Jenkins on my left. Bishop Needly sat at the head of the table. Five of the deacons sat on the right with Deacon Sable and the other three sat on the other side of Deacon Jenkins. Oddly enough, Deacon Abraham Finley was not present at the meeting. Perhaps he was running late.

"Is there evidence to suggest these allegations are true?" Bishop Needly asked

"We have fifty signatures from New Light members that have suggested that they too have heard these allegations about Pastor Stevens," said Deacon Sable.

"I need proof. Do you have any evidence, Deacon?" requested Bishop Needly.

"Why, no . . . I just have these signatures. I do have receipts where over $5,000 of church funds was used to purchase his office furniture," Deacon Sable said. "Our bylaws state the senior pastor cannot spend more than $500 of church funds within thirty days without an approval from the majority of the deacon board." He placed the receipts from the various stores in front of the bishop. "And about $5000 is missing from New Light's general fund," Deacon Sable continued.

"How do you respond, Pastor Stevens?" the bishop asked.

"I did not authorize any furniture, computers, or clothing to be purchased. I walked into my office on last Sunday morning and the furniture was there. Someone purchased a new desk, computer system and everything. I didn't buy the furniture or the electronic equipment," Lance said, implying that this was a set up. "I certainly didn't request that over $1,000 be spent for a pastoral robe and a Steve Harvey suit."

Deacon Williams spoke up next. "Well, we sure as heck didn't authorize it, Pastor. We just renovated the pastor's office over a year ago with our previous pastor. So, I know we didn't authorize more money be spent on that area. Did any of the other deacons authorize this transaction?"

All of the deacons, except Jenkins, shook their hands and said, "No."

"How was the transaction made?" Bishop Needly asked.

"Everything was purchased with cash," Deacon Sable said, glaring across the table at Lance. "If you notice the date, most of the items were purchased over a period of three days last week."

"May I have a look at those receipts?" Lance questioned.

"Yes." Bishop Needly passed him the receipts. Lance looked at the receipts for a few moments, gently raised his head and smiled at Deacon Sable.

"Let the record reflect that on the dates of these purchases, I was 250 miles away in Houston preaching a revival. This is not possible that I could have purchased these items at these stores in Southlake.

Deacon Sable's hot air balloon bubble belly just seemed to deflate in that one moment of time. He turned as red as a Santa Claus suit.

"Excuse me gentleman," Deacons Jenkins intercepted. "I must give you some information that may lead us to the culprit of the new expense items. This information, of course, must be investigated further. It is my belief that Sister Finley and my sister, Betty Jean Pepperdine, may have purchased these items, and then created it to look like an unauthorized purchase."

"Has anyone bothered to ask Deacon Finley for a financial report or ledgers of the transactions?" Lance asked.

"Deacon Finley has been sick with the flu since Tuesday and Sarah won't even let anyone come within ten feet of him. So no, we don't have a record of the last month transactions," Deacon Jenkins said.

"Maybe your sister Betty Jean can get it for us since she and Sarah are best friends," Deacon Williams asked.

"No. I don't want to breathe any of this nonsense to any of our members. Therefore, I have not said a word to her about any of this, and I suggest to you all that you don't spread this poison and vicious lies to any of your wives," Deacon Jenkins said as he wagged his fingers at the other deacons around the table.

"You are right, Jenkins," they all agreed.

"Since there is no evidence to support who made the purchases, we will move on to the other issues of sexual misconduct," said Bishop Needly.

At that moment, I thought I would faint. This was all too much. *Lord, give me strength*, I asked Him.

"Is there any evidence that proves the allegations of sexual misconduct?" Bishop asked.

Deacon Sable pulled out a torn letter from his jacket pocket. "This was turned in to a deacon last Sunday. It was found in the secretary's office. It is a love note addressed to Pastor Stevens."

"I will attempt to read it so that all persons at this meeting will hear. I need one of you good deacons to make sure that you are taking minutes of this meeting," requested Bishop Needly. He cleared his throat and began to read the words on the crumbled up piece of paper that was torn in two and had been re-taped together.

Dear Pastor Stevens,

Every night I think of you. My heart is full of love for you. I wish I was your first lady. I can give you what she cannot. I see how you look at me. I watch your eyes move from my bosom to my ankles. This could all be yours if only you would make your move. I am here for you. I see the passion in your eyes when you look at me and say, 'Good morning, my sister' on Sunday mornings. You know it just doesn't have to be on Sunday mornings? You could say 'good morning' to me every morning if you'd like. I have a condo in Plano, Texas and no one would know it is our love nest. I enclosed the condo key for your pleasure. Meet me there this Monday afternoon at noon and I will make it worth your while. God has given us this passion for one another and you were meant to be mine. I long for your love. My body groans to become one with you. You know who I am because I hear your body calling out to mine every Sunday morning.

Signed Anonymous Sister, just follow the color red which symbolizes my love for you.

Lance was shifting uncomfortably in his chair. I looked over at him and gently caressed his hand. His face was completely flushed and I could tell his hands were beginning to sweat.

Lord, Jesus give me strength and the peace that surpasses all understanding, I thought.

"Would you like to respond, Pastor Stevens?" asked Bishop Needly

"This is a letter I received about three months ago. It is not uncommon for preachers to get anonymous notes from parishioners. I immediately tore the letter up and threw it away. So, I know that someone has been snooping around in my office trash can, if the letter is in your hands. I ignore those distractions however, this note does not prove I have been involved in sexual misconduct," Lance said, angrily pounding his hand on the table.

I slunk down a little in my seat. Another letter? Why didn't he tell me that he received an anonymous letter? How many letters had he received before?

"Where is the condo key, Pastor Stevens?" asked Deacon Sable with a sly grin on his face.

"What? I placed that condo key in the trash as well Deacon Sable, or do you have it?" Lance asked, looking him straight in the eye.

Deacon Sable turned beet red in the face.

Bishop Needly loudly cleared his throat. "Do you have any evidence of sexual misconduct, Deacon Sable?" Bishop asked.

"No, this is all I have. The other allegations of a homosexual pass from Pastor to Brother Ray Joseph, the deacons and I believe is completely untrue. We know Brother Joseph is upset because he was fired. He should have been fired a long time ago," Deacon Sable said with a defeated look on his face.

I looked at him from across the table, and the man could not even look me in the eyes.

"There is just one more thing, it is minor, but since we are here, we might as well bring it up," Deacon Sable said. "Mrs. Stevens took some time off from within the past month without contacting the entire board of Victorious Workers. I don't think that is right or fair. I believe we need to take another look at the policy of Victorious Workers and conduct a review of the procedures and practices. Furthermore, she hired Julie Jones and completely bypassed our long-term member Kayla Barnes, not even for an interview," he continued.

I looked at him like I was Michael the angel and I was going to slay him with my sword. But I remembered my prayer, *Lord, reveal to us our enemies.* Even though Lance and I had been there for Deacon Sable when his son died of a cocaine overdose during the first few months of Lance's pastorship at New Light, here he was betraying us and being petty about small issues.

"Wait a minute, Deacon Sable. We are here to talk about

the request for a formal review of Pastor Steven's tenure as shepherd over this flock. We are not here to malign his wife. That is a question for the board of Victorious Workers," said Bishop Needly. "Is there anymore evidence you would like to present?"

"That is all the evidence we have," Deacon Sable said. "Pastor, you must understand that we, the deacons, are here to protect the sheep and there are a lot of preachers sleeping with their parishioners, stealing the money and making a mockery of the church and we want to make sure that this doesn't happen at New Light."

Bishop Needly loudly cleared his throat.

"I am not trying to disrespect you, Bishop, but we have to be careful that we are not deceived. "There must be a check on everyone, including the preacher," Deacon Sable said as he pointed at Lance.

Lance was silent and just looked Deacon Sable straight in the eye, man to man from across the table.

Bishop Needly reviewed the petition and the evidence presented. The room was eerily silent. After two minutes of silence, Bishop Needly began to speak.

"It is my determination that you have not provided sufficient evidence for a formal review hearing and the request is denied," Bishop Needly said. "Are all of you in agreement?" Everyone in the room responded, "Yes," including Deacon Sable, even though it was delayed and ended up on the carpet floor as he looked defeated.

"There is something I would like to say," I said as I looked within myself and was shocked that I was even speaking. I stood up from my seat and looked the deacons in the eyes. "I want you to know that Lance and I love each other very much. I, for one, do not believe any of these rumors of sexual misconduct involving a man or a woman. He has proven to our family and me that he is a good, respectable Christian man who moves by the Holy Spirit.

"I know some of you may not have liked all of the changes that he has made this year at New Light, but he needs your support, not your venom. If we follow the vision of the man of God, we will all be blessed. But if we fight him, we will not receive those abundant blessings. Women have tried to lead this church from their houses and you have allowed them to do this at New Light for years. This is the 'Jezebel Spirit' that is destroying our churches. God has ordained male leadership within His church. The church is one of the few institutions where the man is still the hero. But where is he? Where is his leadership? Where is his counsel and wisdom to balance the conversation of church women?" I said.

"I want you to know that we love you and we respect your position within the church. But, I must tell you my heart. These allegations hurt. We live in a world where assumptions and rumors are ruled as fact. Proverbs 22:1 says, 'A good name is more desirable than great riches; to be esteemed is better than silver or gold.' Our family will constantly have to defend ourselves against these allegations and rumors long after it has been ruled a lie. True Christianity lies in what you do in life when no one else is watching you. My husband, Lance McClain Stevens, is a man of integrity. We need to stand together in solidarity and stomp these attacks from the enemy. Satan seeks to destroy us all. You are the spiritual leaders and protectors of this church, and in the future, I pray that you all learn to do that together. And learn to pray about conflict before you assume them to be fact to fit your own personal agendas and biases. This is time that we could spend evangelizing or planning to win souls for Christ instead, of taking sides concerning vicious rumors," I said with tears in my eyes.

I grabbed my purse and walked out into the hallway as my heart seemed to explode within my chest, it was beating so fast. I heard Lance begin to speak to the men. I leaned against the wall and exhaled. I couldn't believe that I had just said all of that. Whew!

"Gentleman," I heard Lance say. "Let me begin by saying, these accusations are very serious and my family has been affected by this. I will never again allow my wife to endure the insanity of this type of conference. Brothers, if you want me to leave New Light, then you will have to vote me out, because God has not released me from my call here. Concerning Brother Joseph, the church has the moral authority to talk about behavioral changes. The government cannot and will not tell people morally how to live. It is my job as the 'watchman on the wall' to rebuke and reprove behavior that God calls sin. On the second issue, I am not a perfect man, but I have been faithful to my wife. I try to discreetly deal with women who may develop an admiration that borders on lust or obsession of me, and recently, Deacon Jenkins has dealt with Sister Steele who is now on an official leave of absence from the church due to inappropriate behavior unbecoming of a church staff member in regards to my wife and to the church," Lance said.

I immediately stood up straight at that comment. So my sweetheart did handle that "Steele my Man" daughter of the devil, Marilyn Steele. Thank you, Lord! Another answered prayer! I had learned that there were some things that only the power of prayer could battle. I was so glad that I prayed over Sister Finley's surprise instead of running to Lance with all of that information. Instead I ran to Jesus and He took care of the matter. God knows how to deal with His children better than I ever could. Our prayers and pleas to Jesus will move Him to action on our behalf. Thank you, Jesus!

"Brothers, the Lord says in His Word, First Peter 8-9 "You should all be like one big happy family, full of sympathy toward one another, loving one another with tender hearts and humble minds. Don't repay evil for evil. Don't snap back at those who say unkind things about you. Instead, pray for God's help for them, for we are to be kind to others, and God will bless us for it." Lance said. "I know this has been a period of great change and readjustment for you all. Since the Lord has called me to New Light, 183 members new members have joined the church, Forty-two of those through baptisms and conversion. We average $5,000 in collections and offerings every Sunday. We now have over twelve active new ministries; three of which directly serve our community. New Light has an active 501c3 business, a surplus monthly budget averaging $3500 after expenses. We have $30,000 in financial CD's and a for profit business that generates an additional $2,000 monthly to the church in its nine months of operations.

"God has been good to this church as we follow His will and the vision brought by the man of God. Deacon Sable don't believe the hype. Most preachers are not sleeping with their members, male or female. Most preachers are not stealing the church's money. Most preacher's are not making a mockery of the church. Most preachers labor in the Word for fifty-two Sundays a year. Our vacations and time with our families are robbed from us and very few preachers make the same amount of money as men with similiar vocations, such as medical doctors. We are spiritual doctors, so to speak, who are expected to be at every member's beck and call and then preach a solid Word on Sunday," Lance said.

"Deacons, the preacher is the watchman on the wall, the protector and feeder of the sheep. Apostle Paul said that it would hurt the Word if we did not give the Word proper preparation and so deacons were established to meet the needs of the people. God will hold the man of God accountable for his actions. Believe me when I say I have been whipped by God enough to know that this is true," Lance said with confidence.

Preach, baby, I thought as I raised my fist in the air leaning against the door.

I heard a chorus of Amen's from the deacons.

"Now, men we are to hold each other accountable in love, solidarity and unity. Some of you are not happy that I will call you when you miss a Sunday and don't call me to tell me that you will not be in service. The pastor and the deacon are the two offices in the church that will have to give an account of their stewardship toward the sheep. Would you rather deal with me now or have to answer to God later? But I do really miss you when you are not here at the church. I need you and the people need you. The people of God need to see that we, as leaders of this church, are unified. And still some of you are upset because I am the man that I am as the pastor. I take my calling very seriously. I am not perfect, but I serve a perfect God who can do all things.

"You are the sheep that God has called me to shepherd, and all I can do is my best with God's strength and power. I have asked God to help me to not harbor any ill feelings toward my distractors. I pray that we can now return to the work of ministry and God's business for our church," Lance said. "As for the fifty petition signatures, requesting a formal review of me I resolve to personally call each of them and let them know that the rumors are false and encourage them to pray for our church and their pastor."

"Amen!" said Jenkins and a few of the other deacons.

I imagined Jenkins looking at Deacon Sable like he was a big fat rat. I laughed at the thought.

I heard Bishop Needly lead them in prayer and the men walked out. As the deacons walked past me, they all gave me a hug. I hugged them back. When Deacon Jenkins walked up to me, I fell into his arms in tears.

"I know this was hard, Sister Stevens. But you and Pastor Stevens did great," Jenkins said, as he continued to hold me. His embrace reminded me of my late father's touch and I began to cry even harder with joy as I remembered all that God had brought us through.

Lance came out of the room and we all stood together.

Bishop Needly shook my hand and told Lance that he would have his secretary type the minutes of the meeting and his decision and he would send a copy and file it with the church national headquarters.

In that one meeting, I learned the real pressures of Lance's job. I now understood that our lives were definitely a call from God. And whether I wanted to be included in it or not, I was a part of his ministry. How many corporate wives are called to sit in on their husband's employee discipline hearing? Not too many, I tell you that. I drove home to find Amanda, my mama, Big Mama T, Sister Peterson, and all three of my children playing a game of Scabble at the table. I walked in and they all looked at me and invited me to join in the game, and so I did.

Amanda kept looking at me and finally announced to the children that it was time to retire to bed. I went into the kitchen and made a fresh brew of coffee for our seasoned guests. I toasted some bagels and spread some strawberry flavored Philadelphia cream cheese and made my way to the den where Amanda, Big Mama T, my mother and Sister Peterson were singing some old gospel hymns such as "Guide me Over Thou Great Jehovah" and "Shine on me." Big Mama T rounded off the course in customary booming tenor voice that could rival any man's, my mama and Amanda took the alto note. Sister Peterson and I sang soprano.

Big Mama T belted, "Guide me Over thy Great Jehovah, pilgrim through this barren land!" and we all joined her in the long drawn out call and response notes that were left over from the vestiges of slavery, Jim Crow laws and the tricks of affirmation action. The songs reminded me that although African-Americans were free from the physical shackles of slavery, some of us are still chained to the horrendous psychological, invisible chains of slavery, which cause us not to trust each other and doubt persons with a spirit of excellence. It has split our churches, our communities, and stunted our entrepreneurial spirit. In some ways this slavery mentality has crippled our spiritual growth as we demote God to a God that can only deliver to white people.

I prayed that God would help New Light to look like heaven! That one day, people of all colors could worship together, the true and living God.

My mother began to sing one of her favorite church songs, "God Can."

She sang as she pointed at me and danced in a gospel jig toward me. She grabbed me and we sung and danced around the den as she assured me that whatever was going on in my life, God could fix it and make it right.

Amanda chimed in with her sultry contralto and began singing Sheila Chargois's new song, "Just When I Need Him Most," which had us all on our feet! Then Big Mama T chimed in with James Cleavland's "God Is." God is the joy and the strength of my life. He moves all pains, misery and strife. And finally I sang the Watkins legendary, "Change."

By the time I finished the song, there wasn't a dry eye in the room. There they were, these four women, who had all strengthened me and protected me in some way over the past years of being on this Christian journey.

I thanked God for these angels standing around me. They could celebrate Jesus with me. Weep in hurt and pain and dance in victory as they felt the victory of Christ, even if they truly didn't know the details of the situation. Not one of them asked me about the earlier meeting with deacons, not even my mother. But they didn't have to know everything, because this walk was my walk. They had enough faith in our God that He would see me through. Their songs reinforced to me that I should pray and praise God in advance for the promises of His Word and not focus on the problems. We continued to sing and shared deep into the night about the grace of God and His mercies which are new every morning.

Chapter Twenty-Nine

Jesus Will Work It Out

We walked into the processional together as a family that next Sunday morning. I was dressed in a light green apricot dress with matching hat, matching three-inch high-heeled shoes, and an apricot purse. My mother completed my look by surprising me with an apricot Japanese hand fan that she purchased from Neiman Marcus at the Galleria in Houston. The girls were dressed in apricot lace dresses and Junior had a light green Sean Jean suit with matching Stacy Adams shoes. My husband wore a black suit with matching apricot accessories, silk white shirt, apricot tie and handkerchief, and silver apricot cuff links. I walked down the aisle with my husband with my chin strong and our children by our side.

Today was a day to celebrate that Jesus had protected our family and kept us together during our first year at New Light. I looked up at my husband, Pastor Lance McClain Stevens, and had a new respect for him on this day. He looked at me and smiled. The church programs read, "Pastoral Family Appreciation Day!" across the top. There was a biography about Lance and his vision for New Light. There was a list of all of his accomplishments as a preacher and pastor. There were pictures of our family, a small biography about me and a caption of all of our names. Funny how some things can change over night.

On previous Saturday, while we were having a barbeque with all of our family members at the community center, we received word that Sister Finley had a massive stroke, and was rushed to the hospital. Lance and I immediately left the barbeque and rushed to her side. When Lance arrived, Kayla and a flushed Deacon Finley were at Sister Finley's bedside. Her friend, Betty Jean Pepperdine, sat motionless in a seat by the hospital room door.

"I don't know what happened, Pastor. She was talking on the phone to Deacon Sable late Friday night, and she just started complaining about her side hurting her and then she just slumped over," Deacon Finley said.

"Why didn't you call me on Friday?" Lance asked Deacon Finley.

"I just felt so guilty about not showing up to that meeting, because I knew what Sarah was up to, but I didn't do a thing about it. I was ashamed, Pastor. I found out last night that she is the one who authorized all that furniture for your office. How she managed to get a key to your office and withdraw church funds, I really don't know," Deacon Finley explained, looking like a lost puppy. "I'm sorry that you and your family had to go through all of that."

"Brother, we forgive you. We need to see to Sister Finley's needs right now. She needs all of us," Lance said. We looked at Sister Finley and noticed that she was not able to talk. Her body was slouched on one side and she seemed to have aged by twenty years overnight. We prayed for her that God would heal her and restore the activities of her limbs. Deacon Finley, Kayla, and Betty Jean all cried during the prayer.

As we were exiting, a woman with a new born baby girl and a little boy, probably around the age of seven, entered the hospital room.

"Monique!" Kayla explained. "What are you doing here?"

"I had to come and see about her. My mama called me and told me that Cousin Sarah had a stroke. I had to come and see about her. I know she told me never to set foot again in Southlake, but, I don't care what these people in Southlake think about my children and me. I brought Stewart's new born baby girl for you to see, Cousin Sarah," Monique said as she rushed to Sister Finley's side.

Lance and I quickly turned around as we heard the conversation unfold. Was this the notorious other woman of New Light's former Pastor Adam Stewart? Was this the legendary Monique Howard? The convention whore known from Houston to El Paso, Texas according to the gossip at Heavenly Hands?.

Lance looked at me and we both discovered that Sister Finley was more notorious than we originally thought.

I thanked Jesus that he had protected us from the wiles of the enemy. Satan can use anyone to try to destroy Christian believers who truly love the Lord.

Just then, we heard a loud strange horrid moan rise up from the hospital bed from the lips of Sarah Finley. She rolled her head from side to side and white solid saliva came from her mouth. Kayla rushed to her side. I imagined she knew that her Aunt Sarah was probably having a fit that her torrid distant cousin, Monique, was back in Southlake with her two illegitimate children.

"Say, hello to Auntie Sarah, little Sarah Ann, this is your namesake," said Monique as she cuddled her baby and brought her closer to Sister Finley's bedside.

Sister Finley, let out another loud howl, her one good arm flung from side to side, and Deacon Sable stood to console her and calm her down.

"Let's tell her about our new home in West Texas and how Daddy is home with us every day since his retirement, and we need some help, now," Monique continued with a smirk on her face.

Lance and I looked at each other, shook our heads in disbelief and smiled. He reached out to grab my hand as we headed out of Sister Finley's hospital room.

Before leaving the hospital, I had a wonderful idea.

"Lance, have you ever thought about asking Kayla to be the church's administrative assistant?" I asked him as we drove back to the barbeque.

"You know that is an excellent idea. I'll discuss it with Deacon Jenkins."

So here we are today; walking together as a family in the light of God's love down the middle aisle of New Light. We are a witness that God will take care of His church, His preacher man and his family. I learned through our trials and tribulations that we have been sealed with God's divine protection and favor. God will reward us if we remain faithful to Him. Great is the Lord's faithfulness! I have learned over the years that my tongue and anger can only go to so many places; however, my earnest prayers can go to places that I cannot. Our prayers can reach deep into the spiritual realm where the enemy tries to destroy us and entrap us. I am grateful that I have discovered how to watch over my family, embrace my position post in this Christian army, and spiritually grow. It is through the power of much prayer, reading and application of God's Word in my life that I have learned to fight on my knees in prayer than with hurtful verbal assaults or physical attacks. Now the Lord is going to have to have a little patience with me on my "thoughts" of visualizing knocking them out, because Sister Finley has been cold cocked several times in my thoughts. I am under constant construction. Help me Lord Jesus!

Later that night, I found my journal and told her about the day's events:

Dear First Lady,

Today was a beautiful day! The appreciation service was great! Not because we looked good in our clothes, but because four souls were saved and restored today! Hallelujah! Brother Graves arranged for Luke Mercer Jr. & Chosen to serve as our special surprise musical guests and they took the worship to another level! It was an awesome experience! I am going to have to go and purchase their new CD! And to top it off, gospel artist, Chester D.T. Baldwin strolled in during the service and blessed us with his song, "Another Chance." I don't know how Brother Graves was able to get Luke Mercer Jr. and Chester D.T. Baldwin, on the same platform, on a Sunday morning, But First Lady, as in the words of Big Mama T, "We had some chu'ch, today!" There was not a dry eye in the worship service. The Holy Spirit moved in the place and He helped to unify and strengthen our church by His presence.

A powerful young preacher from LaMarque, Texas by the name of Pastor C.L. Yancy, Sr. served as the guest evangelist. He preached a powerful sermon called, "A Preacher's Job is Never Done," and the entire church was on its feet! That young preacher can PREACH! The Word of God is powerful and life changing. Vivian Daniels tore the church up with her rendition of Vickie Winans' "We Shall Behold Him" during the invitational period. She can give Vickie Winans a run for her money. Ms. Vivian's voice is anointed! She was one of the members who joined our church today! Hallelujah! Jesus will Work it Out!

The kids and I surprised Lance with a painted self portrait of him in his preaching robe by the artist Henry Lee Battle. Lance absolutely loved it and it brought him to tears of joy. It was our children's idea to give their daddy a painted portrait of what he enjoys doing the most, preaching the Word of God!

First Lady, off the record, my friend, Gerald Vaither, came to New Light today as well. At first I didn't think he recog-

nized me with my First Lady regalia on. But after services, I went up to him and introduced myself as Mrs. Jacqueline Renee Stevens and welcomed him to New Light. We hugged and he smiled and said, "I hope this won't stop you from visiting my store Lady Stevens." I gave him a friendly wink and said, "Please, call me Jackie." We shared a laugh and I knew he would one day return to regular church attendance.

Sister Finley is still in the hospital and she is still unable to speak. Betty Jean Pepperdine is totally devastated that her life long friend is ill. Kayla has an interview for church secretary with the New Light deacons on Wednesday. Marilyn Steele resurfaced finally. We heard through the grapevine that she has joined a church in Dallas, Texas. Now, we hear her favorite color is purple. Rumor has it she is still chasing powerful men in the church and causing old church women much grief already. We could not figure out who authorized all of our utilities to be cut off during the early part of the week. Personally, I think it was that green eyed monster, Sister Steele and Sister Finley, of course they were both being used by the devil. Okay, yeah, right. Yes, we've got to love the sinner, yet hate the sin. Lord, give me strength.

Yesterday's barbeque was awesome. We had over forty family members ride in or fly in to celebrate with us. All of the New Light deacons and brotherhood provided the food and games. There was not any hint of tension in the air. There was a sweet, sweet spirit of communion in the air at the barbeque that day. Big Mama T, my mama, and Sister Peterson were inseparable during the entire appreciation weekend. By the time, Big Mama T and my mama loaded up to return to Richmond, they were humming the tune to Sister Peterson's code word song.

I don't know what Jesus is to you.

But I hope He is to you what He is to me. He's my all, my all and all.

He's my chief cornerstone. I don't know what Jesus is to you,

But I hope He is to you what He is to me.

They all had a blast together!

I have discovered that my identity is completely found in Christ. Because I have committed my life to Him; there will be constant trials and tribulations in my life whether I am Mrs. Lance McClain Stevens or not. I have learned to rejoice in this Christian journey and praise God for His blessings that fall like a fresh new rain. True peace is not the absence of trouble, but the presence of God. When Jesus is on board my ship of trials and tribulations, I know that I do not have to panic or experience anxiety attacks; I just have to trust in the presence of God. As long as God is there, I can ride out any storm. I thank God for the seasons of my life as a Christian believer that have come to make me strong. Nothing can separate me from the love of God, not mean and hateful church folks, not conniving deacons, not deceitful women or Lucifer himself. God's love is longsuffering and strong enough to break through my enemies' distractions. I am created to worship and praise God at all times. My new song of praise is "I Know What Prayer Can Do."

Thank you, Jesus! I thank you for the communication of prayer. Now that I truly understand the power, position and purpose of prayer, it is empowering and exhilarating to my life! My walk as a Christian in the position post of a clergy wife is a life of emerging seasons of growth and maturity. It is, in fact, a process. This process is not a sprint, but it is a marathon. I am the student and God is my teacher and every now and then He allows me to instruct the class in the lessons that I have learned from Him; for I am blessed to be a blessing. The evidence of my growth in Christ is found in Proverbs 31: 28 concerning a virtuous woman:

Her children arise and call her blessed; her husband also, and he praises her:

When my children call me blessed and when I can find praise and honor in my husband's eyes, that is the proof of my virtue *as a mother and wife. I thank God that He is true to His Word and He will take care and provide for His own. If Christ loved me enough to die for me, then I know that He will fight for me even today. I know that my name is written in the palm of God's hand. For the scripture says: "Cast your cares on Him, for he cares for you," First Peter 5:7; and First Lady, I know the Lord definitely cares for me.*

Love,
Jacqueline Renee Stevens
And this is my confession.

Chapter Thirty

A New Season

I am now serving on the Praise and Worship Team at New Light. It feels so good to worship God in His sanctuary. Deacon Jenkins and Vivian are officially dating, and Jenkins' sister Betty Jean Pepperdine is having a fit about it. Sister Finley is attending rehab three times a week. She walks with a pearl cane and has regained her speech, although it is somewhat slurred. She now resorts to writing on a big yellow legal pad in church to make her point when she can't be understood. She is still wearing her pretty suits and hats and riding around the city of Southlake in her Pink Cadillac, some things will never change.

Gerald Vaither joined New Light and serves on the Greeter and Hospitality Ministry. I noticed that he and Tammy Benjamin have been spending a great deal of time together. Sister Peterson is holding on and still passing me notes in church about different women. Lance and the Deacon Board are steadingly working toward God's vision for New Light. The vision God gave Lance is coming to pass. We added another Sunday service and we will be implementing a special weekly service for prison families. Lance plans to hold a quarterly job fair to help them find work. We have already been able to place three young men into permanent jobs through our Victorious Workers Temporary Agency.

Lance, Connie, and Jaylyn, are all blessed and growing in Christ. Every three months, the family goes away and does something together as a family. He and Lance Jr. have even learned how to fish and play golf together. It is amazing how a little time with your family can make a world of difference when we face trials in the ministry. We have even booked a cruise to take our kids next year and then we are off to Disney World three months after that.

We discovered that our little Connie has an anointed voice. She has been singing around the city for the last few months at special services. I thank the Lord, for allowing us to grow in grace. Brother Ray Joseph Jr. came to visit New Light last Sunday. We heard that he was fired from his last church he played for. Ray has played for at least four churches since he left New Light. Lance has an appointment scheduled with him this week. We hear that Ray may be ready to go to that counselor and an alcohol treatment center that Lance told him about. He looked a hot mess on last Sunday in church and smelled like one too. But, the church is where we all need to be so that we can be healed, restored and encouraged.

We recently received an invitation to the wedding ceremony of Marilyn Steele, who will be marrying Pastor Reginald Montgomery of Cedar Hill, Texas. He pastors a 1,000 member church called Redeemed Community Church. I pray Marilyn finds what she is searching for. She is in a run for her money being a pastor's wife. You know, life is like a boomerang. What you put into this life, it will come back to you, good, bad or maybe a mixture of both. May the Lord help her . . . the same way He helped me.

Jacqueline Steven's Journal Entry Prayer Map

"And I will do whatever you ask in my name, so that the Son may bring glory to the Father. You may ask me for anything in my name, and I will do it." (St. John 14:13-14)

may ask me for anything in my name, and I will do it."   (St. John 14:13-14)

Prayer: Please allow Lance to finish seminary

Answer: Lance graduated from seminary! We're going to the graduation tonight.

Prayer: The parsonage is not suitable for a family. It even leaks when it rains. I pray for us to have a really nice parsonage in the near future

Prayer: I pray that one day we will OWN our own home.

Answer: It took some time and I have to admit I was getting anxious, but Lance was just appointed Pastor to New Light and God I thank you. The parsonage is absolutely GORGEOUS! Especially with the new paint and the modifications you blessed us to make. I love the prayer nook!

Prayer: I met Sister Finley today and I pray the she grows in Christ. I discerned from our conversation that she has some real issues with wanting to run the church's business.

Ongoing Prayer: Lord, I pray that you would continue to confirm me into your image and mature me so that I can walk worthy of this position you've called me to as a Pastor's Wife, but most importantly as a Christian. I so want to please you in everything I do and say. I have to admit it does get difficult, but I pray that the words of my mouth and the meditation of my heart are acceptable in your sight O' Lord my strength and my Redeemer.

Prayer: There is something not quite right about the new lady, Marilyn Steele that joined our church. Please reveal to me if her motives are pure.

Answer & Prayer: Well, Lord, Sister Marilyn Steele is always in Lance's face and she is moving up rather quickly in the church for someone that is "newly" saved. I thank you that you are revealing to me her true motives. I discern that she and that Sister Finley might be keeping up some mess with our upcoming anniversary program. The kids and I are being completely excluded from the services. They are even acting up about being left out. Especially Junior. He's really mad at his Dad and the church. One more thing, Lord, the Deacon's want to have a meeting with Lance - some sort of allegations. He wants me to go. I pray you go before us and speak through us. I know that no weapon formed against us shall prosper. I thank you in advance for a positive outcome.

Prayer: I went to get my hair done today and Vivian was at it again. Just picking me for gossip. I didn't say a word. She did manage to get poor Sister Wiley to tell all her church's business. I pray that you would grow her up as a Pastor's wife quick. She's so young and naive. Also she seems hurt and troubled about something. Minister to her on a personal level as only you can Father. Also, I pray that Vivian will come back to church.

Answers: Wow, God! Talk about exceedingly above what I could ask or think. The anniversary was wonderful! We had many souls to join the church including Vivian! I am so happy because you have kept us through such a trying year and we came out with VICTORY! You have brought my family closer to each other and most importantly closer to you. I pray that I can be an example to other First Lady's that you are faithful. We just have to trust you completely!

Answers: God, I thank you for moving Marilyn Steele completely out of New Light. She and Sister Finley allowed the enemy to use them with all the anniversary mess and the allegations against Lance. That meeting with the Deacon's was so unsettling but you brought us through it. It's a shame that Sister Finley ended up having a heart attack because of her part in all this. But you did say not to touch your anointed ones. I pray that she will have a complete and speedy recovery and come back to the church with a renewed spirit. This isn't the way I wanted her to grow in you, but Lord you always know what's best. Also, thank you for allowing Sister Wiley to grow in you and I am glad she is no longer angry with me and she's not letting Vivian pick her anymore.

Confessions of a Preacher's Wife

Discussion Questions

1) What influence do you think Sister Finley's growing up with an alcoholic father may have had on her behavior as an adult?

2) Do you agree that pastors' wives live in a fish bowl? What, if anything, can be done so they don't feel so isolated and alone?

3) How important is balance in the life of the believer? What impact might a lack of balance have on a believer's marriage and or family?

4) Deacon Jenkins was called "a friend of the preacher man." How important is it to be supportive of the pastoral family? What are some ways you can show your support?

5) Do you feel that Sister Finley and Sister Pepperdine's views of the younger women in the church reflect the view of older women in the church toward younger, less churched women? If so, why? How can the gap be bridged between the older and younger women in the body of Christ?

6) Deacon Jenkins indicated that New Light is seventy-five percent women. In an age when more and more men are joining churches, why do you think New Light is still comprised of predominantly female members?

7) The subcharacters, Tammy Benjamin and Gerald Vaither, symbolize persons that have one time or another lost their

faith in the church. What can we do for wounded believers that have lost fellowship with the fold?

8) As is the case with New Light, more and more "unchurched" people are attending worship services. How should the church handle this new "unchurched" generation entering its walls for the first time? If you were "unchurched" when you joined your church, what did your ministry to do attract and retain you as a new believer/member?

9) Jackie had her journal as a means of release and a coping mechanism for her daily problems. How important is it to have positive outlets/coping mechanisms? What outlets do you currently have in place? If none, what can you put in place to assist you in dealing with life's challenges?

10) Who or what do you think women in the church like Marilyn Steele are seeking?

11) Jackie is very open and honest in regards to all of her feelings when praying to God. What can we learn from her transparency in prayer?

12) Jackie speaks of nurturing a personal relationship with Jesus Christ. How important is it to go beyond church membership and ritual to truly become intimate with Christ? What are some ways you can deepen your personal relationship with Christ? How can you influence those around you to do the same?

13) We all know that Satan is after the men of God, much like Pastor Stewart, the former pastor of New Light. What are some ways we can cover our pastors and the men of God so they don't fall prey to the enemy?

14) Pastor Stevens established a 501c3 organization and the Victorious Worker's Temporary Agency. The agency had a tremendous impact on the community. What are some way's the church can go beyond its walls and make a difference in the community? What gifts and talents do you possess that could be used to assist your church in this area?

15) Jackie and Lance have truly learned how to take the adversity in their lives and grow from it into more mature Christians. What circumstances has God allowed in your life to mature and prune you? What did you learn from those events and how did they shape you into the Christian you are today? What present circumstance in your life is less than favorable? What godly characteristic might God be perfecting in your life?

16) Why do you think Lance was so secretive when it came to divulging information to Jackie? For example, his past with Marilyn Steele and the anonymous letter he received?

17) What do you think of Jackie's comments during Lance's informal review with the Board of Deacons?

18) The Bible says in I Chronicles 16:22 "Do not touch my anointed ones; do my prophets no harm." Sister Finley violated this biblical warning over and over again; as a consequence she ended up gravely ill. How important is it to watch how we handle the people of God. Have you fallen short in this area? If so, how can you rectify the situation?

19) The triumphant story of the first lady is a testament to the power of prayer. Please share with the group in-

stances where God moved in your life or the life of a loved one as a result of prayer.

20) If this fictional story would be made into a movie, what current actors would you see starring in it? And in what roles and why?

Mikasenoja

(pronounced My-ka-sen-no-jay)

Mikasenoja seeks to empower, equip and educate Christian soldiers to stand boldy for Christ, regardless of life circumstances. It is imperative that we minister to an unsaved generation and repair the wounds of crippled saints. She hopes to invoke serious discussion and biblical solutions concerning the challenges of the modern day church. Mikasenoja possesses a compassionate heart of ministry for clergy wives and women church leaders.

Mikasenoja holds a B.A. in Government and African-American Studies from the University of Texas at Austin. She currently lives in League City, Texas with her husband, Pastor C.L. Yancy, Sr. and their four children, Joshua, William, Jennifer, and C.J. Currently, Mikasenoja is a History teacher, psalmist, and a motivational speaker. Her husband serves as Senior Pastor of the New Hope Bible Baptist Church in La Marque, TX. Mikasenoja is a proud member of Delta Sigma Theta Sorority, Inc. and strives to exemplify Christ in everything she does in her commitment to God and in serving her community. Her scripture of purpose is Luke 1:37 *"For with God nothing shall be impossible."*

For Book Signings, inspirational lectures and appearances contact Mikasenoja's agent:

Kimberly Matthews of Kissed Publications at kissed publications@yahoo.com

Email: mikasenoja@aol.com

Check out Mikasenoja's website at
www.mikasenoja.com

Feel free to sign her guestbook and send in your responses to the discussion questions. Stay tuned for
Mikasenoja's next literary project!

For more Urban Christian books go to
www.urbanchristianonline.net

Urban Christian His Glory Book Club!

Established January 2007, *UC H G y B k C* is another way by which to introduce to the literary world, Urban Book's much-anticipated new imprint, **Urban Christian** and its authors. We are an online book club supporting Urban Christian authors by purchasing, reading and providing written reviews of the authors' books that are read. *UC His Glory* welcomes both men and women of the literary world who have a passion for reading Christian based fiction.

UC His Glory is the brainchild of Joylynn Jossel, author and Executive Editor of Urban Christian and Kendra Norman-Bellamy, author and Director of Talent & Operations for Urban Christian. The book club will provide support, positive feedback, encouragement and a forum whereby members can openly discuss and review the literary works of Urban Christian authors. In the future, we anticipate broadening our spectrum of services to include: online author chats, author spotlights, interviews with your favorite Urban Christian author(s), special online groups for *UC Book Club* members, ability to post reviews on the website and amazon.com, membership ID cards, *UC His Glory* Yahoo Group and much more.

Even though there will be no membership fees attached to becoming a member of *UC His Glory Book Club*, we do expect our members to be active, committed and to follow the guidelines of the book club.

UC H G y members pledge to:

- Follow the guidelines of *UC His Glory Book Club*.
- Provide input, opinions, and reviews that build up, rather than tear down.

- Commit to purchasing, reading and discussing featured book(s) of the month.
- Agree not to miss more than three consecutive online monthly meetings.
- Respect the Christian beliefs of *UC His Glory Book Club*.
- Believe that Jesus is the Christ, Son of the Living God

We look forward to the online fellowship.

Many Blessings to You!

Shelia E Lipsey
President
UC His Glory Book Club

**Visit the official Urban Christian Book Club website at
www.uchisglorybookclub.net